I0847054

Lay Your Heart on the Wind

Doris Gaines Rapp

Copyright 2025 Doris Gaines Rapp

All rights reserved. No part of this publication may be reproduced or transmitted in any form or by any electronic or mechanical means including photocopying, recording, or any information storage and retrieval system now known or to be invented, without permission in writing from the publisher or the author.

Name: Doris Gaines Rapp, Ph.D.
Title: Lay Your Heart on the Wind
Library of Congress Control Number: 2025912836
ISBN: (paperback): 979-8-9885283-7-1
ISBN: (eBook): 979-8-9885283-8-8

Cover design. From Alex (Kyiv, Ukraine) at PIXABAY. @alexbon_com

The cover was put in place by @Debi Lindhorst/The Type Galley, Warren, Indiana.

All Scripture quotations, unless otherwise indicated, are taken from the Holy Bible, New International Version®, NIV®. Copyright ©1973, 1978, 1984, 2011 by Biblica, Inc.™ Used by permission of Zondervan. All rights reserved worldwide. www.zondervan.comThe "NIV" and "New International Version" are trademarks registered in the United States Patent and Trademark Office by Biblica, Inc.™

website: www.dorisgainesrapp.com
contact: dorisgainesrapp@gmail.com

Glossary
For a word with an asterisk (*) beside it, go to the back of the book for information.

Published by Daniel's House Publishing - Huntington, Indiana

in cooperation with Never Alone Publishing - Fort Wayne, Indiana

DEDICATION

This is dedicated to my wonderful husband, Bill Rapp.
God sent you to me many years ago.
Blessed be the name of the Lord.

Prelude

"Lay Your Heart on the Wind" is in response to readers who asked that I expand my Tucker McBride books to include how Bill and I met.

It is difficult for me to write about private issues.

So, I wrote a fictional book that includes how we met during our freshman year at North Central College in Naperville, Illinois.

I also wrote about how Dad asked me why I wanted to go to college, and my answer.

I grew up in Kettering, Ohio. I included fun events during the Holiday at Home festivities on Labor Day weekend.

The book is based on my love for my husband, but the storyline is fictional.

CONTENTS

Premise

Finding an order of importance for your life can be a major struggle or a sacred blessing: faith, marriage, family, career, friends, fun, or community.

Do you toss the dice and wonder where these important segments will land?

Or do you take charge of your life?

This is the story of Sunny Gaynor, a gifted singer and composer, who discovers that she isn't in control of anything.

Is it too late for her to sing a new song?

Chapter One
The Flight Home

She met him in Naperville. That was ten years ago, but she thought of him every day. How could she have been so foolish? But then, she was only nineteen years old at the time. Now, in 2025, her decisions were being put to the test.

She loved everything about her year in Illinois. Naperville was a small college town, nestled among tall old trees, brick-paved sidewalks, and flanked by stately Victorian homes with steep roofs. The "painted ladies" boasted a variety of bright colors. As a singer and songwriter, Sunny interpreted everything with an artistic flair. She believed the tall trees bent low, hugging the houses, were to keep the family's love safely inside.

Sunshine Gaynor and Nick Sullivan were both freshmen when they met at North Central College. Nick was several years older than Sunny because he worked in a factory to make money for college before enrolling. For Sunny, it was a magical year of music theory classes, football games, and weekend dances with Nick. She loved their long walks in Naperville, past willow trees and fluffy, friendly dogs. But that was a long time ago.

It was on one of those walks that Sunny bubbled over. "Nick Sullivan, I love you." She fell into his arms and snuggled close, excited that her dream had come true.

"Shine, I love you so much, I'm about to bust open. I'll be happy with anything you decide to do. But —" Nick pursed his lips and said no more.

"But what?" Sunny couldn't believe it. Nick had taken pride in her singing and the songs she composed.

"I just …." The words caught in Nick's throat. "Don't leave."

"Nick, this may be my only chance to start a musical career." Seeing the broken look on Nick's face, she made a promise, "I'll think about it before I make my final decision. I don't want to leave either." But she did.

~~~~

Everything had changed for Sunny in the years since then. Life had flown by, and she never had time to think about what had happened. When she reached out to grab the key to her future, she let go of the lock that held her together.

That spring, Sunny sang the lead when a music agent attended the college musical on opening night. It was the school's performance of Rogers and Hammerstein's old favorite, *Oklahoma!* Sunny stole everyone's heart as Laurey. The curtain call prompted an uproarious ovation. In the days that followed, while the thrill of performing still had her flying high, music agent Bruce McDaniels offered her a contract with a major recording company miles away from Illinois.

Ten years later, as she sat staring out the airplane's window, her breath escaped her as she remembered
~~~~

holding the contract in her hand. It was the fulfillment of a childhood dream.

On warm spring days, she would sing and dance on the family's porch, facing an audience of dolls in a baby carriage and the family dog, Spotty. But when she accepted the one hope for her future and left Naperville, she walked out on another dream, her vision of love.

It wasn't an equal trade. Would she ever find real love again? At that young point in her life, it was easy to step blindly into a new, unpredictable music career. That dream had been part of her life before she knew the meaning of love. Becoming a music star felt like the right decision, a familiar part of every dream.

Lately, Sunny was beginning to understand what had happened in Naperville. If she stayed, love would have come close. Leaving, she would receive tons of love from strangers, but they would be kept at a distance.

She closed her blue/green eyes and sat back in her seat. Lyrics she didn't want to hear, wheedled their way into her thoughts. *When the rain comes down, my tears start to flow. If I had stayed, we'd never know.*

Stop it, she demanded silently to herself. She didn't want to think about leaving. She wanted to enjoy the thought of arriving. She needed to fill her thoughts with lovely memories of family, friends, and her long-awaited trip home.

But there, on the plane that flew her to her sister's wedding … alone, with nothing to do but reminisce … it all came back.

Robin was two years older and had preceded Sunny to the same college. Now, after teaching fourth grade for several years, Robin would finally marry Gary Foxworth, her college sweetheart. Robin was sealing the commitment she had made years before. Would Sunny ever find that kind of love? All of her time and energy had been dedicated to her music career. As the years rolled by and her memory of Nick's face remained fixed in the past, her hope of finding real love faded too.

The morning sun glimmered through the American Airlines cabin as she looked out over a beautiful sky.

"It looks like it will be a nice day after all," a man in bib overalls and a red plaid shirt said when Sunny opened her eyes.

"Oh, I thought …" Sunny stammered as she looked around. The flight attendants didn't usually allow passengers from business class to wander up front. Yet here he was, where a quiet young woman had been sitting minutes before.

The man smiled. He assured her in a deep, warm voice, "Your friend is talking to someone in the back of the plane."

Why did someone Sunny had never met before look so familiar? The man did. "She isn't my friend. I don't even know her," Sunny denied. The absent, young, round woman who sat beside her was a total stranger, which was usually the case when Sunny flew to the next singing venue. On board alone, she would sleep.

"You often don't know the people around you, do you?" the man asked as he took a cup of steaming coffee from the flight attendant.

"Would you like some coffee, Miss Gaynor?" The woman asked.

"Yes, that would be nice." Sunny took the cup and smelled the fresh, smooth aroma of the blend. "Thank you."

Sunny argued silently. *What does that mean – you don't know the people around you? How does he know if I don't know the people around me?*

She asked him boldly, "What do you mean, 'You don't know?' Is that in the collective use of the word 'you,' or 'you,' meaning me?" She felt a little insulted by a man who didn't even know her. She assertively took over the conversation. "What's your name?"

"Mel," he said with a smile. "Sorry, I didn't mean to offend you."

Sunny sat up straighter. She wondered about his last name but didn't ask. She'd discovered that most people don't want to reveal personal information to a stranger, not even their full name. Sunny hadn't been a stranger to anyone since she had won the award. But they were strangers to her. "My name is Sunny Gaynor."

"I know," Mel answered. "I recognized you right away."

Then she laughed to herself as she thought about it. *That's wild, a Grammy Award winner with a fan holding an old, broad-billed, flat-top painter's hat and wearing coveralls.* "So, you know me?"

"Everyone knows Sunshine Gaynor, the woman who single-handedly introduced the beautiful words of Love-Story songs to new fans." Mel started drinking his coffee.

"Well … thank you." As usual, Sunny let a compliment cloud her judgment. Where had her other no-name flight companion gone? Why hadn't the woman come back? She needed more information before she would feel comfortable. But honestly, there was something about the man that made her feel safe and at home. "Why are you flying?"

"I've seen the big flying machines overhead that Orville and Wilbur built. But I've never flown in one before."

"Orville and Wilbur?" Sunny wondered out loud. "Oh, the Wright brothers. Yes, they started it all."

"You asked about my travel," Mel said as the corners of his mouth turned up. "I'm going home to my wife, Josie. I was out east."

"Josie? That's a cozy name," Sunny said as she rubbed her tongue over her front teeth. "The name kinda tickles the mouth. She wasn't able to go with you?"

Mel chuckled softly. "We have six children and live modestly. There would be no nanny to watch the kids while my wife was gone."

"Six children? Wow. That's quite a few." Sunny caught a mental image of six little ones grabbing her ankles as she kneaded bread dough over a blue kitchen counter. Her entire body shuddered at the noise and hubbub. She added, "Oh my. You have a full house. I'm sure you miss them."

Mel looked around the first-class cabin and smiled. "This is elegant. The cabin has a nice color scheme. Yes, I miss the family, even when I'm at work. I was gone three days this time."

"I don't mean to be nosy. May I ask why you had to be away for several days?" Sunny wondered if Mel had to work, or did he seize every opportunity to be away from a busy, noisy, full house.

Mel patted Sunny's hand. "That's okay. You're friendly, not nosy. I was in the east because I'm a paint contractor and was bidding on a job."

Sunny couldn't mask her surprise as her mouth popped open. "In New York City?"

Mel blew across the surface of his coffee. "The executive offices in the newly rebuilt Equitable Building are ready to be decorated and painted. I heard about it and went east to put in a bid."

Odd, the Equitable Life Building was rebuilt in 1915, after a 1912 fire. "I know an architect who talks about the history of all the buildings in Manhattan." She fished around in her purse for her lipstick, buried at the bottom. Pulling it out, she reapplied a fresh coat. Looking at Mel, Sunny smiled sheepishly and said, "I'm redecorating my exterior right now." Replacing the tube, she asked, "Why couldn't you do a virtual interview on your computer? Or did you need to get away for a while?"

"A virtual interview?" He asked no more about computer video programs and started a different line of conversation. "Your other question was about my family." His eyes brightened. "Family is everything, Sunny. That's what living is about. Do you have any children?"

"Me?" Sunny gasped. "No, not me. I haven't even found a man I could live with day after day."

Mel relaxed on the headrest. "My days are full of my wife and children. I think of them all the time. My oldest son has joined me in the business. I hope they're in my life for a long time."

"You think of them every day?" Sunny thought again of Nick Sullivan. Her heart warmed, and she secretly wept at the same time. She assured Mel, "I understand."

"Sunny," Mel looked out the window with a young, fresh face of amazement. "Look at those clouds gathering in the east. They are perfect. It looks like a valuable painting, created by God himself."

Her heart filled with joy as she turned to the beautiful cluster that stretched across the sky. The fluffy, pale blue and white vapors sat on the very breath of God and filled the sky's horizon with hope. "They are amazing, Mel."

"Mel?" The woman who occupied the seat before Mel showed up put down a book. "I'm Amy, not Mel."

"Oh, I...." Sunny looked around in confusion. "Where?"

"Where?" Amy looked at her watch. "We've been flying for about an hour and a half. So, we're over eastern Ohio."

"Oh, right." Sunny brushed off any further inquiry about the switch of flying companions. "Did you have a nice visit with your friend back there?"

"My friend?"

Sunny sat wide-eyed. "Mel," she repeated. "He said you were talking with someone in business class."

Amy laughed. "Hardly. I was in the lavatory, alone."

"Oh, sorry," Sunny apologized. "I guess I misunderstood." She thought about Mel, his soft, deep voice, and gentile manner. She felt relaxed with him. Why did he leave so quickly? She thought of going back to look for him.

"Oops," Amy exclaimed. "Better stay in your seat. The fasten your seatbelt light just came on."

A flight attendant's mellow voice sounded over the speaker. "Ladies and gentlemen, please fasten your seatbelts and replace the lap tray. We will be gradually descending in preparation for landing in twenty minutes. Enjoy the scene from your window. The clouds are beautiful, but they are making our flight a little bumpy."

"Already? We'll be landing in twenty minutes?" Sunny stretched, looking over her shoulder. "I was hoping..."

Helping passengers with their seatbelt buckles, one of the flight attendants walked past. "May I help you?" she asked Sunny.

"No, thank you. I'm fine. I was looking for Mel, the man sitting with me for a while," Sunny explained as she looked around again.

"Yes, Ma'am," the attendant soothed complacently.

"You served him coffee …" Sunny insisted and checked the attendant's name badge, "Valerie."

"Yes, Ma'am. I can't say I remember."

"He wore bib overalls," Sunny insisted.

"Oh, I think I would have remembered a man in bib overalls." Valerie dismissed the idea as she moved on to help other passengers.

"Bib overalls?" Amy asked with a snicker. "Coveralls would be more appropriate with a horse and buggy."

Sunny didn't answer. She had no answer to give. But one thing she knew, Mel made her feel relaxed, at home. She had given concerts she had always dreamed of, and traveled around the world. But she was lonely out there, far from home, wherever home was, in her empty hotel room, or even in front of thousands of people. People adored her, but they didn't know her. She knew Mel for only a few minutes, but felt more hopeful than she had in years. Where had he gone?

Chapter Two
Home

It was Labor Day weekend. Sunny hadn't been home for the Holiday at Home festivities since she moved to New York. She wasn't avoiding her family. Fans had embraced her and her music so much that she felt trapped on a high note. All the air inside her, her creativity, and her ability to enjoy others' company were squeezed out of her. Singing every day, she had learned to control her breathing and get every note out of the last breath before she inhaled again. But she was suffocating. Her concert schedule got heavier and harder to carry every day. Lately, the demands were more than she could fulfill. She was unhappy in New York but didn't have the energy to take a break from it. Robin's wedding was a lifesaver, an excuse to leave the stage and find herself again.

The plane landed on time at the Dayton International Airport. It felt great to be home. As soon as she stepped onto Ohio soil, she put on a ball cap and pulled down the bill. Walking through the airport, she was glad no one recognized her. Then she began to wonder if everyone had forgotten her. That contradiction controlled her entire life.

The rental car she had reserved would be waiting for her. It wasn't to be a luxury brand like you might expect of a celebrity, or a low, sleek sports model. She certainly had the money to rent any vehicle on the rental lot. She chose a mid-size SUV in incognito black.

Once on the road, she pulled away from the terminal, crossed the Englewood Dam, turned left onto North Main Street, and drove down into the valley of Dayton. On through the city, Main Street became Far Hills Avenue, and then Dayton became Oakwood. The lovely community with its beautiful, elegant homes always took her breath away. A little past the Dorothy Lane Market, Oakwood became Kettering. Sunny laughed, then quietly hummed, *Back home again, in Kettering, Ohio.*

About a year ago, she had Googled Nick Sullivan. He was also from the Dayton area. They hadn't met until that first day in Naperville. But he had chosen to establish a law office in Kettering. The Holiday at Home festivities would make a busy weekend, with crowds of people bustling everywhere. She didn't want to turn around and find him behind her. She would be with family. Sunny enjoyed her time with her parents and sister. Although no one else was in the car, she insisted, "No, Mel, I am not alone a lot." She had never been alone when she lived at home, but that had been a long time ago.

~~*Memory*~~

Sunny remembered a day in New York, months after she had moved there, when she was so lonely she thought she would choke on her tears. Walking around her apartment, she spoke to the furniture. "I have been so busy with recordings and personal appearances, I haven't talked to Nick for months."

She paused with her phone in her hand, then clicked his number. "Nick?" she asked into the phone. Sunny and

Nick had such a close relationship in college that it didn't feel like it was the Nick she knew on the other end of the call. Or had their closeness begun to fade?

Sounds of giggling were all she heard, and then someone grabbed the phone on the other end. Finally, Nick said, "Hello?"

Sunny was shocked and hurt. Her voice was strained and low. "Nick, it's me."

"Me who?" a female voice interrupted, along with the sound of more hand slapping.

"Who are you?" Sunny asked. Unwilling to accept the confusion, she checked her phone to see if she had misdialed.

Then the voice on the other end changed, with what could have been another phone grab. "Sunny, is that you?"

"Yes, Nick." She tried to regain her composure. "I needed to hear your voice, but you seem to be busy," she choked, knowing she couldn't say more. She disconnected the call and turned off her phone. There was no explanation she wanted to hear. Nick had moved on. From that moment on, she blocked his calls. The pain stayed with her … forever.

~~~~

"Stop it," she demanded and slapped the steering wheel. She didn't want to think about Nick and New York and the cold, hard skyscrapers with their turbulent caverns down on the sidewalks where the wind would whip along the concrete and nearly knock her over.

During the rest of her drive, she focused on Kettering's holiday celebration events, which were advertised on placards in front of quaint stores and businesses. The signs brought back memories of family
~~~~

and community activities for those who chose to remain at home for the long Labor Day weekend.

Passing her high school, her second home, she remembered all the laughter and realized why her homesickness had doubled in recent years. She had to bring back a sweet memory of Nick. She owed it to herself and to all they had been together. Memories of more joyous times filled her with excitement and lifted her spirits.

~~*Memory*~~

Sunny was a new freshman at North Central College, enjoying a whirlwind of activities. To bring the students together as a class before the semester began, the college had planned activities and mixers. Everyone dressed casually, but with the intent to impress.

Friday evening was a fun time of folk dancing. Large sweet chocolate chip cookies and chewy, cinnamon and sugar-dusted, snickerdoodles were served, with cold glasses of lemonade. Even though everyone had eaten supper, the cookies were devoured like a swarm of locusts had descended on a field of corn.

A tall, blue-eyed guy easily caught Sunny's eye. As the group danced, she would find him watching her from a distance. One of the dances included a fast step in which they changed partners by reversing directions. *Change, change, there he is again, then,* "All turn around." She couldn't remember the exact words, but she knew as soon as the guy got a few people away, the dance-caller would reverse the line, and off he'd go in another direction. Except for never getting to dance with the dark, wavy-haired guy who grabbed her heart, it was a fun evening. The fresh group of strangers was beginning to form a class.

The last activity of the evening would take place in the music department auditorium. A little before that program, Sunny and several friends left the fun activities and started for the Wentz Concert Hall and Fine Arts Center, where they were to enjoy introductions and singing.

They had barely gotten out the door when one of the male students called out, "Hey, Sunshine. Wait, Sunny." He shouted again, "Nick wants to walk with you."

Sunny couldn't believe it. She had noticed the tall, athletic-looking boy when she and her friends first entered the large residence hall lounge. It was the same guy with whom she never danced. What was there about him? Yes, he was good-looking. But it was more than that. His very presence drew her near him.

"Wait for him," her roommate encouraged. "We're all going to the same place."

Her friends walked on while Sunny waited at the end of the sidewalk for Nick to catch up. "Hi, I'm Sunshine Gaynor. Everyone calls me Sunny."

"Nick Sullivan," he returned. "Everyone calls me Nick Sullivan."

Sunny laughed softly. "So that's the way you are."

"Yep," he admitted. "Where are you from?"

"Kettering, Ohio," she said proudly.

"Kettering?" Nick asked with a wink. "I'm from Dayton, actually Englewood." Nick reached for her and drew her next to him as they walked. "You are definitely Sunshine."

That wasn't too quick for Sunny. She felt at home tucked under his arm. It was as if she had always been there.

~~~~
~~~~

That was then, the end of one of the songs of her life. In her heart, she added lines to her popular hit, "What If:" *If I didn't go, this would have been so, since ten years ago.*

Now, it was the last Friday in August. Sunny drove a few more miles down Far Hills, then turned onto the most familiar road in the world. She half expected to see kids in the middle of the dead-end street swinging at a tennis ball. That's what she and Darcie from across the street used to do.

The home of her childhood wasn't in the fancy part of town, where company executives and white-collar workers lived. Most of the girls in her high school wore cashmere sweaters and designer jeans. Sunny and Robin didn't. Their father was a factory worker, and their mother served macaroni and cheese in an elementary school cafeteria. They were a normal family, and their home breathed life and love.

Sunny had moved to a New York, Park Avenue, apartment, but her parents' house would always be home. She had such mixed feelings. She loved the sights of Manhattan, but she never felt comfortable there. Home was through the door with the three glass windows. Every Christmas, her parents flew to New York to visit Sunny and enjoy the lights and bustle of the holidays. But, in ten years, Sunny hadn't had time to drive down Keystone Avenue. Or, to be honest, she hadn't taken the time.

"I'm home," Sunny called out as she opened the front door.

"I haven't heard those words in a long time," her mother exclaimed as she hugged her youngest daughter.

"You got here," Robin said as she made it a group hug. The trio jumped up and down, bouncing with joy.

Rerun, the family's little cockapoo dog, joined in the greeting. She had been a fifth family member for just two years when Sunny moved east. But Rerun was smart. She remembered the sister who took her everywhere before she left, played catch each morning with a pink tennis ball, and made the house feel empty when she was gone.

"Hi, Rerun." Sunny bent down and scooped up the little black love button. Like replaying a favorite movie, the fuzzy dog got her name from her habit of repeating a routine. If you tossed a ball to her, she would run and catch it repeatedly until you gave up. If you started scratching behind her ear and then reached for your laptop, she'd jump up on your lap and lay her paws on the keyboard until you began petting her again. She was the center of attention. It was fine with her if that meant doing the same thing repeatedly.

"Come, sit," Sunny's mother offered as she led the way into the dining room. "I've made chicken salad for lunch." Grace went to the kitchen as Sunny and Robin sat at the table. Robin brought her up to date on the pre-wedding plans.

"Can I help you, Mom?" Sunny asked.

"I've got it," Grace said as she returned with a tray of croissant sandwiches and small fruit dishes. "Before we begin to eat, let's pray." They joined hands while Grace offered a prayer of thanks. "Amen."

"Did you have a good flight?" Robin asked.

"Yes, I did." Sunny stopped for a minute as Mel's face came to mind. "I met an interesting man."

"Oh …?" Robin drew out. "A new man?"

"No, not a new man. He was just a man I had never met before, a new friend." Sunny took a bite of her sandwich. It had a creamy, tasty combination of chicken white meat, fresh herbs, and onion. "Mom, this is great chicken salad. And as to that man, he was old enough to be my father."

Robin's cell phone rang. "Wait. I'm sorry. I have to get this." Speaking into the phone, she began, "Hi, Quin. Right. The Gala starts at 6, and remember, it's a semi-formal event, with a buffet-style dinner. We'll meet you there. Okay."

"Six o'clock?" Sunny said as she checked her watch. "It's 1 p.m. already. After lunch, I want to unpack everything and then rest a little. How long will it take to get to the banquet center?"

Robin put her croissant on her plate. "It's about a twenty-minute drive. I want to get there early. The wedding party will sit together. We'll enjoy the music and dancing after we eat." She paused for a minute. "The Gala is a big deal. They'll give out the scholarships they supported. Uh … Nick might be there."

Sunny felt her heart flip over. "Nick? Nick Sullivan? Why? How do you know?"

"Well, I don't know for sure," Robin admitted. "But he is on the Events Committee, so I would logically think he'd be there."

"Warn me if you see him," Sunny said.

Robin changed the subject and asked, "Sunny, what will you wear to the Gala, something by a famous designer? Every eye will be on you, so I imagine you will want to dress for attention."

Sunny was embarrassed. She thought Robin knew her better than that. Still, she had to admit, it's hard to watch a person grow and mature, with short clips of conversation in a text. It's too easy to guard your thoughts and feelings when you can hide them behind a small cell phone screen.

Sunny laughed and said, "No, I bought a dress in a department store with a branch right here in your mall." She quickly changed the subject. "How is Dad doing? Is he getting anxious to retire?"

"Retire? Heavens no," Grace said with her napkin to her mouth. "Retirement is a long way off for him. But he has found golf. That's an acceptable outlet. He plays on many Saturdays during this warm weather."

Sunny's eyes popped. "Golf? Daddy? I never would have dreamed it. Will he have to miss next Saturday?" She turned to Robin. "That's your wedding day."

Robin laughed. "Nope. Dad has it all planned. He'll host Gary and the groomsmen on the first tee when the sun comes up on Saturday. Gary's dad will join them. The wedding is in the evening. No problem."

"Ah, no problem?" Sunny chimed in. She recalled all the issues that often arise when she watches Bruce plan and organize a major concert production. For ten years, she had seen her team organize concerts for thousands of people. She knew how many details were involved. With experience and hard work, those events were successful. One challenge she would not be able to manage is Nick Sullivan. "Oh my," she whispered.

Chapter Three
Nick

Red, white, and blue helium balloons floated above the room, and small American flags decorated each table. Colorful banners depicting various fields of work: teachers, plumbers, and builders, hung from the walls. It was Labor Day weekend. The banquet room was already beginning to fill with women in their fancy dresses and men in summer-weight suits. The event committee would honor scholarship winning students they had selected who had excelled in academics, sports, and the arts. Excited, designated winners and their families were seated at the head table, waiting to be presented to the community. City representatives, Monday's parade grand marshal, and various sponsors of the weekend events were also placed at the head table. A joyous buzz filled the air. Sunny took in every friendly smile and laughing couple.

She saw Gary Foxworth slip his glasses into his top jacket pocket, put his arms around Robin, and kiss her like a man getting married in a few days. "Hi, Tweety Bird." Sunny heard Gary call Robin his name of endearment for her.

"Hi, Coach," Robin said, remaining in his embrace. "I'm so glad you got here. Did you and the team have a long practice?"

"Yeah," he said as he rotated his right shoulder. "All the boys worked very hard. And, I'm the one with the sore passing arm." He laughed at himself. "Since we start football practice in August, while it's still hot, we stop often for hydration breaks. Those breaks aren't enough for me, and they sure aren't long enough."

"I can't believe it, Gary," Sunny said with a laugh. "You were a football star all four years of college. I thought you learned how to protect your body."

Robin nodded in agreement. "Well, work out that shoulder kink, fast. Later, there will be dancing," she said, growing giddier about the activities. "I made a great decision, planning wedding activities around the Labor Day events. I didn't even have to hire a band to provide dance music. The city had it all arranged."

"Genius," Holly Blanchart agreed. Holly was the second bridesmaid and a friend of Robin's and Sunny's since they were all little, in the Toddler Classroom at church.

Quindalyn Tuttle smiled and shook her head. "You Gaynor girls are amazing."

Sunny waved off Quin's comment, saying, "Not me. Robin. Things always seem to fall in your direction."

"In my direction?" Robin gasped. "You're a good one to talk. You're the one with two Gold Records, each selling more than 500,000 copies."

Sunny wanted to scream, *But you're the one who's getting married. You're the one who will have a home, not a house. You're the one who's with someone who loves you for being you, not for being a flash in a music video who people think they know, but don't.* But she said nothing, except, "You're probably right."

"Sunny," Holly whispered, "who's the guy who keeps watching you?"

"Where?" she answered, but didn't look. Every day for the last few years, she felt like she lived in a fishbowl. People were always looking in. The only way she could live anything close to a normal life was to not look out through the glass in her tiny circle of safe water.

Holly nudged her again. "Well, like it or not," she covered her mouth with her hand like she was rubbing her nose, "he's coming over."

"Shine?" a soothing, deep voice hummed behind her.

How could she turn to see who it was? She wouldn't be able to tolerate the disappointment if it weren't him. But it sounded so much like a voice from her past. She closed her eyes and tried to compose herself, to calm the fear that her goldfish bowl had suddenly shattered. Fearing she would flounder on dry land; she turned slowly and met his gaze.

"Nick Sullivan," she whispered. She quickly avoided his gaze, fearing her eyes would give away the instant attraction she was experiencing. How could ten years make Nick even more ... more of everything? She took another look into his blue eyes, then quickly looked away. "I had no idea you'd be in Ohio." The fact that she had Googled him would remain her secret.

Nick stood close and took Sunny's hand. She could smell the faint fragrance of aftershave, Nick's favorite, Forest Fresh..

Leaning closer, he said, "I got back to the Dayton area quickly. When you left, I finished my last three years of college in two years and two summers. Then I went to Law School before opening an office here in Kettering."

Sunny looked past him to the area where he had been standing with a few couples. Trying to calm her voice, she asked, "Is your wife here? I'd like to meet her."

Nick gently smoothed the top of her hand with his thumb. "Shine, I've never been married."

"Nick Sullivan?" Robin asked, too far into her own heightened pre-wedding jubilation to recognize the moment that Sunny and Nick were sharing. "Sunny, Nick is one of our up-and-coming attorneys."

"Really?" Sunny asked, surprised. "You never told me."

"It's hard to give you all the news of home in a few short text messages. Those are for 'See you at 7,' and 'Sure, Sis.' Those short clips are not for long news reports about mutual friends who had returned home. Sunny, you have been busy on several continents. When we come to New York, we chatter about all of the events in each other's lives, but can't catch up on everything."

"Right. Hi, Robin," Nick answered. "I haven't seen you since you and Gary graduated from college." He winked and teased, "I see your opinions are still quite sharp. It has been a long time."

"That's right," Robin agreed. "But I read about you in the newspaper occasionally. You have won a lot of cases."

"Now, you're revealing my resume. I'm not applying for a job," he said with a laugh and another wink.

Robin smiled sheepishly. "If you were, what would you be applying for?"

Sunny looked at Nick but said nothing. Their eyes met, and that said everything.

"Nick." Sunny's father, Doug, reached out his hand in greeting. "It's good to see you again."

"Sir," Nick responded with a hearty handshake. "Mrs. Gaynor," he greeted Sunny's mother.

Grace was stiff. She looked shocked by his presence. She swallowed hard, then graciously invited, "If you are here alone, you're welcome to join us."

Sunny was trapped in Nick's gaze. She knew what she wanted, but would she be able to be around him all evening and not wish for the past? But she had to give in since he had already been invited. "That would be nice, Nick. Holly's husband, Phil, had to work late. There's an empty spot with us. We'll add another chair when he arrives."

The group had politely waited for the rest of the wedding party and had seated themselves at the table. Those who had already found their spot moved to create an open space beside Sunny. Nick sat down and leaned toward her. "I can't believe this."

"Me either." Sunny had to admit that this was a time in which she was not in control. She would have had each place setting identified ahead of time, ready to be occupied by the named guest. Here at home, she was not in command of the situation. She was one of many.

Robin tapped the side of her water glass with the tip of her fork. "Now that everyone is here, and the line has gone down, let's all fill our plates at the buffet table."

Many in the room had already started eating. At the buffet tables, people circled the food and greeted friends they may not have known were there until they stood up. To Sunny, it was like a high school reunion, with friends she had known all her life. She was glad few had noticed she was there. It was the beginning of a joyous evening all around. It all felt so normal.

Sunny smiled as the three groomsmen eagerly lined up at the feeding trough. "Are men of this age always hungry?"

"Men of any age are always hungry," her mother agreed. "But the extra food often settles in their stomach rather than their biceps. Except, of course, your daddy." She smiled at Doug. "He's been the right size since I met him."

Sunny blushed when Nick winked at her. In the past, he had been around Sunny's family enough to remember that Grace and Doug appreciated each other.

Nick nodded to Sunny in the direction of the food. "Come on." He stood up and led her to the buffet tables laden with salads, vegetables, chicken strips, meatballs, and a large shrimp platter.

"So, Robin and Gary are finally getting married," Nick stated in a low, private conversation as they each took a plate from the stack.

Sunny looked around to see if Robin or Gary were nearby. "They were together all through college. After graduation, Gary went into the Marines. You knew Gary well enough to know the Marines were always his plan. Robin knew he was going to enlist, but she was still crushed. She got a teaching job here in Kettering and settled into a life of teaching. They wrote letters to each other every night."

"I'm glad to hear they stayed together," Nick whispered close to Sunny's ear.

His tone sounded like a double meaning, but Sunny didn't dare think about that. However, she wondered if Nick was only talking about Robin and Gary. Stepping aside to let Nick get in front of her in line, she teased, "You'd better fill a plate. It sounds like you're one of those men who need food."

Nick gave in and moved ahead. "Thank you, my dear. I know you. You'll make a major decision about every dish on the buffet. I'm too hungry to wait to see how you, a jury of one, will vote on each shrimp."

Then, a familiar voice spoke from behind her. "It's a great spread, don't ya think? The food looks delicious."

"Mel, it's good to see you again." Sunny was surprised. "When I met you before, you didn't say you were from Kettering. Or are you here only to enjoy the festivities? Grab a plate. I'll let you get in front of me."

Mel's smile was sheepish. "I'm waitin' for Josie. Besides, I wouldn't want to get between you and your beau." He looked around the sparkling room.

"My beau?" Sunny couldn't believe that someone she had just met could have had such a misperception. "Oh, you mean Nick? Well … I haven't seen him in years. He's not my boyfriend. He's just an old friend."

Mel walked beside her as she chose the reddest strawberries for her plate. He teased, "You could have fooled me." He said, exaggerating an expression of shock. "You two look like a great couple. Like you've been together for a long time. I would suggest you rethink your relationship, or lack of one, with Mr. Sullivan." Then he seemed to see someone he knew. "Oh, my. Nick and Mr. Drummond are in the same room."

Sunny stopped. "Mr. Drummond? Who's Mr. Drummond?"

"Drummond is the Superintendent of Schools here in Kettering," Mel explained in a secretive tone. "Gary's principal is being investigated for embezzlement of school funds. Something about a Boosters' Club. The superintendent might put Principal Stafford on unpaid leave until the investigation has been completed." Mel looked around to see if anyone was listening. "Rumor has it that Principal Stafford is hiring Nick Sullivan to represent him. Appearances are everything. It may be awkward for Drummond, Stafford, and Nick to socialize this evening."

That seemed odd to Sunny. "Has Stafford been arrested? Is he even accused of anything? I don't see how Principal Stafford could be suspended if the investigation is only beginning. Robin didn't tell me about any Teachers' Lounge gossip. But then, maybe Gary hadn't told her the most recent chatter, or she recognized it as gossip and chose not to spread it. How is it possible to lose your job due to gossip?"

"It may not be gossip," Mel said. "But I would think it would be uncomfortable for them to be together tonight."

"There's a little more to it than that," Sunny added. "I remember, Robin told me that she had invited them to the wedding. After all, Mr. Stafford is Gary's boss. Once the job interview is over and the teaching contract is signed, teachers have little contact with the School Administration Office. They probably would not have invited Superintendent Drummond and his wife to their wedding. But the Drummonds were invited because they are also friends of Robin and Gary from church. They are personal, not professional friends. Nick showed up this evening because he is a community leader and is involved in many activities around the city. How can that be a conflict of interest?"

"I suppose not," Mel said with a knitted brow. "But I'm so glad we talked about it." Then he smiled while looking over the fresh fruit on the buffet table. "There she is."

Sunny followed his gaze to the far corner of the room. "Where?"

"Where, what?" Nick asked as he looked around the banquet space.

Sunny stuttered as she tried to make sense of Mel's appearance. "Where … ah … do you live? I heard you live in Kettering. But I wondered why you didn't choose to settle in the area where you grew up?"

She held her breath to stay calm, not wanting him to see how flustered she felt by his presence. She had to calm down. Nick might feel uncomfortable if she blushed every time he looked at her. One of the calming songs she had written, to relax her nerves before a performance, ran through her head as Nick answered her question, and they talked together.

Nick turned to meet Sunny's smile. "I do live in Kettering. I bought a house I like a lot, on Far Hills Avenue." As he piled spare ribs on his plate, he turned and added, "You probably passed it when you drove in from the airport. If you're going to be in town for a few days,

I'll invite you to my home for dinner. I make a mean lasagna. You can see the house then."

Sunny hardly remembered that Mel had left to meet his wife. She was too focused on Nick to have divided attention. Nick's smile filled her with the same old feelings of belonging, of being home, that she felt in college, and fueled the excitement she was feeling even more now. *My home,* she repeated his words silently. It would be wonderful to experience home. Mel's wandering off again was forgotten.

Nick looked at the buffet and back at Sunny. "You taught me about wall colors and draperies, Shine. I remember our walks on wintery evenings when it was dark outside, but inside, Naperville living rooms were softly lit by the cozy flicker from brick-lined fireplaces. You would point out the elegant decorations you saw through their front windows, or the mistakes you thought the homeowners made in their decor. 'That color is too dark for the light that could come in during the daytime.' Or, 'Those drapes are way too gaudy. They don't match the furniture.' You called yourself the sidewalk interior designer. Shine, I decorated my house like I thought you would like."

Sunshine didn't know what to say, or if she should say anything. She loved his words, "I decorated like I thought you would." But it scared her, too.

Chapter Four
The Gala

Everyone at the Gala banquet laughed and visited with those around them as they ate. Some even returned to the buffet for second helpings. Nick made a return trip for dessert. There were too many offerings to resist the temptation to sample several tasty treats. Strawberry ladyfinger cake stood proudly in the center of the table. Blueberry cream pie and double chocolate brownies were just a few more that beckoned Nick to the table.

"You'll share, won't you?" Sunny coaxed. "All I want is a nibble." Sunny settled for one bite from each of the desserts Nick had selected. They ate, shared, and made a game of being together.

"You know I'll share anything with you." Nick broke off a piece of strawberry cake and slid it across the plate to Sunny. "There ya go. Goodness knows, when my spending money ran low in college, you would share with me." He handed her a napkin and pointed to some cake crumbs on her mouth. "We'd walk downtown, just to be alone for a while. My jeans pockets were empty, but my heart was full. You would say you were hungry for a banana split, and would I mind stopping? You'd say you would be happy to share with me. Then you'd eat a bite, claim you were full, and push it over to me."

Sunny looked down at the cake, needing to hide her true emotions. "I remember, Nick."

The clang of dishes being removed from the table signaled the transition to phase two of the evening's program. "I'll take that," a young volunteer offered as Nick nearly finished the pie.

"Let me have the last bite, Lannie," he said as he scooped the thick crust into his mouth.

"Lannie?" Sunny asked. "You know her?"

"I sure do." He chewed on the last blueberry. "She's my secretary's daughter. Lannie belongs to the Career Professionals Club at the high school. It gives them work experience."

Sunny scooped up the cake Nick offered, smiled, and popped it into her mouth. "Please leave my plate. I'm not quite finished with the chicken. Thank you, Lannie," Sunny said as the high school junior wiped off the table in front of them.

"You are very welcome, Sunny," the girl said pleasantly, and left Sunny's plate with a few bites of chicken left on the bone.

A man at the microphone broke into the final cleanup. "Ladies and gentlemen, girls, and boys, before we begin the program we had already planned, we have a surprise for you. We had no idea earlier, so you won't find this on your program, but ... Sunny Gaynor is with us this evening."

Those in the room erupted into hometown cheer, as they clapped their hands and stretched to see her. No one had asked for her autograph, and there were no uncomfortable stares. It may have been such an impossible thought that a music star would be in their midst that no one noticed Sunny among all the other people. Nick put his hand on her shoulder.

The emcee asked with a tone of hopefulness. "Is there any chance you'd bless us with your award-winning song, 'What If'? We've a pianist in the room who was scheduled to play for us later, and our guitar player will perform after we've eaten. The gang's all here," he said to a familiar-looking guitarist. "I'm sure he'll be willing to rearrange the program and play as planned, after Sunny entertains us."

"Sure," a man in a beige Western shirt said as he stood up halfway. He leaned his knuckles on the table and admitted, "But I don't know how anyone would hear me, following a voice like Sunny Gaynor's."

The audience clapped enthusiastically, with cheers of welcome. Two pre-teen girls in fancy party dresses bounced up and down on their seats.

Sunny didn't believe she was ready for a solo. Her constant performance mode had been turned off. She had almost allowed herself to forget that she was an internationally known singer. When she got off the airplane and drove into Dayton, she was just Sunshine Gaynor, Doug and Grace's daughter, a real person.

Sunny jumped up, faking the energy she always demonstrated in her music. In every performance, she was a powerhouse on stage, even if the song was slow and melancholy. Drawn back from the freedom of anonymity into the world as a public figure was like being sucked through a knothole in the fence that she had built to keep oglers from seeing her. Once she was dragged through the fence barrier, she found herself in the world of a thousand eyes.

What would Nick think of her song? She guessed he may have heard it, but she had never sung it in his presence. She wrote the song with Nick on her mind. He was always on her mind. She even had an inkling of him before they met. Sunny instantly remembered the evening before she left home for college.

~~*Memory*~~

The memory led her back to the summer after high school graduation. Upstairs, suitcases and cardboard boxes were filled with all she would need for her freshman year in college. Outside, the hot air was toasting the backyard grass, turning it a crisp beige. Sunny and her family were sitting around the table in the breakfast nook, eating dinner. Rerun was under the table with her head resting on Sunny's feet, ready to catch any bites that might fall.

Her dad teased, "Sunny, you just want to go to college to find a husband."

It wasn't true. She wanted a degree in music, not an M-r-s. Degree. But she knew something else. Deep inside, where ideas lay softly on her heart, she knew she would meet a guy in college and marry him. She laughed and joined in her father's fun. "Last Christmas, Santa told me I'd meet a guy named Nicholas and get married."

After she met him, she found it strange that Nick Sullivan's full name was Nicholas.

~~~~

</div>

There at the Gala, Sunny made her way to the microphone. She took a deep breath and began. "Good evening, everyone," she greeted warmly. "It's so good to see you all. Many of you are old friends." Scanning the audience, she brightened. "Darcie, hi!" she greeted with a
~~~~

wave. "Everyone, Darcie was my best friend. The girl across the street. How's your tennis game?"

"Good to see you, Sunny," Darcie shouted from a table near the back. "Thanks for our practices when we were kids. Last year, I placed third in the US Open Tennis Championship, my first year to compete."

"Fantastic! You'll show 'em all next time," Sunny said with a laugh. She turned to the emcee. "I'll be happy to sing if your guitar player will accompany me, too, and join me in the song."

"Guitarist and pianist will sing along." A woman in a red sundress slid onto the piano bench. She ran her fingertips over the keys, playing the major chords of Sunny's song, with runs and elaborate chords.

"Jenny!" Sunny squealed. When the man strummed the six strings of his Gibson electric guitar, she gasped again. "Frankie? It's you. Friends, when we were in high school together, Jenny, Frank, and I sang at weddings and even some Holiday at Home events. We were in the high school musicals together. Ladies and Gentlemen, it looks like we got the band back together again." Sunny laughed. "I never thought I'd be able to say those words."

As everyone laughed and clapped, Jenny began to play the introduction to "What If,"[2] the song Sunny had written and performed. It won her two Gold Records and, after several years, was still firmly planted at the top of the charts. Frankie softened the tone with the deeper bass chords of his guitar into a romantic song of love.

The lyrics raced through Sunny's mind. She had written each word for Nick. It was now many years later. She hoped he wouldn't make the connection. But Nick was the only man who found a place in her heart and stayed there. She was convinced he would know the song was written about him if she sang it there during the Gala. She would have to avoid looking in his direction. As the music played the familiar introductory bars, she closed her eyes and dreamed of "What If."

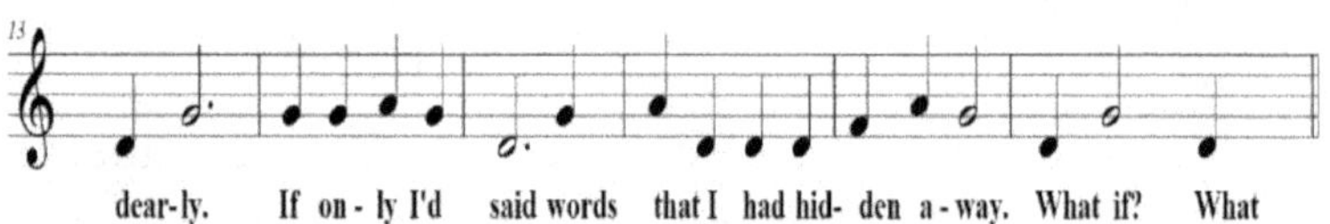

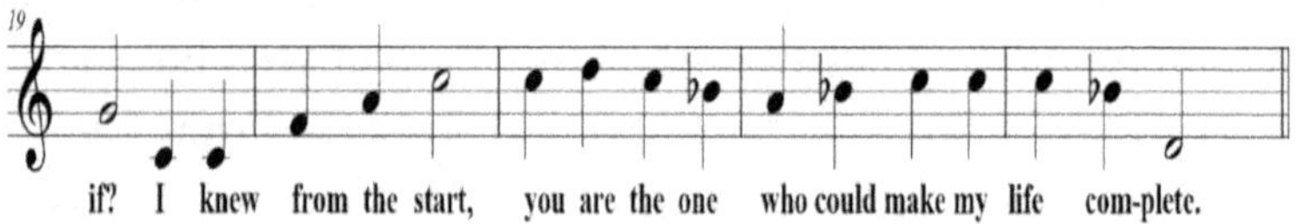

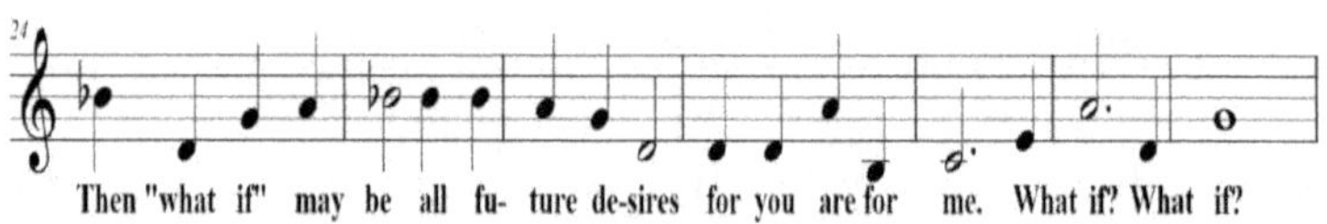

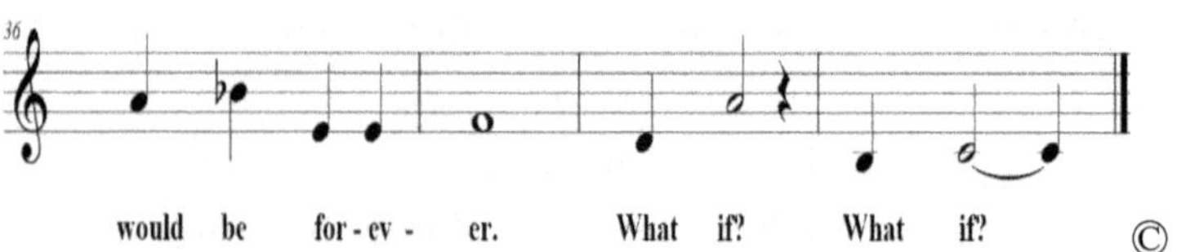

48

She couldn't help it. Sunny had to get Nick's reaction to her song. Would he know it was written about him? Would it please him, or would he feel trapped, or embarrassed? Maybe he'd even leave the Gala.

She opened her eyes as she let go of the last melodic note. Everyone cheered, but Nick said nothing. Tears rolled down his cheeks, refreshing his smile. When Sunny returned to her seat, Nick grabbed her, wrapping his arms around her.

"Shine, that was wonderful," Nick whispered in her ear. "I heard a message in the song. For tonight, I'd like to pretend the message was meant for me."

Chapter Five
The Evening

"Nick," a female voice interrupted before Sunny could respond to Nick. "I had no idea you knew Sunny Gaynor."

Nick turned and blinked. "Oh, Alissa, I didn't know you were here."

The woman smirked at him, then turned to Sunny. "Nick, aren't you going to introduce us?"

"Sure, sure," Nick stuttered. "Sunny, this is Alissa Bowser. She teaches English at the high school."

"Well, that's a fine introduction," Alissa snapped back. "Sunny, let me explain. Nick and I are often dinner partners at these events. Obviously," she glared discreetly at Nick, "not this one."

"Oh, yes." Sunny suddenly felt very awkward. She wondered if she had come between Nick and his girlfriend? She looked around at her family and blustered, "My mother asked Nick to join us."

"Of course," Alissa said in a superior tone. "I'm going home. Steven brought me this evening. If you're ready, Nick, I'll let you drive me home."

"I'm sorry, Alissa. I'm not ready yet," Nick apologized.

Sunny didn't know what to say or do. She hadn't seen Nick for so long; she would have loved to chat more. She wouldn't stay in town for long and didn't want to interfere in his life. She looked at Nick, then said in a pleasant tone, "You're welcome to join us if you want to stay."

Alissa seemed to search across the room. "There he is. I think Steven is ready to go, too. Nick, I'll see you at the Arts and Crafts Festival, perhaps. It should be a lovely day. Just taking a walk in the sunshine would be nice." She offered her hand to Sunny. "I'm glad I had a chance to meet you."

"Me, too," Sunny said as she took Alissa's hand. Her grip felt limp and distant. Sunny thought, *I feel the same way, Miss Bowser, teacher of high school English.*

A small ensemble gathered to the left of the head table and began playing bouncy music. Some couples started to dance, but not at the Gaynor table. Sunny played with her fork, tapping it on the edge of her plate. Bones from three chicken wings bounced a little as she kept time with the music. Another teen server came over and gathered up Sunny's dirty dishes.

"I'm sorry we missed your plate and silverware when we first cleared the table, Miss Gaynor."

Sunny smiled and touched her arm. "You didn't miss my plate. I am a very slow eater. And … Miss Gaynor is my sister. I'm Sunny."

The server raised her eyebrows in a surprised smile. "Yes, Sunny, thank you. I told my mom you would be a nice person."

"Thank you," Sunny said. Then she thought of how she had snubbed Alissa in her thinking and her interaction with her. *I guess I'm not always nice.*

Nick placed his hand on Sunny's. "I thought the hip-hop music would get you going, Shine. You love music with a beat. Those chicken bones got into the rhythm. They were bouncing on your plate and flying all over the table."

"Don't be silly," Sunny teased. "Chickens can't fly." When Nick removed his hand, she started twirling the straw in her glass of soda. Then she added, "Robin said the Staffords will be coming to the wedding." She stopped to study Nick's expression. "I also heard that Superintendent Drummond will be there, too, and you will represent Mr. Stafford in a legal matter. Will that be a problem, a conflict of interest, with you and the other two being there?"

"Thanks for the warning," Nick said. "It won't be a problem, but I wouldn't want Harrison or Ed to be surprised seeing me at the wedding. I'll call them and let them know what to expect."

Sunny was glad she told him. She didn't want to intrude on his business. Quietly, she swayed to the music the ensemble was playing.

Nick watched as Sunny bounced the ice around in her glass, first clockwise, then in reverse motion. He said, "The music will slow down to my speed in a few minutes. Will you want to dance?"

Sunny couldn't control the smile that snuck out on its own. Twirling a curl from her long, golden, auburn hair, she felt vulnerable. Would she give away how much she missed him if she allowed him to take her in his arms as they danced? He had to know after she sang her song. But Nick hadn't left Naperville. She had.

Nick didn't ask again. With only a smile, he stood up and offered his hand.

Sunny let him lead her onto the dance floor, a large circle with polished hardwood and a mirrored globe overhead. Neither Sunny nor Nick spoke. But she remembered.

~~*Memory*~~

She remembered that first evening at college when Tyler called for her to wait for Nick to walk with her to the auditorium. They chatted smoothly during the casual walk. Once inside, sitting beside Nick, with both of them leaning on the same armrest, they sang old familiar songs and learned some new ones. Most of all, she remembered the timbre of his baritone voice and how it blended with her own.

<div align="center">~~~~</div>

That evening at the Gala, dancing with Nick, it felt good in his arms just as it had so long ago. Now, their embrace felt the same. He wrapped his hand around hers and laid it on his chest. He was warm and solid muscle. They danced to the holiday music the rest of the evening.

Chapter Six
Sunday Morning

Sunny woke up the next day and gazed out the window. Sunday morning was glorious. The sparkling blue sky seen through her upstairs bedroom window had always been marvelous. As a child, she would lie at the end of her bed and watch the clouds and listen to the songs of birds. Now, it was eight-thirty, according to her faithful Barbie Alarm Clock Radio. She wondered why her mother kept the "wake me" timepiece. But it did make her room feel homey.

The church service would start at ten. Grandma and Grandpa Gaynor would meet them at nine forty-five in the church parking lot.

Her grandparents didn't usually attend the Church of the Cross on Wilmington Pike. Living in Greenville, about fifty miles north of Kettering, they worshiped in Darke County every Sunday. Grandma taught an adult Sunday school class. That weekend leading up to Robin's wedding changed everyone's schedule. The Labor Day activities made it a fancy, wedding destination, but Robin and Gary didn't have to go anywhere or arrange anything. An experienced city committee had already planned each event.

Sunny was soon ready for the day in a pink and red flowered sun dress and a white short-sleeved cardigan. Downstairs, she had enough time for a half cup of coffee.

"Honey, coffee isn't enough for breakfast," her mother reminded her. "When you were still in school, you wouldn't even eat cereal. Coffee has no nutritional value."

Sunny threw her head back in mock surrender. "You used to say that my glass of orange juice wasn't enough."

Grace winked. "Today, I would be happy with orange juice over coffee."

Sunny blew across the surface of her cup. "Robin, what's on your schedule after lunch? I have forgotten the usual holiday activities. It's been a while."

"It is all planned, lunch and even after that," Robin said as she finished her last bite of scrambled eggs. "Mom, these eggs are especially fluffy. Later, you'll have to show me how you do that." She blotted her mouth and added. "We're going to the Arts and Crafts show. Lucky for us, they'll have food trucks with all kinds of food for lunch."

"That sounds like fun." Sunny finished her coffee and took the cup to the dishwasher. "I don't know of any food trucks near my place in Manhattan. There's Tony and his hot dog wagon, a few blocks from my apartment, and the salted pretzel guy, but no trucks with several items on their menu. This will be a field trip for me."

Grace nodded and wiped off the kitchen counter. "We won't get to the food trucks until almost 1 o'clock. Everyone will be faint by then." She looked at Sunny, but didn't acknowledge that it would apply to her.

"Mom, I'll survive," Sunny said with a soothing smile in her mother's direction. "Maybe they'll serve doughnuts or chocolate chip cookies in the fellowship hall after the service like they used to."

"They still do," Doug said, putting his breakfast dishes into the dishwasher.

Sunny smiled as she watched the dance of the kitchen. "Mom, it looks like you have Daddy well trained."

"Arf, arf," her dad barked. "And this dog knows where the cookies are kept in the church's Fellowship Hall. I have sniffed them out."

"Let's go." Robin grabbed her napkin and tossed it into the wastepaper basket. "Gary and the rest of the wedding party will meet us at the church in a few minutes."

Grace checked the clock above the sink. "Your grandparents will pull into the parking lot in ten minutes."

John and Claudia Gaynor married at a young age and moved to a farm in Greenville, Ohio, down the road from Grandpa John's aunt and uncle. Grandpa met Grandma through his cousin, who grew up on the farm across the road from his uncle's home, in the rich, dark soil of Darke County. One summer, Grandpa spent four weeks with his aunt and uncle to help them on the farm after Uncle George had a farm accident with his tractor. Grandpa's cousin's best friend was Claudia Sanders, in the white farmhouse across the street. His uncle's cows had to be milked, fed, and their bedding replaced daily. That's why Grandpa John was there. But he believed his visit was more of a blessing to meet Claudia than to muck out the barn.

Grandpa originally grew up in the Beavertown area of Kettering. The red brick church of his boyhood, with its stained-glass windows and cross-topped bell tower, was the center of his life. His morning high school Sunday school class and evening Youth Fellowship met in the room nestled high in the bell tower. But that was long ago. The red brick church had been torn down to make space for the new, modern church sanctuary and classroom complex.

The old brick church had been torn down long before Sunny was born, but she missed it. Maybe it was the stories her grandfather told, of happy family Sundays, that tugged at her heart. Or, perhaps it was her aging grandparents and what the years ahead would bring that held her feelings trapped inside. The only safe way for her to express her love was through the hymns she sang as a child, the songs she wrote, and the love that spilled out when she sang them.

Sunny's dad pulled into the parking lot, and they all watched as people came to worship. Seeing the members again was exciting for Sunny. They were indeed a family.

"Grandpa!" Sunny squealed when she jumped out of her car with Robin behind her. "Grandma!" she added as she embraced them both. "It's so good to see you. You both look amazing."

"Gary," Robin said as he pulled in a space and parked his car. When he jumped out, Robin gave him a polite, church parking-lot-hug.

Sunny kissed Gary's cheek. "Thanks for loving my sister." What she didn't say was how much she had recently become aware that there was no one in her life to hug at the end of the day. Loneliness had caught up to her.

Gary returned a peck on Sunny's cheek. "I thought you might have brought a plus-one with you."

"There are too many pluses," she admitted as a joke. "They're everywhere. But there's no plus-one-and-only."

Gary looked surprised as they walked into the church. "Not even a plus-maybe?"

"Not even a plus-not sure." Sunny took Robin's other arm as the sisters locked step and walked inside.

As the service progressed, Sunny thought about how much every aspect of the bulletin meant to her. She occasionally attended church in New York, but her schedule made it difficult. Or, her many hours in the air were a good excuse for staying in bed on Sunday morning. Just like her entire life's work thus far, it was the choir music and congregational singing that touched her heart and allowed her to express love.

Pastor Tom Morton's message hit a spot Sunny needed to soothe. The scripture from Matthew 6:24 meant the most. "No one can serve two masters. Either you will hate the one and love the other, or you will be devoted to the one and despise the other. You cannot serve both God and money."

Sunny felt uncomfortable hearing those words. *But I don't serve money*, she argued inside. *Yes, I earn a lot of money, but I love to sing. It makes people happy. For me, the verse should read, "You will love applause and hate silence."* Tears gathered in her eyes. She blotted them with a tissue to block their escape. A few lines of the third verse to "O Love That Will Not Let Me Go" brought more tears to her eyes. She didn't know why.

I trace the rainbow through the rain,

And feel the promise is not vain that morn shall tearless be. [3]

Chapter Seven
The Gathering

The church's fellowship hall hadn't changed, yet it had. The room had been freshly painted, and new banners decorated the walls with messages of faith. For the holiday weekend, one banner had red, white, and blue flags with the inscription, "Blessed is the nation whose God is the Lord, the people whom he has chosen as his heritage!" Psalm 33:12. It felt familiar and homey.

"Are you Sunny Gaynor?" a cute little girl with long blond hair asked. She appeared to be about seven years old.

A second girl, with shiny black pigtails, nudged her friend. "Of course she is. I'm Shaneah. I'm seven, and this is my friend, Lizzy. Can we have your autograph?"

"Shaneah!" a woman gasped. "Don't bother Miss Gaynor." She turned to Sunny. "I am so sorry."

"But, Mom," Shaneah whined.

"No complaining. It's not ladylike," Shaneah's mom warned her in a quiet tone and eyes that were loving but firm.

"Rebecca?" Sunny couldn't believe it. Rebecca had been one of her best friends in high school. Now here she was, answering to "Mom" to a seven-year-old. "Oh, my goodness. It is you."

Rebecca's eyes brightened. She put her hand over her mouth in surprise. "Sunny, do you recognize me?"

"Rebecca, are you kidding? Of course, I do." Sunny started to hug her and then waited as she studied her friend's reaction. Would her longtime friend accept the friendship of someone whose face appears on magazines in the checkout lane of the grocery store?

"It's so good to see you, Sunny." Rebecca finally exhaled and hugged Sunny first. "I'm surprised you knew my name."

Sunny returned her embrace, then reached down and hugged Shaneah. "This is your daughter?"

"She sure is, Sunny," a tall, handsome man joined in, "and she looks just like her dad, me."

"Kevin?" Sunny was doubly surprised. "Rebecca, you had a thing for Kevin all through high school. Now look at you two."

"It was mutual," Kevin admitted. "Hi, Sunny. It has been a long time." He gave her a side hug. "Rebecca and I got married the summer after we graduated from high school, when you went off to college. Rebecca and I got our degrees at Wright State University, here in the area. After a few years, Shaneah came along. Rebecca and I took turns working and babysitting. It was hectic but wonderful. We both knew we were building a life together, a family. I teach middle school, and she has a successful real estate business. And, look again. We'll increase our family with a second baby in six months."

"Rebecca," Sunny hugged her again, "I'm jealous."

"Of me?" Rebecca gasped. "You have to be kidding. Sunny, how can someone who is known by most of the people in the world be jealous of me? You're the one who has everything."

Sunny became quiet, then said softly, "That's the second time I've heard something like that. I love singing the songs I write, but that's not everything. The longer I'm home, I'm discovering that there is much more to life than a music career. And you and Kevin have found it. You're building a life together. I am so happy for you two."

Lizzy handed Sunny the two three-by-five cards her mother gave her to take Sunday school notes. "When Mama gets home from work, we make cups of really good hot chocolate with marshmallows, sit at the kitchen table, and I teach her the Bible lesson from this morning." She searched her pocket. "Do you have a pencil? I can't find mine."

"I have a pen," Sunny said as she pulled one from her purse. "Now, let me think. Something special for a special girl." On Lizzy's card, she wrote, "Dear little Lizzy, dance 'til you're dizzy. Twirl and twirl. God loves you, Lizzy girl. Sunny Gaynor." Shaneah's words were similar: "Shaneah, loved by your father above, and your parents here. Let God know you love him, Dear. Sunny Gaynor."

Both of the girls beamed. "Thank you," they sang out in a duet.

"And I thank you," Sunny echoed back. "When you asked for an autograph, that brought your mama over. I'm glad to see her again." She looked around, asking Lizzy, "Are your parents here?"

Lizzy's gaze fell. "No," she dragged out. "My daddy died, and Mama is a nurse. She works all weekend at the hospital. Then she works at Doctor Billy's office during the week. Shaneah's family picks me up for church."

"Well, I think it's wonderful you're here," Sunny said, smiling at Rebecca. "Becca, you already increased your family by two more, Lizzy and her mom."

Rebecca nodded lovingly. "We are a part-time eclectic family."

"There's my breakfast." Sunny pointed to a table with platters full of delicious-looking cookies. She selected a cookie from the closest serving plate and bit into a chocolaty treat. "You are a loving family, Becca."

Rebecca also selected one of Mrs. Baker's fantastic chocolate chip cookies. "I know they have to be Mrs. Baker's," she said as she closed her eyes and melted into its goodness. "She's the only one who can make cookies this good." Becca took another bite. "Are you going to be in town very long?"

"I wish I could stay longer," Sunny said as she chomped into her breakfast cookie. "But I'll only be here through next weekend, for my sister, Robin's wedding."

"I know she's getting married. We have been attending the same Bible study group. She invited Kevin, Shaneah, and me to the service and reception." Shaneah and Lizzy started counting the cookies by putting their "pointy" finger on each one. Becca took Shaneah by one hand and Lizzy by the other. "Girls, settle down. The Gathering after church is where you practice being a lady, not a baby dog. Puppies will lick every treat until they decide on one, then devour them all."

The girls' expressions dropped. Lizzy asked, "Do I act like a lady with a sad face like this, Miss Rebecca?" She exaggerated a droopy smile and wrinkled forehead.

"No, Sweetheart, look around. Being a lady doesn't mean being sad. It means being happy in a polite way, respectful of the other people around you."

"I like you, Miss Rebecca," Lizzy giggled and kissed Becca's hand. "You explain everything. Sometimes, Mama's too tired."

"I like you, too, Lizzy. In fact, I love you," Rebecca said with a little hug. To Sunny, she added, "Isn't it great that we are safe to love everyone?"

Sunny was amazed. "Love everyone? What if it isn't safe to love everyone? What if they don't love you back?"

"Love was never intended to be given only if you get it back," Rebecca said as she looped her arm through Sunny's. "You taught me that. Some of your songs describe not being afraid to give love away."

"I know." And Sunny did know this on a surface level. "What if you love someone and they don't love you? Wouldn't that hurt?"

"I'm a realtor, not a theologian or psychologist," Robin admitted. "But, to me, we are surrounded by a sea of love. We inhale love and exhale love. The more we try to hold it in, so we don't get hurt, the more we clog ourselves physically and emotionally, with stagnant emotions that fester inside as disappointment, anger, fear, pain ... you name it, as well as physical problems."

"Wow," Sunny said in amazement. "You're a therapist, Becca."

"No," she laughed and shook her head. "I unlock doors and let people into their new homes, and into the possibility of changing their future."

"Hi, Rebecca," a blond-haired beauty greeted. "Good morning ... Sunny," she cooed sarcastically.

Sunny looked at the woman up and down. Her clothes were expensive, and her necklace was a good-sized solitaire diamond. Sunny recognized her right away, but how could that be possible? "April? April Commons?"

The woman smelled like an expensive Dior perfume, with opulent, sensual tones. Even though Sunny could afford it, with so many people allergic to scents, she rarely wore perfume. She decided that fans couldn't smell her from the back of a packed arena.

The woman didn't smile. Looking down her nose, she answered, "I'm not common anymore, Sunny. I'm Mrs. Harrison Stafford, April Stafford. My husband is the principal of the high school."

Sunny was shocked and felt a hot blush crawl up her neck. She remembered a strubbly-haired, dirty-blonde girl in a tattered shirt and pants who got on the school bus near the end of the route. She and Sunny were twelve years old at the time. April had pierced her ears. The hole had dirty string hanging out of it, streaked with blood. The self-pierced earlobe was infected and oozed pus. On Sunday mornings, April and her five younger brothers and sisters were dropped off at the church for Sunday school. Sunny didn't know who brought them. She tried to get to know her, but it was a slow process. April pulled herself inside her turtle shell and only came out occasionally.

The new April Sunny saw that Sunday morning, so many years later, was amazing. She was still an introvert. Sunny suspected April never let others see her when she projected the pain and embarrassment she experienced as a child. Sunny gently took her arm. "It is so good to see you again, April. I have been admiring your lovely necklace."

"Isn't it beautiful?" a professional-looking man said. He appeared to be at least ten years older than April. But she held herself in such a tall, elegant manner, when he came over, she surprised Sunny. The man added, "Tell Sunny about your new financial adventure and the rewards you receive."

"Sunny, I'd like you to meet my husband, Harrison Stafford." April's eyes beamed as she linked her arm in her husband's. "Honey, you tell it so much better." She smiled, embarrassed again.

"If that's what you want," he said in fun, and put his arm around her waist. "We've been saving a lot for a summer cottage. April wanted to have extra money to buy some beautiful jewelry. She said her mother's pieces were divided among all six children."

April's eyes darted to Sunny. In Sunny's polished manner, dealing with erratic fans and pesky paparazzi, she learned to interact with a wide variety of people without a change in her expression. Sunny wondered if April had ever told Harrison about her humble beginnings.

Harrison gently touched April's necklace. "Some of the teachers got together to form an investment group. Those who know how to invest are there to help those new to the adventure. Investing as a group, they can get into opportunities they wouldn't have been able to invest in with less money. April invests a little of the money her parents left her each time the group meets. She buys a new bobble about every three months." He gestured to her brilliant necklace. "Gus Walters, the group's leader, is a friend of mine from high school. He certainly knows the investment business. He has an office suite in a building downtown, Walters' Wallet Investors, and a podcast."

April smiled and admitted, "Harrison, Gus told me you two weren't such great friends in high school."

"My goodness," Rebecca said with a knowing look of surprise. "Long-abandoned secrets are finally coming out."

"That's the truth, Rebecca," Harrison agreed. "It all comes out eventually. Indeed, we were not close as teens. We both wanted the same leadership positions: president of the senior class, and quarterback on the varsity team were just two of them. There were more."

Sunny nodded. "It seems like you both managed to secure community leadership roles as adults. You just chose different songs to sing."

April finally smiled at Sunny. "Music is the language of your life, isn't it?"

Sunny threw her head back in surrender. "It is, April. I hadn't thought about it in those terms."

Rebecca let go of the little girls' hands and pointed them to their Sunday school teacher as the teacher herded the incoming second graders to their class.

"We'd better go too, April," Mr. Stafford said as he checked his watch. "We're new to this church." He explained, "April said she and her family used to go here for a while. She only returned after we were married. We haven't chosen a Sunday school class yet. We promised to go to my parents' home in Centerville for lunch. We'd better get moving."

"It was good to see you again, April," Sunny said and smiled. She liked the new April. "It was nice to meet you, Mr. Stafford."

"Please," he responded, shaking Sunny's hand. "Call me Harrison."

"I will, Harrison," Sunny saluted.

Rebecca watched as Sunny said goodbye. "Are you sure you don't need a lovely home, here in your hometown? Must you live in New York?"

Sunny blinked, realizing that she could be a real person. She began to entertain a completely new thought. "I have always thought I should live in New York, near Central Park. It would be a symbol of success. But it's not. It's a lonely place for me. I have no family there. I'm not in

New York long enough to become active in the neighborhood, so I don't know anyone except the people in the recording studio. Most of the time, I'm only in my apartment to rest up after a long concert tour."

"You could do that anywhere." Rebecca reached into her pocket and pulled out a small card. "Here's my office phone and address. We could have a girls' day out if you want to go house hunting. Looking at beautiful, clean, polished homes, all prepared for sale, can be a lot of fun."

Sunny was speechless. Perhaps, where she lived would make no difference in today's music scene. That had never occurred to her before. She knew she had heard someplace: "If you want to be successful, move to New York City." She smiled, remembering some old song lyrics: *If I can make it there, I'll make it anywhere. It's up to you, New York, New York.*[4] But she had made it, everywhere, and had only used the living room wall of her New York City apartment to hold her Gold Records.

"I'll think about it," Sunny said as Becca started to walk toward one of the adult classes. Sunny's cell phone rang with Bruce's unique ring tone, and the image of her agent appeared on the screen. Flipping her phone to Do Not Disturb, she said, "I'll call him back later." She waved Rebecca's business card in her direction. "I don't have to think about the girls' day out. That's a definite yes. I'll call you. But I'll have to think about house hunting." She thought to herself, *A home at home. Wow.*

Chapter Eight
A Trucked-in Lunch

Sunny was excited to be the soloist and maid-of-honor in Robin's wedding. She even liked the beautiful, fun dresses Robin and the other two bridesmaids, Holly and Quin, had selected for the attendants. It was a sleeveless, soft robin's egg blue dress with a flared skirt and a modest neckline. The fun part was the lightweight, sparkling white denim, Levi-style jacket with traditional, highly polished silver buttons. Sunny's dress didn't even need alterations. Everything was perfect. Well, not everything. Her solo was a problem. She hadn't finished writing the important song.

She had promised Robin she would write a new piece for the ceremony. And she tried ... over and over, she tried. Nothing seemed right to her. She didn't doubt Robin's love for Gary. By the time Sunny enrolled in college, Robin and Gary were already in love. Sunny's inability to write the new song for the wedding had nothing to do with doubting their relationship. It had everything to do with her fear of getting too close to real love.

Guilt overwhelmed her as she rode home from church that Sunday. She wouldn't be writing the song that afternoon either. Everyone in the wedding party, her parents, and her grandparents, were all going to the craft show. Gary's parents would meet them there. It wasn't Robin's fault that Sunny had no time to create. She knew the itinerary for the wedding party and all the fun that had been planned long before she left New York.

Everyone had decided to change their clothes. Returning to the house, Sunny began wondering what she would wear for the afternoon. She only brought the number of tops, pants, and dresses that would fit in her suitcase. Still, she was ready in a flash. Learning to change her costume rapidly had been a talent she had learned a long time ago, while changing costumes for various themed segments of her concerts.

Fraze Pavilion in Kettering was the perfect place for the Arts and Crafts show. And the day couldn't have been better. Jewelry makers and those gifted in creating items of earthy-smelling leather were only a few of those who had set up merchandise displays. Even if no one purchased anything from the creative crafters, the day in the sun would be enough to make it a perfect outing. Finally, after walking around the Pavilion and, enjoying each booth she passed, Robin made an announcement.

"Gather around, everybody." When all the chatter stopped, she said, "I know we're all hungry. We'll find our lunch here, among the various food trucks. You decide what you want to eat." She pointed to a cluster of picnic tables under a stand of shade trees. "We'll gather over there. When everyone finishes eating, Gail Schmidt has a wonderful booth of handmade pottery items. For your wedding party gift of appreciation, I invite you to select one of Gail's amazing pieces. She has items that will interest both bridesmaids and groomsmen. Gail and I have already worked out the financial end of the transaction. They are my gift of thanks to you. But now, let's eat."

The group spread out among the food trucks of tacos, chicken wings, and pork chops. A variety of side dishes included a strange mix of elephant ears, loaded potato fries, and giant pretzels with warm cheese sauce for dipping.

Behind Sunny, a voice said, "I hear the fries are great."

She was startled. "Nick, I didn't see you anywhere. You always manage to sneak up behind me." She got in line to place her order at one of the trucks.

Nick winked. "I would find you anywhere."

"Anywhere?" Sunny asked and poked his ribs. "There was a morning at a laundry mat in Naperville, if you remember. Granted, we had only met the week before, but we had spent every available moment together after that." She twirled a curl around her finger. "That day, I had my hair in curlers and wore no makeup. I planned to try a vintage hairstyle when I returned to the dorm. You and Tyler came in the Speedy Wash to do your laundry. I kept smiling and winking at you. It took Tyler to tell you that the 'flirt' on the other side of the room was actually me." She laughed and poked him again.

"I needed glasses back then," Nick excused himself.

"And now?" Sunny teased. "Do you still need them?"

"Contacts." He batted his eyes. "I have contacts."

A seven-year-old girl with bright blue eyes interrupted by pulling Nick's hand. "I finally decided. I want chicken wings."

Sunny's smile faded. "You said you weren't —" Her heart sank as an entire scene of Nick's probable happy home life, with his wife and child, unfolded in her imagination.

"Married?" He watched the little girl bounce over to get in line at the Wings Over Dayton truck. "No, Shine. She isn't my daughter. That's Maddie, my niece. My sister and her husband are touring England and France, celebrating their fifteenth anniversary. Maddie is spending those two weeks with me."

Sunny felt like her heart had been freed from the anvil that sat on her chest. "Oh." She finished coming up for air and redirected the conversation to the adorable little girl. "School will be in session on Tuesday. Does Maddie go to school here in Kettering?"

"Yep," Nick said as he held up his index finger to notify Maddie that he would be right there. "Beavertown Elementary. I take her to school on my way to the courthouse on days I have business there. Then I leave the office early to pick her up at the end of the day. I could call the bus garage and have a school bus take her and bring her back, but I enjoy chauffeuring her around town."

Sunny was surprised. "You can just walk out of the office whenever you want to?" There was no opportunity for her to take time off. Once her demanding concert tour schedule was planned, there were planes to catch, ticket times to honor, and fans to entertain.

Nick laughed softly. "It's my office, Shine. I can keep whatever schedule I choose. And my office is attached to my home. Maddie can come to the office with me if I have appointments that can't be changed. I have a variety of coloring books, crayons, markers, and colored paper in project packets in a kids' cabinet in the waiting room. She can create whatever she wants on the low table near the couch. The glass surface holds up well with the use of scissors and paste. Or, she can go into the house and watch television until I finish. My secretary watches her if she's in the living room. It's no fun to be in an empty house alone."

"Or an empty apartment," Sunny whispered under her breath. She was amazed at how Nick had worked it all out. She had no children around to mentor or enjoy. This was the same Nick she had known before, but even so much more. He had matured evenly. "You are a devoted uncle."

He tipped his head a little. "Shine, family is everything."

Sunny looked back at her family, who had already started eating. *Family is everything.* Then she continued arguing with herself. *Then why haven't I been here and cherished the years they have?*

She stepped up to the order window as he attended to his niece. "Nick," she called after him, "why don't you and Maddie join us?"

"Sure," he agreed as their eyes met. His voice softened, "That would be great."

"We're going to the pottery booth after we finish," she told him. "You and Maddie can walk along with us for that, too, if you want."

"Oh, yes, yes, yes," Maddie jumped in. "The kids at school won't believe I spent Sunday afternoon with Sunny Gaynor."

Sunny stole a look at Nick. Would he agree, or look for a way to escape? "It's really up to you, Uncle Nick." She quickly dreamed up an excuse for Nick to bow out graciously. To Maddie, she explained, "Maybe he has some important work to finish before Monday in court."

Nick smiled a teasing grin. "Tomorrow is Labor Day. The courthouse is closed."

Sunny said nothing at first. Her heart warmed as she thought of Nick's humor. She remembered the "Nick jokes" well, so she created her own. "Whereas the afore mentioned Attorney Sullivan hath consulted the authentic calendar of the day, and found tomorrow's date to be the first Monday in September, and whereas Congress created a national holiday in 1894, a day of rest, and called it Labor Day, a bill which President Grover Cleveland signed into law, and ordered that it be celebrated on that date in September, it is determined that Attorney Sullivan is correct. Tomorrow is Labor Day."

Nick's eyes glistened in fun. "Now you're making fun of my career."

"Me?" Sunny gasped. "Never."

Maddie was still waiting, with her hands folded together. "I don't know what you said, but, Uncle Nick, can we hang around with Sunny today?"

Nick patted the girl's shoulder. "Okay. We can hang. If Sunny agrees not to bully me anymore."

"I never bully anyone, Nick Sullivan, as you should know." She squared her shoulders. "I was just trying to learn your foreign language so we can communicate."

Nick winked at Maddie. "Let's get our food and eat. Later, we have tickets to tour Hawthorn Hill, the home of Orville Wright. Our tickets are for the 3 p.m. tour. I'm sure, you being who you are, that you could get in with us."

Sunny wasn't sure. "I hate to jump the line."

"Okay," he decided, "you can have my ticket, and I'll jump the line. I'm not above pulling rank."

"You can call them and add me to your party."

"Good," Maddie said, "Uncle Nick, maybe they have a family rate."

Sunny only smiled at Maddie. Words were stuck in a spot between fear of love and fear of letting go.

A server in one of the trucks handed Sunny her plate. It was piled high with crisp, sizzling chicken wings, coleslaw, and a side order of an elephant ear as big as Dumbo's and dusted well with powdered sugar. "Nick, I'll sit here while you and Maddie get your food." She threw her leg over the picnic bench and watched for Nick to return. *Was he just being polite? Will he slip off and eat somewhere else?*

"You can sit beside Sunny," Nick said to Maddie as they returned to the table. "I want to be across from her so I can see her beautiful face."

"You are pretty, Sunny," Maddie agreed. "I hope I'm pretty someday."

"Maddie, you are pretty now," Sunny said, putting her finger under Maddie's chin. "I know you will grow up to be a beautiful woman."

Maddie was wide-eyed. "I will? How do you know?"

Sunny paused for a second and smiled. "Because God is love and love is beautiful, and you are a child of God. That makes you beautiful, too."

Nick put down his fork and mouthed, "Thank you." Then he pointed to Sunny. "Beautiful."

She mouthed in return, "Thank you."

"Thank you for what?" Maddie questioned.

"For your uncle being a gentleman. He said that I am pretty, too."

"See, I told you," Maddie confirmed.

Sunny's agent rang again, but she didn't want to answer his call while enjoying Nick's company. "I'll answer that later."

"Why don't you take your call over there?" Nick said as he pointed to one of the other tables. "I'll go back and pick out a dessert."

Nick took Maddie's hand as she pulled him toward the food trucks. "Slow down," he said with a laugh. "We'll both get dessert. But don't take long to decide. Our food will get cold."

"Hi, Bruce," Sunny spoke into the phone. "What's so urgent?"

"Great news. Fantastic!" Bruce continued to bubble over. "The producer of a new film called me. They want to use your song, 'What If,' in the movie they're planning. We have to let them know right away. They want to start filming soon, and the music will be a major theme in the movie."

"Wow!" All kinds of questions and possibilities flooded her mind. "What does that mean for me? Will I have to be involved in any way?"

"They'll want you to leave Tuesday and fly out to discuss your involvement. It would take a special musical arrangement of 'What If.'"

"No, Bruce, no." Sunny was more than impatient. She was angry. "I am here to participate in my sister's wedding."

"She'll understand." Bruce's tone was so smooth it was almost oily. "If she truly loves you, she'll know what you need to do."

"Don't you dare manipulate me, Bruce McDaniels." Her anger mounted. "Is this how it's always been? Have you twisted me around your finger for —?" She saw Nick and Maddie returning to the table. "Gotta go."

"Wait—" Bruce called out before she disconnected.

"Sunny?" Nick questioned as he put the sweet-smelling treat on the table. Seeing her face, he asked, "What's wrong?"

"I got a call from my agent," she said, but said no more.

He spread out the various food items. "Bad news?"

"The worst and the best," Sunny said, pushing her food around on the paper plate.

"Oh, my goodness," Nick said as he studied her face some more.

"It'll be okay, Sunny," Maddie soothed. "Good food heals all things. At least that's what Mama says."

Sunny knew she would have to shake it off. She didn't like the way she felt, and she certainly didn't want someone to take all the fun out of her trip home. "Maddie, I think you're right." She pulled some meat off the chicken bone and popped it in her mouth. "And, this is very good food."

Nick smiled supportively. "Do you want to talk about it?"

"The chicken or the phone call?" she asked, mischievously.

"I'd say the chicken, but you know I'm talking about the phone call."

"Absolutely not," she snapped back. Gasping, she put her head down and her hands to her forehead. *What have I done? I've just shut him out.* "No, Nick, no. It's not that I don't want to talk to you about it. I'm afraid I'll throw up my lunch, or throw it at someone."

"Yuck," Maddie sighed and stirred her food.

"My thought exactly." Sunny squared her shoulders and sat up straight. Tearing off more chicken, she popped it in her mouth. "I'm not going to think about my silly agent. I will dwell on the good news and decide if I'll accept the bad with it. Now, I am going to enjoy my meal. How about you, Miss Maddie?"

"I'm almost finished," the little one boasted.

Nick stared at her plate. "How did you do that?

"I ate," Maddie explained. "You guys talked."

Sunny laughed. "That would make a difference." She dipped her fork into the coleslaw. "This is good." Looking at Maddie's plate, she added, "You didn't get any."

Maddie boasted. "I ate three chicken wings, and I'm half done with this big soft pretzel and cheese."

"Are you sure you chewed as you ate?" Nick asked as he nearly finished his meal.

"Look," Maddie said as she opened her mouth. "See. I'm chewing."

Sunny set her discomfort aside and laughed. "I can't keep up with you, Young Lady."

She wanted to talk about the movie offer. Nick would be the perfect one to ask. As a lawyer, he could answer any legal questions. As a friend, he could sort out the family stuff. But she would not allow Bruce to ruin any of her vacation time. And there was a time, long ago, when Sunny wondered if Nick would be there for her. She cleaned up her plate, folded her hands in her lap, and said, "I'm done."

~~Memory~~

"I'm done," Sunny remembered saying over ten years ago as she finished her lunch in the dorm. "Gotta run. Mr. Zimmer wants everyone there by 2 p.m. for the choir concert this afternoon. I still have to change into my white blouse. That's the uniform of the day, white shirt and black skirt or pants."

It was her usual Sunday afternoon. Lunch in the dormitory dining room with all her friends. But this time, she had arranged to meet Nick after the choir program in the front lobby of the large college concert hall.

Sunny and several choir members walked down to the auditorium together. She didn't see Nick before they all processed onto the stage. But he said he would be there. She was used to her family doing as they had promised. When, after the concert, Nick wasn't anywhere around, she was brokenhearted.

After the last song was sung and the lobby gradually emptied, Sunny was finally left alone in the dim light of the entry hall.

When Tyler darted through, he stopped. "Sunny?" Seeing her cry, he asked, "What's wrong?"

Ordinarily, she wouldn't have spoken negatively about a friend, or in this case, a boyfriend. But she was hurt, and everything tumbled out. Music was how she spoke, how she breathed. "Nick promised to meet me here after we performed. He hasn't come."

Tyler was a good guy. "If you're going to the dorm-lounge party at our place, I'll walk with you."

As they walked, Sunny was quiet.

~~~~

That may have been when she started holding important feelings in even more tightly. She continued to have a lot of practice, as fans approached her, interrupting conversations, meditation time, and making plans. She learned to hide in her apartment, away from everyone and everything, to think and create. She became more and more alone in her thoughts as she stood more and more in the spotlight.
~~~~

Chapter Nine
Throw Me A Pot

"Where are we going now?" Maddie asked excitedly as they walked through the Arts and Crafts booths. There were hand towels for the kitchen, unique, handmade jewelry pieces, and pottery in the area around the food trucks. Maddie pointed to a booth labeled "Cathy's Creations." Running her fingers over the stacks of doll clothes, some for Barbie, many for American Girl dolls, and knit booties for baby dolls, caused her to dance around the exhibit. "Can I? Can I? Can I?" she begged.

Nick tipped his head back and laughed. "Well, yeah."

Sunny enjoyed Nick's generous reaction and asked Maddie, "What kind of doll do you have?"

"Mama gave me the American Girl doll she had when she was a kid—Molly." Maddie sifted through the clothes and found the perfect attire for her beautiful doll: a gold exercise outfit, a soft red dress, and a tan woolen cape. "Are these too many, Uncle Nick? Molly could use a new pair of glasses, too."

Nick said, "That's fine."

Sunny's mind darted back to the day they took the commuter train into the city. "Do you remember when we went into Chicago and shopped at Marshall Field's? We went to a baseball game at Wrigley Field, then shopped until the stores closed. I was looking for a special dress for Mom and Dad's twenty-fifth wedding anniversary. I bet I tried on a dozen that day."

"Really?" Nick said. "I could have sworn it was more like two dozen."

She looked at him, perplexed. "Are you serious?"

"Yep," he leaned close. "The one you bought was amazing."

Sunny got lost again in precious memories. "Thank you, kind Sir."

"No, I thank you," Nick said. Then, looking past Sunny, he added. "I see someone I know."

Sunny turned as Harrison and April Stafford came up. "April? I've known her since her family moved into a house on my school bus route when we were about twelve."

"We've known each other for a long time," April said.

Nick raised his hand, greeting the Staffords. "Good to see you."

April reached out her hand to Nick. "I'm April … Mrs. Stafford. Harrison just met Sunny today at church."

"Yes, I'm glad to meet you," Nick said. "Your husband has told me about you. I'm Nick Sullivan, his attorney."

"Oh yes," April answered. A slight blush crossed her face. "I wasn't able to come to the first meeting you had with Harry. I was in Columbus."

"It's good to see you, Nick," Harrison said. "I'll see you next week."

"Right," Nick answered as the couple left.

"She is a beautiful woman," Sunny whispered. "She was a mess as a kid." Then she stopped when she realized how that sounded. "I'm not saying that to be mean. April was born before her dad left for the war. When he didn't come home, her mother remarried. She and her new husband had five more children, but her stepdad wasn't a good provider. He drank heavily, and that tore him apart inside and mentally. He worked off and on, but not steadily. And the drinking continued. Their house was like the city scrap yard." Sunny paused and shook her head. "Now … she is amazing. Both of her parents are gone now. But I don't think April told her husband about her youth."

"Oh, wow," Nick gasped. "Everyone in your graduating class would have known about her past, wouldn't they?"

"Sure. And her dad hid nothing. Why do you ask?"

"The police," Nick answered with a furrowed brow. "And the prosecutor may say that Stafford embezzled money to let April make up for all she didn't have as a kid."

"I hope not. I like them," Sunny said. Then she offered, "If there is anything I can do, just let me know."

"I will." Nick nodded toward another craft table. "Look at those fussy, fowl. I didn't realize people were dressing porch-geese again. I think I'd rather talk about geese than glitz."

Maddie sorted through all the goose outfits that hung on rods inside the tented booth. "Do you have a porch-goose, Sunny?"

"I don't actually have a porch," she admitted. "I have a small balcony. My porch-goose, if I had one, couldn't greet anyone on my apartment balcony. I live on the twelfth floor."

"Oh, that's sad." Maddie patted Sunny on the back sympathetically. "Look at this one." She pointed to one complete outfit on a plaster goose model. It was dressed as Abraham Lincoln, with a tall, black top hat and button-down jacket. Another figure was outfitted as Little Red Riding Hood in a bright red cape and carrying a basket of flowers. Then Maddie asked the big question, "Don't you ever want a home, Sunny? One that's on the ground? You could have a goose that's dressed like a guitar player. There's a house on Uncle Nick's street that has a For Sale sign in the yard."

Sunny shrugged a little and protested, "I have a home, Maddie. Many people are envious of my beautiful apartment. It's right on the edge of Central Park. There are trees, and there's a playground just across the street."

"Do you have nice neighbors?" Maddie pushed a little farther. "That helps to make a house a home."

Sunny stammered, pulling on the bill of her hat, "I don't know —"

~~Memory~~

After Sunny's Music-of-Love career exploded on the world stage, Bruce convinced her to buy a place in Manhattan, overlooking Central Park. He claimed it would be large enough for her to have a practice studio in her place, and it would be a monument to her success. At the time, she saw no need to be a monument to anything. She would, however, benefit from a larger home base.

Home. But it never felt like home. Long flights from France, Italy, or even California brought her back to a super polished, hollow museum of an apartment that seemed to belong to someone else. Maybe Bruce.

Late one night, when the grandfather clock on the first floor's main entrance chimed twelve, the doorman helped drag her suitcases onto the elevator. When the lift rose and opened again, the twelfth-floor hall was empty. She thought she could hear an echo, despite the luxurious, deeply piled carpet that stretched out on the friendless hall floor. Bright, brass wall sconces lit the way to her door. A blond, ten-year-old boy opened the apartment door down the hall, on the courtyard side of the building. He took two steps outside his home, still gripping the doorknob.

"Can I help?" he whispered.

"It is late," Sunny whispered back with as warm a smile as her exhausted body could produce. "Shouldn't you be in bed?"

"I woke up when the blue alien from the planet beyond the purple rainbow used his globus gun to attack the Star Team. It was loud," he explained as he yawned.

"Oh, my." Sunny pretended to be caught up in the thrill of the space story. "If you can bring in the two smaller cases, I'll get the big one. Ah, what's your name?"

"Jonathan," he said, and picked up the two.

She grabbed the large, heavy case, dragged it to her door, and pulled her key from her pocket. "Thanks, Jonathan. I'm Sunny."

"Well, yeah, of course," Jonathan spoke in a matter-of-fact tone. "Everyone knows you, Miss Gaynor."

"Jonathan," a woman hollered from his apartment. "Get in here. You know not to talk to strangers."

"But, she's not—" he started to protest.

It was no use. Sunny was always a stranger in her own building. Jonathan would wave a little when the family would go out. He'd even share a few words about how school was going if he were in the hall. Still, it was clear. Sunny was always alone.

~~~~
~~~~

Nick saw Sunny's reaction to Maddie's questions and jumped in to rescue her. "I have a plan. If Sunny buys a house here in town, she will let you know, Maddie. Then you can visit her. You could take her a gift to welcome her back to Kettering. How is that, Sunny?"

Sunny smiled weakly, unsure of what to say. "I haven't thought about it, but if I buy a house in Ohio, maybe Kettering, your uncle will be the first person I call. He can tell you. How's that?"

"I love it," Maddie squealed as she jumped and laughed. "We could have a sleepover. Oh, and you could teach me how to play the guitar, not the goose. I've always wanted to play a musical instrument. Maybe the piano. I'd love to play the piano."

"That sounds like fun," Sunny agreed. "I could move my piano from New York back home. Or, better yet, you could go with me to buy one of those fancy grand pianos. I've always wanted one of those."

"It sounds like fun to me, too," Nick admitted in a low voice.

Sunny asked herself, *How is it possible? Several people have brought up a topic I haven't even considered. I never thought of moving out of Manhattan. Why haven't I thought of that before?*

"Sunny," her grandfather called out and waved. "Are you having fun? Have you found a goose gown you can't live without?"

When Grandpa John got to the dressy goose table, Sunny hugged him again. "I am having a lot of fun. Maddie has convinced me to buy a porch-goose." From four booths down, she saw a familiar man and waved.

Her grandfather followed her gaze past others as they browsed the craft booths and saw the man. He had turned and started walking the other way. With his hand to his brow to block the sun's glare, Grandpa John tried to follow the man. "That fellow looks familiar."

"I met him on the airplane yesterday. He—"

"There you are," Robin said as she caught up to them. "Did Grandpa tell you that we've all decided to go back to the house to rest? We're getting sunburned."

"Okay," Sunny said. "Take a nap for me. I'm going with Nick and Maddie to Hawthorn Hill."

Robin looked at Nick up and down like she was inspecting a new vacuum cleaner. "That sounds like fun. I'll see you at home." When Nick looked away, Robin brightened in a go-for-it expression.

Sunny couldn't help thinking of Maddie's suggestion to buy a house that sat on the ground.

Chapter Ten
Hawthorn Hill

Sunny grew up less than four miles from Hawthorn Hill, but she had never been inside, and never remembered driving past. It was a straight shot down Far Hills Avenue into Dayton, with no deviation east or west, so the estate lay hidden off on a side street. She was as excited to see the Wright home as she was the first time she saw the Statue of Liberty. Both are monuments to the greatness of the American people. The Statue of Liberty represented a welcome to people from all over the world.

The beautiful white Georgian-style house, with its four pillars and two porches, represented the inventiveness of Americans. Hawthorn Hill was located on Harman Avenue in the beautiful community of Oakwood.

As she walked through the craft show, Sunny Googled the house on her phone, always eager to know what she was "getting into before she got there." Her research found a picture of the stately two-story house with its 4,864 square feet of living space. The home of Orville Wright, his father, Bishop Milton Wright, and his sister Katharine, was named for the hawthorn trees on the three acres that surrounded the house. Orville and Wilbur designed the house in the style of the beautiful homes they had seen on a trip to Virginia. Orville's brother, Wilbur, had planned to live there with the family, but he died of typhoid fever before he could move in. It was a beautiful place where historic figures, like Henry Ford, Thomas Edison, and Charles Lindbergh, visited Orville Wright after it was completed in 1914.

Sunny left her car parked near the Arts and Crafts bazaar and rode to the open house tour with Nick. It only made sense. Transporting three people to the same location in two cars was silly.

Sunny sat up front with Nick, and Maddie sat in the back. Sunny didn't occupy the passenger seat because she wanted to be near Nick. It was simply the adult thing to do. Or, that's what she told herself. Nick drove past the amazing, relaxed homes of Oakwood to the Carillon Historical Park. The plan was to leave the car in the lot and take the museum's shuttle van to the Wright home.

Nick's car was nice, with maroon leather interior, and all the fuss most people had grown to expect in a car. It appeared to be a nice-sized vehicle before she got in. But next to Nick, it felt to Sunny like she was riding in a Matchbox car. She knew it was probably her own misunderstanding. She felt overwhelmed being so close to Nick and chose to redirect her thoughts. "The car still smells new," she said, filling the thundering silence.

"It is rather new. I bought it this past spring."

She cleared her throat and began again. "About your case with the high school principal." She stopped, remembering the legal responsibility of an attorney. "I know that you have to maintain attorney/client confidentiality and not discuss his case with anyone outside the office, but—"

"You're right," Nick agreed. As he used the floor shift to his right, his hand brushed Sunny's. Neither acknowledged the contact. "But you had met Harrison earlier today, and we were just sharing pleasantries."

"I'm not talking about when we saw them a little while ago." Sunny adjusted her skirt. "I learned something that may be important, but I'm hoping it's not."

Nick glanced her way. "Say that again."

"April is in an Investment Club. It's mostly made up of teachers. Together, the group invests their pooled funds in short-term investments, makes money, and then receives a quarterly payout based on a percentage of the total they invested. If I put in one-fourth of the total pooled amount, I would receive one-fourth of the total earnings. Each quarter, April buys a piece of jewelry with the money she makes. She had on a beautiful diamond pendant this morning."

"And ... where does she get the money to invest?"

"I don't know. What I know is, her family was dirt-poor," Sunny whispered and looked back to see if Maddie was listening. She was asleep. "April would get on the school bus in a coat that was either way too big or too small, depending on what was available in the donation box at church. She didn't even have her face washed and her hair combed for school. She seemed to get out of the house as quickly as possible."

Nick pulled into the Carillon parking lot and nearly slammed on his brakes. "That beautiful woman I met back in the park?"

When Nick screeched to a stop, Sunny found the grab bar over the door and hung on. "The same one. But now, with Harrison, she is so much more than she ever was when she was at home. I am so proud of her."

"We're here." Nick parked the car, turned around, and nudged Maddie, who slept. "Wake up, Honey," he said. To Sunny, he added, "I want to hear more about this later. I have no idea how it may or may not connect to the missing money. But I also don't know if April Stafford is the fashionable, gracious person I saw today, or the person who grew up always needing money."

"I suppose she could be both," Sunny speculated as she reached for the door handle. "I prefer to think she has grown into a special person."

With its motor running, a van sat in the shade of massive trees in the Carillon Park area. Families still clinging to their summer shorts and flip-flops, walked along the paths that stretched in front of many of Dayton's transplanted historic buildings. The structures revealed the creative, industrial ingenuity of those who developed the city.

Sunny, Nick, and Maddie got into the van with other families. Maddie sat on Nick's knee to make room for others. Two teenagers were on the bench seat opposite Sunny and Nick. They kept looking in Sunny's direction, but were polite enough to say nothing. Soon, the driver drove up to the Hawthorn Hill estate.

"Oh, look." Maddie pointed out the window. "That house is big."

"Yes, Maddie, the house is amazing," Sunny agreed.

When the driver released the door, the tour began. They strolled toward the mansion through the gardens in front of the property. Orange and yellow fall blooming flowers lifted their blossoms and fragrance from the beds at the front of the house.

The entry opened to a beautiful two-story foyer with a grand, white staircase opposite the door. Sunny was thrilled. The living room, study, dining room, and kitchen were all decorated with the furniture and appointments in the house when Orville Wright lived there.

As the guide led the group up the steps to the second floor, Nick whispered, "Do you remember that red brick house near campus? We always passed it when we walked to the football field. Sometimes you would stop and stare over the fence."

Sunny's mind wandered back along the brick sidewalk, walking hand-in-hand with Nick. The swirling leaves of fall danced around them, as they strolled along on evening walks, happy to be together. Colors of gold and crimson made a carpet under their feet, like the colorful rugs in the Wright estate.

"Oh, I remember," she said, lightly touching his hand. "Every minute of it."

"How about that dog?" he asked.

Maddie wrinkled her nose as she asked, "What dog?"

Sunny explained, "There was the tiniest Yorkshire Terrier," and shaped her two hands into the size of a grapefruit. "That Yorkie yapped incessantly as anyone walked by. She seemed to think she could take on a six-foot-six basketball player and a two-hundred fifty-pound linebacker. The Yorkie was so little that she could escape through the fence intended to keep her safely in the yard. One day, she skittered through a low spot in the ground at the fence line and charged forth as fast as she could. When your Uncle Nick saw a car coming, he knew the little fuzzy thing could have been mistaken for a few leaves on the road. He ran out into the street and snatched up the tiny dog just as a car was nearly upon her. The doggie-mama thanked him over and over."

Nick smiled a satisfied smile. "The dog's owner ran back into the house and brought out a plastic bag with six chocolate chip cookies inside." He patted his stomach. "They were still warm and so good."

Interrupting the memory of their stroll through their college town, one of the teenagers on the tour, wearing a state high school vocal ensemble winner's t-shirt, excitedly asked, "You're Sunny Gaynor, aren't you?"

"No," Maddie jumped in. No one had told her Sunny didn't want to be recognized, but she had seen Sunny's expression each time her normal life was interrupted. "Sunny Gaynor is a music star. This is our friend Sunshine."

"But ..." the girl looked at her and squinted her eyes. "Why are you wearing Sunny Gaynor's face?"

Sunny laughed. "You girls have been very polite. I appreciate that. Yes, I'm Sunny Gaynor."

The taller girl with a large turquoise cross around her neck squealed. "I knew it. I knew it."

"This room was Orville's," the guide said. He kept his eyes on the teenage fans who were bubbling with excitement. Without calling attention to Sunny, he glanced back at her, nodded slightly, and smiled.

Sunny had seen that expression before, an acknowledgment of recognition. Touching the bill of her hat and smiling, she had to admit that she enjoyed knowing that others appreciated her work.

Orville and Wilbur Wright made the first successful airplane flight at Kitty Hawk, North Carolina, on December 17, 1903, nearly one-hundred twenty-five years ago. They are famous to this day. My fans may forget me tomorrow and go on to cheer another singer. Then the wheels began to turn faster: *Is it the music I like, or the fame?*

When Sunny first arrived in New York City so long ago, she was immediately overwhelmed with a whirlwind of planning, activities, and personal appearances. She trusted her agent to have her best interests in mind.

Sunny remembered her first recording session: the studio filled with electronics she had never seen before in one place, and the huge microphone that waited for every sound she made. Everything about it was a fascinating, new experience.

Jimmy Lustering, the internationally popular country and western singer, happened to come into the studio one day as Sunny recorded, "Where Did You Go?" He was amazed by Sunny's vocal range, the pure tone to each note, and the amazing new form of songs she sang, the Love-Story song. Country music had always told a story. Sunny's songs did the same without a country sound.

Lustering was so impressed with Sunny's voice and her new creative style he talked to Bruce about her singing the song as the warm-up artist at his concert at Madison Square Garden in New York City. Jimmy's star billing brought in all of his fans. There were over sixteen thousand music lovers there that night. It was Sunny's privilege to glow in his shared spotlight and launched her career.

Sunny peaked out over the massive audience. "Bruce, look at them all. Even Mom, Dad, and my sister Robin are out there somewhere." Then the Garden went dark.

She took the center spot on the darkened stage by following one thin beam of light to illuminate her steps. The beginning chords of her song began in the dark. The spotlight slowly increased to a glorious blaze as Sunny sang the next few bars. Every word she sang came from her heart. She held the last note a few extra beats, then the room went silent.

Finally, an uproar erupted from the audience and thundered in her heart. Sunny Gaynor was an instant star. Would she admit to herself where she had transferred her love?

<center>~~~~</center>

Sunny listened to the guide as they all walked around the Wright house. She slowly realized that she didn't want a mansion or an apartment in the clouds.

Those from the van enjoyed a few minutes in the backyard when the tour ended. Sunny stood in the shade of the covered patio and inhaled the perfume of the garden. "It's wonderful out here. The air is clear, and people you pass on the sidewalk smile and sometimes even talk for a minute."

Maddie wrinkled her nose. "Don't people talk to you in New York?"

Sunny didn't tell Maddie she was afraid to talk to those she saw in the city. Maybe it was just her fear of coming out of her thinking-and-creating mode and finally interacting with those around her. Whatever the reason, being questioned by Maddie in the inviting garden forced her to be honest with herself. "No, I don't talk to strangers very much. Most people in the city walk around with their eyes on the concrete, or focused on the next responsibility directly in front of them, and mind their own business."

Nick wrapped his arm around Maddie. "I'll bet seeing all the city's sights is fun."

The guide gave an altered plan. "Folks, we'll go back through the house rather than around it. The side yard sprinklers are on right now."

Sunny wasn't sure she wanted to continue their conversation. "I'll have to admit, the city didn't become my home, because I didn't claim it as mine. I did the usual tourist, or new resident, things when I first moved there. I went to the Alice in Wonderland statue in Central Park and to the top of the Empire State Building. But later, I didn't have time to see what was around me."

Nick started to speak, then didn't. Instead, he gave her that old, familiar side hug. He was "with" her.

While Nick seemed to guard how much he wanted to push Sunny, Maddie was there and unafraid to ask the hard questions. So, Maddie asked, "You didn't have time to walk around your neighborhood in ten years?"

Sunny looked down, studying the freshly mown grass in the yard. It smelled sweet and earthy. Above a planting of zinnias, butterflies flitted here and there. "Ten years? That sounds silly, doesn't it, Maddie?"

Sunny was quiet as she walked with the group through the house to the front of the building. Sunny turned and took another look before going out the front door. The beautiful staircase swept down to where it gently placed a family member on the first floor. Color was everywhere. The soft, pastel shades of blue, delicate pink, and muted green, all part of the Edwardian era, warmed her heart. "It is beautiful."

Nick asked in awe, "Could a house like Hawthorn Hill substitute for your New York condo in the sky?"

Sunny knew exactly the house she had always dreamed of. "No, not this one. It is magnificent. But if I were to trade in my place in the big city, I would want a comfortable home, in a neighborhood with kids. I'd want a house with a fireplace in the living room, and a coffee pot that is always warming in the kitchen. A real home."

The driver raised his hand. "Okay, folks, let's get back in the van."

Chapter Eleven
Together

Back at the Carillon parking lot, they picked up Nick's car. Sunny rubbed the top of Maddie's head and drew her close. "I'd better go home. I don't know what Robin has planned for this evening."

Nick pointed to Sunny's floral purse. "I'll bet there's a cell phone in there. Call Robin and get the details. If you have time, there's still half an hour left at the car show. I'd love to share that with you."

"Cars? Okay. I'd like to remember what they look like. I don't even keep a car in New York. I rent one when I'm out of town." She pulled her phone out and called.

"Robin?" Pause.

"We just finished the tour of Hawthorn Hill." Pause.

"Yes, it was beautiful. What's happening this evening?" Pause.

"We thought we'd go to the car show for the last part." Pause.

"Right." Pause.

"Okay."

She put the phone away. "Sorry, Nick. Robin said everyone is going to play games in the yard, and then we'll have supper about six-thirty."

Nick put Maddie into the car and closed the door, then he helped Sunny with her seat belt. Bending low, he reached across in front of her and snapped the closure into place. She could hear his breath near her ear.

Nick had another idea. "How about the parade tomorrow? The parade marches north on Far Hills Avenue beginning at Stroop Road. It ends before they get to Dorothy Lane. The entire parade route is a little under a mile. The parade will go past my office. It's located in a big house with a large front porch. You and your family are welcome to watch the parade from there." He stopped and laughed as Maddie started bouncing up and down in agreement. "Maddie is anxious to see you some more, Shine. School starts again on Tuesday. Then the normal routine begins."

Maddie? Only Maddie? Sunny wondered about Nick's interest in her, but didn't ask. She wanted Nick to be the first to talk about *us,* if there was to be an *us.* She would not allow herself to be the one to bring it up. But Robin had said something else.

Nick smiled. "I would like to see you more, too."

That picked up Sunny's spirits, but she still couldn't clear her head. Maybe she would feel more hopeful if she knew what she hoped for. "Robin asked me to invite you and Maddie to follow me home. She has planned for us to relax, talk, play games, and have a picnic supper. Both of her bridesmaids, Holly Blanchart, and Quin Tuttle, are bringing their spouses and children. The little girls seem to know one another. Quin said her daughter knows you, Maddie. She's Pammy Tuttle."

"Pammy? She's a friend of mine." Maddie giggled and clapped her hands.

"Rebecca Raddner, Kevin, and Shaneah might come. I heard Robin invite them this morning at church," Sunny added.

"Shaneah, too?" Maddie asked in excitement. "I get to spend my day off from school with two of my best friends."

"It looks like Maddie has decided for us." Nick bowed at the waist, like he was surrendering. "She knows everyone," Nick said, then added, "But we're not part of the wedding party."

"You can be my plus-one," she whispered.

"Plus-one, plus-one," Nick corrected her and grinned. "Is that okay?"

"That will be twice the fun," Sunny teased and winked at Maddie.

Chapter Twelve
A Time to Relax

Nick was quiet as he drove Sunny back to her car after the Hawthorn tour. Sunny tried to figure out why no one was talking, and her mental study only added to the silence.

Finally, Nick patted Sunny's knee. "This has been the best day in years." He paused at a stoplight. "I have you to thank for that, Shine."

"Thanks. I had a wonderful day, too." She gazed out the window and added, "Even the sky is the color of the bridesmaids' dresses, and the trees seemed to hum music in the light breeze."

"Your descriptions are poetic, Shine." Then Nick added slowly, "Here we are," as he pulled parallel to Sunny's rental. "Looks like a nice car."

"It's comfortable," she said, looking at it more closely. "If I had a car of my own, that model would be a contender. Although, I might like a different color."

Nick shook his head in disbelief. "It's hard to think of you not running around New York in your own car. Leaving all of the driving to a taxi driver doesn't sound like you. You're more independent than that."

Sunny thought of all she could see from her apartment balcony. Tall trees and delicate, colorful flower beds lined a grassy meadow where children ran and played, and lovers met for a day in the sun. But for Sunny, it was an artistic picture or movie for families and sweethearts. Sunny rarely went outside by herself. There were days when she wished Jonathan would walk with her in the park. His mother made it clear that wouldn't happen.

When they got to her parents' house, Sunny pulled up first. Nick stopped out front near the edge of the road. White spirea bushes bloomed all across the front of the house and, under the sunroom windows. Sunny saw Robin coming toward her car and called out the window, "We're here. Hey, thank you, Sis, for letting me invite Nick and Maddie."

Robin rolled her eyes and smiled. "Of course, Sunny. I'm glad they could come. They'll have fun."

"Maddie!" Shaneah hollered as she ran up to her. "We're going to play croquet in the side yard." When the car stopped, Maddie reached out of the car window and tried to catch Shaneah's hand. "Come on," Shaneah begged impatiently. "With you, me, Pammy, and Bobby Blanchart, that makes a perfect four."

"Can I go play?" Maddie begged her uncle.

"Of course," Nick answered. "That's why we're here, to relax and play."

Maddie jumped out of the car and followed Shaneah across the driveway, past the sleeping peony bushes, and into the yard. Nick opened the door for Sunny, but continued watching Maddie.

Sunny took Nick by the arm. "She'll be fine. Robin told me we also have a badminton net in the backyard and a small drone back there, too. There will be plenty for her to do to have fun with her friends."

"A drone?" Nick stopped and looked to the sky. "Oh, wow. I feel like I'm twelve again."

Sunny was so glad Nick had come. But she hadn't sorted out her new reality. She didn't even know what her new reality was. She lived over six hundred miles from her parents and Nick. During her trip home, she had become aware that she was full of contradictions. So, for that day, she would try not to worry about it. "The drone has a small video camera loaded on it. Gary programmed it so the kids could remove the chip from the camera. We'll put the chip in his computer, and the kids can watch what they filmed."

Nick raised his eyebrows. "The attorney in me has awakened. Did the neighbors sign off on possible lawsuits? Like the invasion of privacy?"

Sunny laughed. "Funny you should ask. Rebecca Raddner, Shaneah's mother, is a realtor. The drone belongs to her. She films her house listings to give buyers a complete picture of the property they're considering. Becca created a form that states the kids have permission to fly over neighbors' property. Gary took it around to each of the houses and got their signatures. The people were great about it. They even asked to see the video."

Nick shook his head a little. "It helps that you have fun-loving neighbors. It also sounds like you covered everything."

"They sure did," Robin said. "And, Nick, Gary could use some help setting up more tables."

"I'm your man," he said. "See you in a minute, Shine."

"See you in a minute?" Robin asked with a tone of mischievousness. She straightened her shirt collar with a teasing attitude. "How long can he be away from you? When you were in college, if I saw you, Nick Sullivan was at your side."

Sunny nudged her sister's shoulder. "Okay, Okay. It was a magical year," she admitted. "As for today, we're having a nice afternoon."

Robin paused, then said, "Invite Nick to the wedding next weekend, Sunny. You don't have a plus-one."

Sunny went through the back door with Robin, up the few steps, and into the bustling kitchen. Rerun wiggled and pranced as they entered. The little dog had to be included in everything. She wanted to be the center of attention, have a lick of everything each one ate, and grab a bit of contact whenever anyone bent near her.

The women gathered in the kitchen, helping prepare the picnic-style supper. In the small room, everyone wiggled past one another. They lifted their elbows to find their way to the refrigerator on one side of the room or the sink on the other. The important thing wasn't the food. It was the joy of being together, talking, laughing, and sharing. The men were in the yard, setting up tables and chairs. The children had already started their game.

"Hi, Gran," Sunny greeted with the joy of seeing her again. "Whatcha doin'?"

"There you are, Sweetie," Grandma Claudia said, and kissed the air around Sunny's cheek, since both hands were full of a pickle relish jar and a small bowl of cooked and cooled hard-boiled eggs. "I'm making my special dressing for your mom's potato salad."

Sunny reached past the many ingredients and kissed her grandmother on the cheek. "Make sure I get the recipe. You know how much I love that yummy potato salad."

"I'll put together a cookbook of family favorites," her grandmother said. "I have some handwritten cards in my recipe box from generations past. There's a luscious, spicy date pudding that's been in the family for over two hundred years, and the secret code to a soft, sweet sugar cookie my mother used to make."

"You write the cookbook, Grandma," Sunny said as she patted her back. "I'll see that it's published."

"Oh, Sunny," Grace said as she flipped around, "that would be wonderful. Mother Gaynor, I'll help you find and select the recipes."

"We could all join in the fun," Robin bubbled. "I'll make a list of all the great dishes you've made over the years." She paced in the few inches of space she could move and tapped her finger on her hand, taking mental notes. "Mom can provide all the dishes and desserts she has enjoyed since she married into the family. And so can Grandpa's sister, Aunt Marge, and his brother, Uncle Andy. They can let you know what they enjoyed eating when they were growing up."

"You could call the book, Grandma Gaynor's Cookbook," Sunny sang out, painting the air with large sweeping musical direction gestures. "Grandma's food is super fun. Every dish is number one," she sang.

Grace started to fold in the tangy Miracle Whip-based dressing Claudia had made for the potato salad. She added, "Sunny could write an introduction."

"I'll do it. The cookbook sounds like fun," Grandma Claudia stated, concluding the project with a final decision. "Now let's finish this meal."

Sunny tried to continue the conversation based on what Robin had said before. "You said I should ask Nick to be my guest at your wedding. Would plus-two work with your seating arrangement? Maddie is staying with her Uncle Nick through next weekend. Her parents are in Europe and will get home on Monday."

"Of course, Sunny. I'll create a space for her. We'll scoot some of the guests down if necessary. She won't take up much space." Robin took some celery from the refrigerator and bit off the fresh, green end.

"Thanks, Honey," Grace said as she took the crisp green stalks to the sink and began washing them.

Sunny added with some excitement, "Nick is creating a space for all of us tomorrow during the parade." She selected a tiny sweet pickle from the jar Grandma Claudia opened and popped it into her mouth. "He said his law office and his home are in a large house with an inviting front porch. His place is located along the parade route on Far Hills Avenue. We can all go over in the morning to watch the entire parade. He'll have donuts, coffee, and juice for the kids. We'll also have the one luxury other parade watches won't have, a restroom in the house. Bring your own lawn chair."

"You seem to be having fun with our wonderful attorney," Holly said as she opened a bag of mini carrots and arranged the sweet, crunchy orange nuggets in one of the spaces on a vegetable platter.

Sunny thought about Nick as he was in the present. But her mind was swirling with memories of the Nick she knew from the past. She kept forgetting that time had moved on, and people flow on the rhythm of its passing. She shook her head to clear out the old brain dust that hadn't been touched in many years. She asked Robin, "Our wonderful attorney?"

Holly opened a jar of salty, briny green olives that Grace had set out, drained the liquid, put the little

pimiento-stuffed green fruit on the platter, and popped
one in her mouth. "Nick has only had his office open for a
few years and has become quite successful. Not as
measured by a big bank account, although he does quite
well. However, he's also part of an Innocence Project
called the Wrongly Convicted Task Force. A friend's
husband had been in prison for seven years. We've all tried
to help her and the kids until her husband could be
paroled. Nick and the Task Force were able to prove he
was wrongfully convicted and got him released. Yes, he is
our wonderful attorney."

"He has certainly made a selfless life for himself,"
Sunny realized more and more. She watched the kids'
outdoor activities through the kitchen window, and her
heart sang. She saw the possibility of a full life for herself
through that glass. The children played and laughed, as
family and friends worked to set up tables, talked, and
fellowshipped together. She began to feel whole, as if the
hollow spots inside were being filled with belonging and
love. A new awareness came over her of the emptiness
that had been there all along. How was it possible that she
had never allowed herself to experience her isolation
before she came home? She was aware for the first time
that she had spent years in emptiness. And the fascinating
thing was, she realized that she felt full, more complete,
whether she left New York or went on a concert tour. *Why
have you been hiding?* she questioned herself. *No wonder you
built a professional career so fast. You worked hard every moment
of your life, so you wouldn't have to experience the reality of the life
you had been living, or tolerating.*

Chapter Thirteen
Monday, Labor Day

Labor Day morning opened with excitement. She would spend the day with Nick. The sun made her feel warm inside and out. As a teen, she would have slept with the window slightly open to let in the freshness of the day. But as a professional singer, that was one more joy that had to be set aside. She couldn't risk getting laryngitis. She'd have to sing tenor if she were hoarse, and none of her original songs were written in that range.

When she came downstairs, the family was sitting in the dining room, drinking their second cup of coffee. "Good morning, all," she said as she breezed through the room on her way to the coffee pot.

Her dad sat at his assigned seat at the head of the table. Putting his cup down, he reminded everyone, "The parade will begin at the corner of Stroop Road and Far Hill Avenue at 9:55. But we'll have to get there early since Far Hills will be blocked. We can cross Far Hills south of Stroop and zigzag north, parallel to the highway, until we come up behind Nick's house."

"His house?" Sunny wondered. That wasn't what he said. "He invited us to his office," she corrected him.

"Right," Doug agreed. "Remember, his office is attached to his house."

Sunny was amazed. Nick had an office building in a pretty part of town. "I'll bet his girlfriend likes the setup."

"Girlfriend?" Grace asked. "Did he tell you he has a girlfriend? I never see him out and about with anyone, and I haven't heard talk about a love life."

A love life. Sunny cringed at those three words. Why? She hadn't even sent Nick a text saying, "Hi, thinking of you."

"Well, let's get going." Doug stood up and started toward the door. "Robin, Gary, and the bridal party will beat us all there. Besides, I want to be one of the first to check out Nick's choice of donuts."

Once the car was fully packed with lawn chairs in the trunk, the ride over to Nick's office was snug. Sunny's mom and dad were in the front of the car on one of the two bench seats. Sunny, her grandmother, and grandfather were wedged into the back seat. It wasn't very far. Sunny could convince herself she was comfortable for a short drive. And this week was all about spending time with family.

Sunny was stunned when her dad pulled onto the street beside Nick's house. The houses along the shady street were elegant and provided a 1940s cinematic experience of home and community. Her dad stopped beside a beautiful, red brick, two-story house with green climbing ivy on the chimney. It was a large home with willow trees and mighty oaks in the front and back yards.

"There you are," Nick announced as he came out to the car, opened the back door, and helped Sunny's grandmother out.

"Here we are," Sunny said slowly, amazed by the beautiful home. "But where am I?" She looked toward the front of the house and the familiar buildings across the street. She got a mental picture of her location with those points of reference.

Nick took her arm. "I told you. It's my office."

"This whole place is your office?" She couldn't believe it. How could a lawyer, and solo occupant in the office, need that much structure around him? "Did I misunderstand? Do you have other attorneys working here with you?"

"No, and my office is not the whole building. A larger portion is my home. Do you want to go inside?" Nick gestured toward the door. "It's not Hawthorn Hill, but it's mine."

She thought for a minute. Was she getting too close to Nick again? Would it all explode when she left to go back home, like it did the last time? Would that final leaving be too painful? But … "Thanks. I'd like to see where you live," she gave in spontaneously.

They went through the outer entry into a wide foyer with two solid doors, made of finely-grained exotic reddish-brown wood, and no windows. Nick opened the door on the right, the one with a copper name plate. Written on the plate was, Nicholas Sullivan, Attorney at Law. Inside was a comfortable waiting room, professionally outfitted with ten blond wood chairs, featuring deep red leather cushions. Dark hardwood floors and bright windows lined the long end of the room.

"There's a public restroom in here," Nick said, opening the door to fun wallpaper and large floor tiles. "Our parade watchers can use this restroom if they need to. The waiting room door will be unlocked."

"Great." Inside, she thought, *Grandma will appreciate it."*

Nick continued, "This door is one of the ways into my secretary, Corene's office." Once inside, he pointed to a window between the area and the waiting room. "Since there are no windows in here, I had the contractor install an opening into Corene's space, so the light and view from the front window on the opposite wall could flow in."

Sunny circled the room and took in the warmth and welcome of it all. "What a great idea."

Nick led her into his inner office through the third door off the waiting room. It was very professional, with rows of books on the shelves. It looked just as Sunny had always imagined his office would look. Law books were everywhere, shelved beside some of the non-fiction books Nick enjoyed.

Sunny smiled a superior smile. "You do know you can look things up on the internet. You don't have to have walls covered with multiple volumes, a complete law library."

He bowed slightly. "I like the touch and aroma of real books. I like the feel of holding a volume in my hands."

Sunny nodded. "Many people do."

"Sunny?" Nick touched her shoulder. "Would you like to see my home?"

"You're inviting me in?" Sunny winced inside. She wondered if Nick had gotten the double meaning of inviting her into the private side of the house that he called home and the even more private space he called his heart.

Nick whispered, "I never kept you out, Shine."

She didn't answer. What could she say? Nick was right. He didn't keep her out, but Sunny hadn't either. She just left. Just like the day she walked out the door of her residence hall and through the door to her future, she walked toward the left door in the entry and waited for Nick to unlock the door to his home.

"I'll leave this door unlocked, too," he volunteered. "If anyone needs anything from the kitchen, they can get it." He was so close she could feel his breath on her neck. "You are welcome to make yourself at home anywhere in the house, Shine."

Sunny was both amazed and envious. How did Nick do it? "Do you always open your life to people?"

He looked at her quizzically. "Sunny, those who will watch the parade from my porch today aren't just 'people.' They're your family." He teased a little. "Do you have a serial killer among the Gaynor clan? No one has asked me to represent them."

She rolled her eyes. "No, none that I know of." Then she remembered. "We have some Revolutionary War generals. Maybe some of those ended in military prisons. I haven't heard about that."

Through the door, the living room was elegant and casual. Large pillows, which men are said to dislike, were fluffed along the back of the couch. "Beautiful pillows," Sunny acknowledged.

"I like this one the best," Maddie said as she came bubbling in and picked up a throw pillow with a large yellow sunflower embroidered in crewel stitches. "Mama made this one for Uncle Nick. Isn't it pretty?"

Sunny laughed and gave her a little hug. "There you are, Miss Muffet. It is very pretty. Where were you?"

"I was in my room. I changed my shoes." She looked down and wiggled her toes through the ends of her sandals. "I like my new shoes, don't you?"

"Yes, I do." Sunny studied the red and white, candy-striped leather for a minute. "Do you think they have them in my size?"

Maddie shrugged. "I don't know. You take me along with you, and I'll show you where we got them."

"That sounds like fun." Studying each pillow again, Sunny added, "I like that blue pillow too, the one with the fancy musical staff and notes stitched onto it. Nick, you do have quite a few."

Nick smiled. "My mother is rather short. She needs pillows at her back or she'll lie down on the couch when she sits up."

Sunny repositioned a pillow. "Yes, I remember Dotty. She's about my height. Your dad is tall, like you."

"Right. Dad and I are both six feet, two." He smiled at the pillows. "I'd show you the kitchen," Nick said, apologizing. "But it's a mess. I don't seem to know how to organize it." He paused a minute. "If you're in Ohio long enough, maybe you can set it up like a kitchen should be."

Sunny smiled but didn't know what to say. She would love to help Nick in his kitchen. Finally, she stated the obvious. "That would be fun."

"I'll help you, Sunny." Maddie jumped up and down. "Us ladies will know where things go."

Sunny joined in the fun. "That would be perfect. Two ladies will get the work done fast." Then, she thought it best to change the subject. "Nick, are your parents coming to watch the parade today?" Sunny hadn't seen Mr. and Mrs. Sullivan since that long-ago Christmas break.

"They should be here any minute."

Chapter Fourteen
~~Memory~~

Christmas break, ten years ago. How could she forget? They would both be going back to the Dayton area for the holiday. Sunny didn't have a car in Naperville, but Nick had brought his back after Thanksgiving.

It was later in December, near the beginning of the holiday break. It had been snowing for several days. Sunny thought it looked magical, like Mother Nature had spent the night sculpting the bushes into snowy masterpieces. But it wasn't safe underfoot. All the sidewalks on campus had been shoveled by 9 a.m., but the concrete and brick walkways beyond the boundaries of the college were still deep with snow and ice. Sunny was concerned about the long drive home.

Mia, Sunny's neighbor in the residence hall, was also from Ohio—Columbus, Ohio. It was a few weeks before Christmas, and Mia wanted a ride home with Sunny and Nick. Sunny tried to be polite and tell her that Columbus was northeast of Dayton and not on their route home.

Mia had been interested in Nick and tried to find ways to come between him and Sunny. When she approached Sunny about the ride, she wore tight slacks and a Christmas-red sweater with a plunging neckline, hardly the type of clothing to keep the chill out in northern Illinois in December.

Sunny smiled warmly, but guardedly. "Mia, I'm sure you know that Columbus is not close to Dayton." She explained how inconvenient and possibly dangerous it would be to drive farther east on such a snowy day.

"I know Columbus isn't a suburb of Dayton, Sunny," Mia had sassed back. "Don't you remember fourth-grade Ohio history?"

"Cute," Sunny snapped back in the sweetest tone she could dig up. "And, Tyler Walsh will be in the back seat," she added to her explanation. "You know Tyler. He'll probably fall asleep and be all over back there."

Mia turned up her nose. "Well, that won't bother me. I get car sick. I'll have to sit in the front."

Nick walked into the conversation, totally unaware of the high-pressure interaction. "Who is sitting where?"

"Me, Nicky," Mia gushed. "I can't sit in the back due to motion-sickness, so I'll be riding in the front seat with you."

Nick looked at Sunny quizzically, then back at Mia. "Where to?"

Mia opened her mouth to speak, but Sunny quickly jumped in to explain. "Mia was asking about a ride home for the holidays. She's from Columbus, Ohio."

"Ah, good old Columbus, the capital. Sorry, we aren't going near there. Maybe you can take the bus if no one else is going to Columbus." He looked at Sunny's expression and hugged her. "Come on, Shine."

Sunny waited until they were out of Mia's hearing. "Nick, did you say anything to Mia about her riding with us to Ohio?"

"Me?" Nick stepped back in surprise. "No. I didn't even know she lives in Ohio."

"Then, how did she find out?" Sunny asked. She didn't want to doubt Nick. But she always got a negative, off-key impression from Mia when they talked. She didn't trust her at all. "Did you … have coffee with her. Or walk to class together?" Sunny almost bit her tongue. How could she ask Nick questions like that?

"No, I didn't have coffee with her." He drew closer. "Shine, she could have been in the coffee bar when I was there, but I didn't see her. Maybe she heard me talking to someone else." He ran his fingers across Sunny's forehead, brushing her hair back from her beautiful eyes.

Sunny wrapped her arms around his body and hung on. She was safe in his arms, even from someone like Mia. "She did it again. She wheedled herself into my friendliness, then turned on me."

"Don't ever stop being kind." Nick kissed the top of her head. "It's better to offer love and have it rejected than to never have loved in the first place."

Sunny remembered his words all those years. Hoping she would never forget, she rehearsed it frequently. That beautiful winter day ten years before played over in her head like a rehearsal tape, repeating the words that needed to be buried deep inside.

They had talked about the trip for two weeks. She had agreed to let him drive her home for the holidays. She may have sounded reluctant at first, but that was what she had wanted all along: a long, quiet ride, on a day covered in crystal white.

A few days after they planned the route, she heard Nick and Tyler talking. Nick asked him if he wanted a lift to Van Wert. It was on the way to Dayton, and he would have an empty car. Is that what he said, an empty car? Had Nick withdrawn his offer to take her home? "I thought you changed your mind," she admitted her disappointment.

In the three months since she had met him, Nick had become her everything. She felt bonded to him from their first meeting and every day that passed. "But you told Tyler that you'd have an empty car."

Since Sunny was an independent young woman, Nick approached her slowly. He put his hand on her shoulder and gathered her in his arms when she didn't recoil. "I don't know exactly what Tyler and I talked about. But I know I ended up encouraging him to ride with us because I'd have an empty back seat. Half the car would be empty."

"Oh," Sunny said, relieved. "I needed to hear that, Nick. I guess I'm afraid you'll get lost and slip away without a word."

"How in the world could I slip away from you? You shine in my life like a beacon. I could never wander off. I'll be able to see your light forever."

She guessed at the real problem. It was that choir concert on that Sunday afternoon. When Nick didn't come to the program, it was devastating to her. It may not have bothered others. But she wasn't "others." She was the girl who had wrapped her life in music since she was a young child. For what seemed like "forever," when she couldn't think of the right words to say, the lyrics of a song would come to mind, either her own lyrics or those of another composer. Perhaps the words were inspired enough to prompt a new piece for her playlist. She finally understood that others don't hear the songs playing in her heart unless she writes them down. She had spent the last ten years doing that, composing the lyrics and music that express her deepest emotions.

That Sunday on campus, she shook off her doubts and put into practice the lesson that she had begun to learn. *Be patient. Others can't hear the music that I hear.* She remembered telling Nick, "The last day of class before break, I'll be ready after I close my textbooks. You make sure Tyler is packed and waiting by the door. From what you've said, he's usually the last one to show up."

"I'll take care of Tyler." Nick laughed, then he held her tighter. "I can't wait for my family to meet you."

"I hope they like me," she said as she buried her head in his shoulder.

He threw his head back and howled. "Like you? Shine, they will love you."

She needed reassurance and grabbed his shirt. "How do you know that?"

"Because I love you," he said. He put his finger under her chin and tipped her lips toward him.

Sunny was filled with love, and joy overflowed. Her best Christmas gift that year would be Nicholas.

~~~~
~~~~

Chapter Fifteen
The Parade

During the days leading up to Robin's wedding, Kettering was jammed with thousands of people enjoying the year's Holiday at Home festivities. Children ran beside the parade participants, waving American flags and singing familiar songs with the bands.

Since Nick's home and office were near the end of the parade route, Sunny's family and his parents had a chance to enjoy the lemonade, coffee, and donuts he provided before the trumpets announced the parade's approach. Nick's parents came about fifteen minutes before the leading band got to Nick's corner.

"Mimi!" Maddie shouted, running toward Dotty Sullivan with her arms out.

"Maddie." Nick scooped her up before the child reached her grandmother. "Be careful. Mimi has a bad back. You'll knock her down."

"Oh, right," Maddie slowed and spoke softly. On tiptoes, she crept closer, carefully putting her arms around her grandmother and hugging her. "Hi, Mimi. I missed you."

"I'm not a China doll. You can hug me tighter." Dotty hugged her while swaying back and forth. "I missed you, too, Maddie."

Nick's parents continued into the living room, looked around, and took in the beautiful open space. When Mrs. Sullivan saw Sunny, she grabbed her and gave her a bear hug. "Sunshine, it's wonderful to see you again."

"You remember me?" Sunny asked, not as a music celebrity known worldwide, but as a woman drawn to their son in mythical ways, even Shine didn't understand. She was overjoyed at being accepted.

"Sunny, of course, I recognize you," Dotty Sullivan said, her eyes beaming.

Sunny held her breath. What could Nick's mom say? *The whole world knows Sunny Gaynor.*

"Sweetheart, I remember when Nicky first brought you to our house. I had hurried to finish setting up the Christmas tree after he called to say you were coming. I thought, *Oh my! The way Nicky bubbles like the sun is shining every day, I want the house to be decorated nicely for you.* And it worked. You came in with sparkling eyes and said, 'Mrs. Sullivan, your home is like a Christmas card. It is beautiful!' I was so pleased that you noticed all my hard work."

Sunny closed her eyes and released all the pent-up fear of being seen solely as a musician, relieved that Mrs. Sullivan remembered her, not the celebrity everyone thought they knew. "Mrs. Sullivan, it's so good to see you again."

"Call me Dotty," his mother insisted. She entwined her hand into her husband's and asked, "Remember Nicky's father, Miles?"

Sunny started to put out her hand to him, but he quickly gave her a friendly hug. Miles greeted her with, "Welcome to the family."

Sunny looked at Nick. He didn't appear embarrassed. Instead, his smile set her heart pounding. She changed the subject quickly, "Aren't Nick's home and office wonderful?"

"We haven't seen it yet. This is the first time," Miles said as he looked around.

"Nicky just moved into the house a few weeks ago," Dotty explained. "We were in Florida, visiting my parents. Mom had just gotten out of the hospital after knee replacement surgery and rehab. I wanted to make sure the visiting nurse and physical therapist were beginning their visits."

"Oh, yes, I remember your mother—Mrs. Ferrari. She is so funny. I hope she's doing well." A memory picture of everyone gathered around the dinner table that Christmas, and the lovely older woman who made Sunny feel welcome with her warm humor. "So, Nick moved into his house while you two were in Florida?"

"Yes, to both." Dotty took Sunny's arm and led her to the porch. "Mother is healing well, and my dad helps around the house. And, yes, Nicky moved in while we were gone. We went through the house when Nicky first found it. His former office was far too small and the house was barely adequate. But this is our first tour since he furnished it, added all of the pillows, and selected new paint, except for the kitchen. It isn't done. Nick is puzzled by that room. "

"That's what he told me," Sunny agreed, and was glad Dotty had brought it up. If Sunny had told Robin before Dotty had mentioned it, her sister might have made something bigger out of it than it was. Or bigger than Sunny assumed Nick had thought it was. Or… she had so many ores in the water she felt like she was paddling off in all directions. She left the conversation with, "He asked me to help him."

"Me, too," Maddie jumped in. "Sunny said I could help her. We're going to put glasses in the cabinet where they belong, and silverware in the best drawer. You know."

Dotty patted Maddie's cheek, then Sunny's. "I can't think of two better people to help him."

Sunny's eyes flashed to Nick. She watched his face as he took in every word. Why did she react to Nick's every expression as she did when she was eighteen? Immediately, a musical theme ran through her mind—*I remember when you and I had been … sweethearts.*

Quickly, she snapped back to Dotty's words.

"I'd like you to meet my parents, Doug and Grace Gaynor, and my sister Robin, the soon-to-be Mrs. Gary Foxworth. Robin teaches fourth grade, and Gary holds down a high school science class. He's also the varsity football coach."

Maddie kicked her foot. "Those football guys can kick far! We go to the games because Daddy played football in high school."

"Children, I love them." Dotty smiled mischievously at Nick. "When are you—?"

"Mother…" he reminded, with a playful warning in his eyes.

"Okay, okay," Dotty surrendered. "I was only wondering. Life's short. Ask your grandmother."

Nick quickly changed the subject. "Let's enjoy the parade. The routine world begins again after the holiday.

I'll be in my office. Maddie, Shaneah, Pammy, and Bobby will be back in school. Let's enjoy the rest of the day!"

The fun procession approached with their Holiday at Home banner leading the parade, followed by the high school band. Everyone on Nick's veranda quickly took their seat. Sunny and Nick sat together on the wooden porch swing, with Nick's arm resting on the back behind Sunny.

The high school band sounded amazing as it always did. Following the Marching Firebirds, the floats slowly flowed down the road. Churches, community organizations, and businesses spent weeks designing and building creative floats testifying to the town's excellence. Sunny especially liked her home church's float. There were four vignettes, a scene in each corner of the flatbed trailer behind the truck. In one scene, children chased creative white doves on bouncy wires, laughing and having fun. In another scene, a couple carried food to a shut-in. The third depicted the pastor, holding an open Bible, and visiting a man behind bars. The last quadrant thrilled Sunny the most. A simple trio dressed in jeans and T-shirts sang the old hymn, "The Church in the Wildwood"[5]

> O come, come, come to the church in the wildwood.
> Oh, come to the church in the dale.
> No spot is so dear to my childhood,
> As the little brown church in the vale.

It was a precious morning. Sunny had forgotten how much "belonging" had meant to her, belonging to her family, her friends, her church, and her community. Why had she stayed away so long? Sitting there beside Nick, watching a community festival, she didn't know why. But a thought was beginning to sneak its way into her consciousness. Maybe, if she had been at home when her music career began, she wouldn't have had the courage to go around the world in song. Maybe she had to be uncomfortable, seeking a place to land her feet, before she could finally know where she wanted to set down. That Labor Day morning, Sunny was comfortably settled. It felt like she and Nick were the only people on the porch.

Chapter Sixteen
A Post-Parade Lunch

The parade had started with the full high school band and ended with a small brass ensemble. Sunny was thrilled with their rich and powerful, close three-part harmony. Together, the instruments complemented each other with a blend of bright, high trumpet sounds, mellow, lyrical French horn tones, and the warm, resonant low notes of trombones.

After the parade passed, everyone on Nick's front porch began to realize how hungry they were. "I'm ready to eat," Gary said, rubbing his stomach, "and I could eat anything they put on my plate."

With their lawn chairs folded and stashed in their trunk, they all hopped in their car to go for food. Sunny got into Nick's car with Maddie in the back. "Maddie, are you hungry, or did you eat a couple of Uncle Nick's donuts?"

"Yes, and yes," she answered with a firm nod. "Yes, I ate two and a half donuts on Uncle Nick's porch. And yes, I am hungry."

The little caravan drove several blocks to the wonderful restaurant Robin had selected. Parade goers were still walking along the sidewalks, carrying chairs, chattering, and enjoying the day. Sunny enjoyed the spectators' joy of being together. Why had she never seen the evidence of her own loneliness before? There were signs all around her. She said no more, but absorbed the day around her.

The restaurant was a rugged place with a western theme. Any cowboy with a love for smoky meat would have reveled in the "saddle-up" decor, the outdoorsy aroma of meat cooking on the grill, and the faint sound of western music in the background.

Sunny ordered baby back ribs loaded with barbecue sauce, and a side salad. After the second bite of ribs, she suddenly realized that even the food tasted better with family and friends. Calm, loving conversation seemed to assist digestion. In New York, people appeared to avoid glances from other diners at nearby tables.

Nick ordered the meal he always talked about in college, but didn't have the money to buy in a restaurant. A New York strip steak and a giant baked potato smothered in butter, sour cream, and cheese. A salad snuggled up beside his dinner plate, but it was obvious to Sunny that his steak was the main attraction of his meal.

"How's your steak?" Sunny asked as she wiped some southwestern barbecue sauce from her hands.

Nick swooned, "I'm not talking while the flavor lasts.[6]"

"It sounds wonderful," his father said with a chuckle. "I'll stick with my lemon butter mahi-mahi."

"How many of you are going to the car show after lunch?" Sunny's dad asked. "I'd like to go but prefer not to go alone."

"We're going," Nick offered as he put his fork down for a minute. "Sunny, Maddie, and I." He looked at Sunny quizzically. "We are? Right? We talked about it yesterday."

"Oh, please, please, please, Sunny, please," Maddie begged. "It will be fun. Uncle Nick said he'd show me a real old car. There will be some as old as I am."

"You mean…like a 2019 Ford? A 1997 Chevy would be really, really old. In fact, it would be as old as I am," Sunny teased.

"I don't think so." Maddie's nose wrinkled. "I think it was older than that."

"Robin and I want to go to the car show," Gary offered as he put down a thick, browned pork chop.

"That sounds good to me," Doug chimed in.

"Me, too," Sunny's grandfather said with a smile and a large swallow from his raspberry-flavored iced tea. "I think Claudia wants to go back to your house, Sunny. She has a project she wants to start."

Claudia spoke up. "Now let me explain. Grace and I are going home to go through her recipe box and pull out the dishes she especially likes. That cookbook sounds like fun. I want to get started on it. She's also going to look for some family pictures, picnic meals, and grand holiday dinners. And, I could use some quiet time in the shade."

"I understand, Grandma." Inside, Sunny wondered if that was where she got her need to re-knit her interior, as she called her quiet time, with fewer people around.

"Thanks for understanding, Honey," Grandma Claudia said as she blew her a kiss.

Sunny kissed back, then turned to Dotty. Sunny leaned forward through all the people around the table. "What about you and Miles? Are you going to the car show?" She stabbed a slice of cucumber with her fork and dipped it in the tangy ranch dressing.

"Well," she began slowly, "if you don't mind, Nick and Sunny, your dad and I will go on home. We got in late last night from Florida, and I'm ready to take a nap. We'll see you next weekend at church."

"That makes all kinds of sense to me," Nick said.

Robin perked up. "Gary and I are getting married Saturday evening. Nick and Maddie are coming to the wedding. Dotty, you, and Miles are welcome to come, too, if you are rested by then."

Dotty looked at her husband and then at Nick, both were smiling. Then she studied the happy, relaxed expression on Nick's and Sunny's faces. "That would be nice."

Robin put down her fork, still pierced with a piece of amazing filet mignon, and said, "The wedding is at our church, and the reception is in a big tent in Mom and Dad's yard. The wedding is at 5:30."

"That sounds like fun, Robin." Dotty folded her hands in her lap, like a job accomplished, and winked at Nick.

Sunny pretended not to notice the unspoken message between mother and son. But she had, and she wondered.

Chapter Seventeen
The Car Show

The car show[7], with its multitude of vintage cars, antique cars, and classic/muscle cars, was lined up, and waiting for car lovers to point and praise. It began at the entrance to Lincoln Park Boulevard Commons near Shroyer Road. Sunny remembered that area very well. It was near her high school.

She rode with Nick, with her dad and grandfather in the back seat. Maddie was wedged between them. Sunny's mother drove Grandma Grace to their house.

An antique luxury Duesenberg was the first in the line to greet car enthusiasts and those who simply love beautiful elegance. Sunny wanted to touch it, and to run her fingers over the deep, shiny finish. But she didn't.

Colorful, fragrant flower beds that were near the line-up invited honey bees to dart from blossom to blossom. Taking off her hat, she brushed a bee from the surface of the old car's hood. "This isn't your hive," she said with her jaw set, and laughed.

"Is that your new car?" Nick teased.

"No, it is beautiful. But that car would never meet my needs. How do you haul the children to their music lessons and Little League games in that? They would have peanut butter all over the seats."

Nick stopped abruptly. "Children?"

Sunny was embarrassed. She had revealed a secret wish. "Well, I'd like a family someday." It was like a young deer had been caught in the middle of the road, and she quickly steered around.

"This is a beauty," Grandpa John said as he circled the Deusie. "It was an antique car when I was a kid." He looked down the row of antique and classic cars. "Wow, there's a Model A Ford." He walked off to inspect the car, which was complete with an open rumble seat in the back. Sunny remembered that her grandfather often mentioned his fourth-grade teacher, Mrs. Sherena Harvey. She drove a Model A. Her husband had died in WWII, leaving her as a widow with two boys to rear alone. Mrs. Harvey had no money for a newer car, so she drove the old A Model her father had given her.

"Sunny Gaynor! It's you, right?" a young woman asked. A lady who appeared to be her mother came up beside her.

The mother added. "I have listened to all of your songs. They are so comforting. I lost my husband last year, and your Love-Story songs have helped release the pent-up emotion that got trapped within me when he passed."

"I am so sorry to hear of your loss," Sunny said, touching the woman's shoulder in comfort. "Music has helped me through deep loss, too. I'm glad my music helped you in some small way."

"You'll never know." The woman took Sunny's hand and looked deeply into her eyes. "I see that you do know."

"Can we have your autograph?" the younger woman asked. She opened a new journal with the price tag still attached.

"It looks like you just bought this journal. I'd be happy to initiate it for you." Sunny took the notebook and paused over the paper. "What's your name?"

"Jewel," she said as she handed Sunny a pen.

"That's a beautiful name." She thought for a minute before she wrote. She often had a long line of fans waiting for an autograph. When she had the time, she made the autograph very personal. She put the pen to paper and wrote, "To Jewel, may your sparkle encourage all those around you. Shine on. Sunny Gaynor."

Jewel read the message, closed the journal, and hugged it close. Her voice broke as she said, "Thank you, Sunny. I haven't shone very much since my father died. You're great. Thanks again."

Looking at the older woman, Sunny asked, "Did you want an autograph?"

"That's okay. What I'd like is a picture with you." She nodded toward Nick. "Would your boyfriend take it for us?"

"He's—" Sunny began.

Nick quickly intervened. "I'd be happy to. I'd love the role of Sunny's photographer." He eagerly took the woman's cell phone and prepared to snap a picture, but said nothing about the boyfriend label. Sunny and the women posed while Nick snapped.

Sunny continued with her arm around the woman's waist. "Take another, Nick. Let's get Jewel in this one, too."

Nick took a few more, one to use and one to blur. Once the picture was taken and everyone expressed their pleasure in the outcome, Jewel and her mother moved on.

"Uncle Nicky, come look at this," Maddie called. She pointed to something beyond the Model A. Nick walked over and joined Maddie as they enjoyed the amazing something that had caught the child's eye.

"It is a good day for this, isn't it, Sunny?" a voice came from behind her. "You're having fun with your young man."

"He isn't my young man," Sunny corrected as she turned. "Mel? It's good to see you again." She put a hand on her hip. "Like I told you at the Gala, Mel, Nick isn't my boyfriend. He's an old friend."

"It's always good to see you, Sunny." Mel looked down at the fancy car. "Few people had cars when I was young. Things with motors were expensive. Our family needed transportation that would hold the entire family, and, I'd be able to use it for the business. When we moved up from Kentucky, the kids were in the back of the wagon I used for work. Josie, with two-year-old Carrie on her lap, sat up front. The four in the back were comfortable. They were piled on top of the blankets and pillows we put back there to get them north. My Josie was even expecting our sixth child and had to ride for days in that horse-drawn wagon. Our youngest son was born in Ohio."

"How exciting!" In her mind, Sunny compared Mel's move to her relocation to New York City, leaving everything she knew behind. The complete transplant was exciting and terrifying at the same time. "Did you have a job waiting for you in Dayton?"

"I sure did." Mel looked over to where Nick was showing Maddie a bright red car. Nick was motioning for

Sunny to catch up to them. Mel encouraged Sunny. "It looks like your boyfriend is waiting for you, too."

Sunny put up a scolding finger. "Now I said, Nick is not my boyfriend. He was my boyfriend a long time ago. This weekend is the first I've seen him in many years."

Mel smiled and said, "But you missed him."

Sunny started to shake her head in agreement, then stopped. "I have to admit, I missed him every day."

"It sounds like you're admitting to a crime, Sunny," Mel said with a chuckle. "Love is never a crime. It's how we act on that love that makes it either right or wrong." He touched her shoulder. "Is it wrong to love your young man?"

Sunny looked away. "No. It never was and it isn't now." She took a tissue from her pocket and wiped her nose. "I guess I'm just afraid to let go."

"Shine," Nick called as he started to walk back to where she stood talking to Mel.

Sunny turned back to her friend, but Mel was gone. Looking around, she circled in place looking for him, but Mel had disappeared, just the balloons and those enjoying the antique cars remained.

"Who was that?" Grandpa John asked as he craned, trying to see where Mel had gone. "He looks so familiar." He took a few steps away from the cars. "I have no idea where I've seen him, but… I don't know. Maybe he has one of those faces that reminds you of a lot of different people, a universal face."

"I just know his first name, Mel." Sunny raised on her tiptoes and searched in the direction she supposed Mel had gone. "I don't know where he went."

Her father rejoined the group, and once again, Mel dropped from her awareness. "You were having a nice talk."

Sunny looked at her dad, nodded, then at Nick and Maddie. "Well, my girl, how many cars did you and Uncle Nick see?"

"Not all, but a lot. There was a funny little one with a seat in the trunk. Your grandpa said he had one when he was young."

"I sure did," Grandpa John agreed. "Isn't remembering the past fun?"

Maddie nodded eagerly. "But my past isn't very long. None of these cars have been on any of the streets I've been on."

Grandpa John added wistfully, "They were on my streets, Maddie. Remembering is fun."

Sunny met Nick's eyes. They were dancing as she said, "It sure is."

Chapter Eighteen
An Evening of Music

Sunny was glad Nick didn't let the last holiday event pass by without them. The sun was setting as Sunny and Nick stood facing the windows near the dance floor at one of the music venues. The crimson and violet hues lit up the sky with the brilliance of the sun, trying to hold onto the day.

It was eight o'clock, and Nick had told Maddie that she could stay up even though it was a school night. But she had to promise to get up in the morning without a fuss.

Sunny was filled with music as she and Nick danced around the floor. The Labor Day weekend's activities closed with entertainment in three locations around town. Live band music played a variety of musical styles. Everyone could choose the tunes and dance steps that pleased them.

"It's my turn to dance," Maddie interrupted as she playfully tried to pull her uncle and Sunny apart.

"Okay," Sunny surrendered and stepped back. "I'll sit this one out if you want to dance with your uncle.

"No," Maddie insisted. "I want to dance with you, Sunny. We could do the Bunny Hop. We did that dance in gym class in the spring. I got pretty good with it."

"But, Maddie, they aren't playing Bunny Hop music," Nick said, laughing at her playfulness.

"We don't have to dance in the middle. We can go over there in the corner and do our own dance," she begged. "Nobody would care if our dance steps matched the music or not, if we weren't showing off in the middle of the room."

"Let's go," Sunny agreed as the three of them moved over.

Maddie stood still and looked behind her. "Sunny, you grab my waist."

"What about me?" Nick asked in fun.

"Well, okay," Maddie went limp as she gave in with theatrical surrender. "You can hold on to Sunny."

Nick put his hands on Sunny's waist, moved in close, and whispered, "Will it do any good if I hold on?"

Sunny didn't answer.

"Here we go," Maddie announced. "Da de da, de da da, jump, jump, jump."

"Can I jump, too?" Bobby Blanchart tapped on Maddie's shoulder. "I know how to do this."

"Us, too," Shaneah and Pammy joined in.

"That would be great!" Nick encouraged. He let go of Sunny's waist and pulled the three children into place. "You kids do the Bunny Hop over here, and I'll do a different dance with Sunny over here." With Sunny's hand in his, he twirled her around and pulled her close. "I can't think of anything better than to dance with you this evening."

Sunny managed a polite distance. She didn't allow herself to be drawn into his arms. *Light conversation that will fill the silence. Keep it simple.* "You will be back at work tomorrow, right?"

"Right," Nick said. "I'll be at the courthouse in the morning and in the office in the afternoon. I'll plan to research the case of Elmer Hollingsworth. I believe he was wrongly convicted last year."

"And you can help him?" Sunny was in awe of all the things Nick did for others.

"I hope so." Nick became animated as he talked about people who have been wrongfully convicted. "I'm part of an Innocence Project here in the Miami Valley. With the help of University of Dayton students, we research every aspect of information concerning a case, and then petition the court for a new trial, or even an innocence ruling."

Sunny didn't know if she should ask, but did anyway. "What was he convicted of?"

"A third-degree felony, with a five-year sentence. They said it was a hit and run resulting in death," Nick answered and shook his head in disbelief. "He was a well-respected morning drive radio personality on WACK. I've tried to make an appointment to talk to the station manager, but he can never work me into his schedule."

Sunny patted his arm. "If I can be of any help, just let me know. He might be willing to talk if you had Sunny Gaynor with you."

Nick's face lit up in genuine surprise. "Shine, I never thought of that. Thanks."

"You're always ready to help someone." Sunny knew Nick was good at interacting with people and how much he enjoyed helping them. Her mind wandered back to a

time when Nick helped her with someone in need. It was
late in the evening in Naperville.

~~Memory~~

Sunny had returned to her dormitory after an evening
of study in the college library when she was stopped.
"Sunny, will you help me with a problem?" Mrs. Grantham
asked as she coaxed Sunny into the Residence Hall Office
next to her small apartment.

Sunny had just gotten back after completing a music
theory assignment. She had written a melody, as the
professor had instructed, and in her usual need for words,
added some lyrics. Nick was writing a composition for
English class. "What do you need, Mrs. Grantham?" Sunny
asked.

"Thalia, who lives on your floor, is … missing." The
resident hall director's hands shook as she brushed hair
from her forehead.

"Missing?" Sunny gasped.

"Thalia left a note, saying she was exhausted and
didn't want to go on anymore." Mrs. Grantham forced her
trembling hands into her pockets. "Someone said they saw
her down at the gymnasium." She pulled a tissue from
where she had it tucked under her bra strap and blotted
her eyes. "You know her well. And you're so good with
people. Would you go down to the gym and bring her back
here? I'll have the clinic staff come and check her out
when you return. Her parents are on their way."

"Of course I will," Sunny agreed. She was worried
about Thalia, too. The dark-haired, thin freshman had
been looking gaunt and had stayed in her room a lot. It
appeared that she had been attending classes. At least, they
continued to walk together to English 102 most days.

Mrs. Grantham cautioned, "It's dark. I don't want you to go alone. I don't know Thalia's current mental state. Her behavior may be erratic, or she may dissolve into depression and tears. Take your nice young man with you," she insisted as she reached out her hands. "I'll keep your backpack here, so you don't have to take it to your room. You call Nick, and see if he can walk down with you, or someone he would recommend."

"Yes, Ma'am." Sunny handed over her gray backpack and pulled her phone from her pocket. "I'll leave right away," she said as she punched in Nick's number. "Hi, Nick," she said as she started out the door. "I know you just walked me back here, but can you help me some more?" She explained Thalia's note and the depression she must be in. She told him of Mrs. Grantham's urgent request.

"I'll be right there." Nick agreed. "I hadn't even gotten back to the residence hall when you called."

Sunny fastened her coat, pulled her wool stocking cap down a little, and stepped out onto the front steps. The snow was falling harder, and the steps felt slick. She marveled at how fast the conditions had changed. It would have been nice to loop her hand through Nick's arm and hold on tight, to steady her. It was February that evening so long ago. The sidewalks were also covered with fresh snow and a little ice, and it was getting deeper and slicker. Sunny knew that it might get more dangerous underfoot if the snow continued. She was glad to see Nick coming toward her. He would be her rock, the balance in her life. They met in the middle of the Quad.

Sunny grabbed Nick's hand as soon as he was close enough to reach him. It was always safe there. His hands even felt warm through the knit in her gloves.

"Thalia Merchant is missing from her room," she explained, breathlessly. "She's been spotted at the gym, and Mrs. Grantham is worried. They found a note Thalia left. Nick, Thalia sounded so depressed, like she was giving up. Mrs. Grantham has requested that some people from the health center meet us back at the dorm. She had called Thalia's parents, and they're on the way. The clinic people should get to the residence hall by the time we return. She wants us to try to bring Thalia back calmly."

When they got to the gym, the side door of the building was unlocked. "I imagine they're still cleaning up after a full day of classes and activities," Nick said as he opened the door slightly.

When one of the janitors brought out some full trash bags, Sunny and Nick slipped in. They looked around, but Thalia wasn't in the basketball court area.

The large, empty gymnasium had a hollow sound. Sunny felt like they were trespassing and hoped that no one would see them there.

"Let's try the women's locker room," Sunny said, quietly. At the door to the locker room, she opened it a few inches and called, "Thalia, it's me, Sunny. Nick and I are coming in."

Nick leaned on the chrome bar of the door. Together, they slipped in and walked past the rows of vertical metal lockers and wooden benches. It didn't look like the staff had cleaned in there yet. A few white towels still lay in the corner of the room. Further inside, they heard muffled crying. When they approached the shower room, they found Thalia curled up in a ball in the corner of one of the shower stalls. The tiled floor was still wet. The water had soaked Thalia's jeans as she lay in the corner with her knees pulled up and her arms wrapped around her legs.

When Sunny approached her slowly, she sat up a little. "Go away, Sunny. It's hopeless."

"What's hopeless, Thalia?" Sunny asked softly as she eased a little closer, trying not to make Thalia feel cornered. Sunny found a dry spot on the floor on Thalia's right side and sat down slowly.

Nick sat on Thalia's left, where the shower stall was still standing in water. He didn't look at her at first. He was just "with" her. Then he asked, "Can you tell us about it?"

Thalia raised her head a little and whispered. "Tony … Tony broke up with me. And I'm … failing. At least, I failed a test in Psychology. I'm doing all I can. I am so tired, I can't do more. It just isn't worth it anymore. I work hard."

Nick spoke even softer as he sat there with water soaking the cuffs of his pants and his hip pockets. "One test is not the entire semester. You can make it up. And, you are so much more than Tony. I've seen you walking with him. I know him."

Sunny touched Thalia's arm and massaged her muscles. "You are so talented in so many things. You have many friends; you're normally a good student; you're funny; and you're great with a basketball."

Nick added to Sunny's attempt at opening the future for Thalia with bright possibilities. "Thalia, I saw you playing basketball. You could make the team if you try out. In fact, I heard the lady's team coach say that she had her eye on you. That would be great next year, wouldn't it? I can help you make an appointment to talk to her about the team, if you want me to."

Thalia looked up. Sunny could see her body begin to relax a little. "Basketball? Would you, Nick? I love to play."

Sunny saw a light go on in Thalia's eyes. Where there had been emptiness, there was a glimmer of possibility, something to look forward to. Nick had been able to plant a truly possible plan in Thalia's heart that evening, all those years before, sitting in puddles of hope on the locker room shower floor.

<p style="text-align:center">~~~~</p>

That Labor Day, on the dance floor in Kettering, Sunny patted Nick on the shoulder. "You will save Mr. Hollingsworth, just like you gave new life to Thalia back at college."

Nick kissed her hand. "I remember that night." Then he focused on Sunny. "And you, what will you be doing tomorrow?"

"I promised Robin I would write a new song for her wedding," Sunny said as she buried her forehead on Nick's shoulder. "I want it to be special."

Nick smoothed her hair. "I imagine it is perfect."

Sunny looked up. "Thank you for your belief in my music. But to be honest," Sunny rested her forehead on Nick's shoulder again. "I haven't finished it."

Nick didn't let her pull back. He didn't force her either. He invited her to stay by humming the song the band was playing. He whispered, "Don't run away again."

Sunny bristled. It felt like Nick had discovered her secret, a secret she had even hidden from herself. "I didn't run away, Nick. I ran to."

"Are you sure, Shine?" Nick whispered, "I've listened to your song 'What If' so many times, I think I can sing it backward."

"I know," she blurted. "I know." Sunny pulled away and ran from the entertainment area. Afraid and pent up with feelings of love, her only expression had been her music. Now, she was being exposed by that which had saved her. *I wasn't running away.* She argued with herself. *I was fulfilling my lifelong dream.*

She had no idea when she left Naperville that the dream would isolate her from everyone. Or, maybe, she let the dream become her master. Nothing else mattered. But it did.

She could hear Nick's voice behind her. "Shine, wait."

But she couldn't. She had to keep going. She had been running for ten years. Her entire life, since college, had been a straight line, no deviation, no turning back. She was sure that if she didn't fix her eyes on the prize and never blink, she would lose it all. But was that "all," really all there was to life?

She had earned more fame and recognition than she ever dreamed she would want. Once she had it all, she felt like she was standing precariously on only one leg, holding it all over her head. She couldn't put it down, and she couldn't hold it up.

Sunny continued her single-minded escape, zigzagging across the dance floor, hoping that Nick wouldn't see where she had gone. She couldn't answer any more questions. When she got to the doors leading outside, she looked out onto the darkening yard and the sidewalk lit by street lamps. It didn't matter. She had started on the path home, and she would stick to it.

She started walking more slowly the farther she got from the event center. In the cool night air, she heard an owl and its hoot from a tree ahead of her. Sunny was amazed. She had never seen an owl, or heard its call before. When she finally became aware of how tired her legs were, she sassed back to the night bird, "Who? It's me, and I am nowhere near my nest."

She hadn't gone much farther when Rebecca Raddner drove up and rolled down her car window. "Hi, Sunny, where are you going? It's dark out here."

Sunny couldn't think of a clever thing to say, so she told the truth. "Hi, Becca. I've been talking to an owl. I am going to try to walk home."

"Walk home?" Rebecca barked back. "Girl, your parents live miles from here."

"I know," Sunny said. She also knew that her plan sounded silly. Of course, she knew how far it was to her parents' house. As a child, she had walked everywhere, just because she could.

"For Heaven's sake, get in. I'll run you home." Rebecca sounded emphatic. It seemed pointless to argue with her. She would no more win that argument than the one she had been having with the owl.

"Thanks." As Sunny slid into the car, she wondered what she could say. Would she tell Becca she was running away again?

"What's going on?" Rebecca slowly moved on. "It'll take a little while to get through all of the crowd, with so many people walking around. Even out here, blocks from the center of activities, people are still on the side of the road." Pausing, she asked, "Where's your car?"

"I rode with a friend and his niece." Sunny was guarded about what she would let slip out. Walking home from the high school area was a task she would have easily tackled when she was fourteen. Now, she was embarrassed and wearing shoes with high heels.

"Does Nick know you're walking home?" Rebecca asked with a cautious tone.

"No, I guess not. I'd better text him?" Sunny removed her cell phone from her cross-body purse and texted, "I started to walk home. Rebecca Raddner saw me walking, and is driving me. Sorry. Shine."

Immediately, he texted back, "Can I see you tomorrow?"

With a glimpse at his text, Sunny quickly looked away. She didn't answer because she didn't have an answer. She had to think. But she was so off balance, she couldn't process his question. She felt wobbly and might lose her footing if she continued to see Nick. And yet, Nick was all she wanted to see.

Becca sounded cautious but asked, "Tomorrow, I'm going to put some Open House signs in the yards of a few listings. I want to announce Sunday afternoon's events in advance. How about it? I'll pick you up at 10 a.m. Maybe you can help me install the signs, then we'll go to lunch?"

Sunny jumped at the invitation. "That sounds perfect. I haven't dug a hole in a long time." And it was perfect, for a much different reason. She could explain to Nick why she wouldn't be able to join him for lunch without pushing him away, while she tried to figure out their relationship.

"I'll teach you how to install a realty sign. We don't dig any more. See you tomorrow," Rebecca said, dropping Sunny off at her parents' house.

When Sunny got home, she picked up her phone and typed, "Thanks, Nick, but Rebecca has asked me to help her tomorrow and then go to lunch. I hope to see you before Robin's wedding on Saturday. Shine." Then she clicked, SEND.

Sunny wondered why she had signed both texts, "Shine." No one called her that, except Nick. Was she trying to tell him how much he meant to her, how she had missed him every day? Then why did she leave the dance? And the way she stepped back was more symbolic than she wanted to admit, even to herself. She had left ... again.

Chapter Nineteen
Tuesday

The next day, Sunny watched for Becca to pull into the Gaynor's driveway. When she arrived, they drove back up to the main road and started toward the center of last evening's activities.

They turned into the area of the first listing, and Sunny smiled. "This neighborhood is beautiful," she said, looking up and down the street. Each lawn was groomed and polished, ready for the holiday weekend, and seemed to welcome those who drove by.

Rebecca smiled and slowed down as they neared the house she would show. "It's comfortable, isn't it? The house is right up there."

"Becca, this house is as cute as can be." Sunny took it all in as they neared the home on a quarter acre of garden. "I love how they have planted the yard with the right balance of tall and short flowers, and those magnificent trees out front are wonderful."

Rebecca pulled into the driveway and turned off the engine. Sitting there for a minute, she surveyed the roof and windows. "I had a contractor come out and replace the roof. It looks good. And the front window pane had a crack in it. A window replacement team installed that new section on the left. It looks like they did a good job of cleaning up."

Sunny got out of the car and stood by the edge of the sidewalk. "It's just the right size to make a wonderful starter home for someone. Does it have three bedrooms?"

"Yes, do you want to go inside?" Rebecca asked as she pushed the button on the garage door opener. "Kevin said he left the signs in the garage. But we can go in first and look around if you want to."

"Let's do it," Sunny announced boldly with a conquering fist in the air.

They entered through the garage into a small laundry room with coat hooks and cubbies for boots. In the kitchen, Becca said, "It looks a little small. But everything you need in a kitchen is here. They even have a narrow freezer in the corner. That would be handy. Let's see the living room."

A red brick fireplace with a rough wooden beam for a mantle graced the north wall. "This house is sweet," Sunny said as she ran her finger over the mantle. "I pay a fortune for my apartment in New York, but it's not much bigger than this house."

"Do you think you might be interested in a house like this, here in town?" Rebecca asked carefully.

"I've been thinking about finding a new home base," Sunny said as she felt the grain in the wood. "But I think I'd like a bigger place than this. I'm cramped where I am in the city." She wandered into the first bedroom and checked the size. "I have a soundproof studio for writing, practice, and sample recording. That takes up a lot of space. Besides a studio, if I were here in Ohio, I'd want to host my family and friends. I'd need a large room with a lot of overstuffed chairs."

Rebecca touched Sunny's arm and pointed to a door leading to the basement stairs. "The basement has a lot of room. Maybe you could have your studio down there."

"Maybe," Sunny agreed.

"Kevin will host this open house for me. I'll be greeting prospective buyers at the other one." She turned toward the garage door. "Let's put up one of the signs. It's nearly noon. After lunch, we'll go to the other place."

Becca pulled the sign out of the garage. "Okay, let's plant this by the road, out from the front door." It was obvious to Sunny that Rebecca had it all planned. Becca pushed the frame into place, then added the Open House insert and the one announcing the date and time. "That will stay in place."

Once the sign was securely upright, Becca announced, "I'm hungry. Let's go eat."

Chapter Twenty
The Historic Pizza Place

Sunny picked up a square piece of deluxe pizza, just like the ones she ate as a teenager. And, according to Grandpa John, just like the ones he ate as a teen. The piece was deluxe indeed, with a mix of savory and sweet flavors on a tomato base. The various meats, cheeses, onions, and peppers satisfied every eager taste bud.

She rolled her eyes in a swoon. "This is magical. New Yorkers brag about our pizza, but nothing can compare to this scrumptious deliciousness. The original owner got the recipe from his mother-in-law and built a pizza empire on it. I would curtsy in his court any day."

"I agree, one hundred percent," Rebecca said with a mouth full, but Sunny understood by the satisfied look on Rebecca's face. Becca paused before picking up another square. "Yesterday, when you were walking home … what was that about? Do you want to talk about it?"

The thought of releasing all of her longing, fear, and trapped love was too much for her. At least, today it was. "My main goal today is to eat half of this pizza."

Rebecca nudged Sunny and cracked, "Touché."

Sunny focused on the food, her conversation with her old friend, and her small world at the table. As she filled up on pepperoni and the rest of the magical pie, she began to relax and feel the presence of those around her. Suddenly, the awareness of everyone in the restaurant came tumbling into her world. She realized that the eyes of many of the diners were on her.

Becca glanced around the room, sat back, and smiled. "Is it fun, Sunny, seeing how much you are loved? Without them, you wouldn't have the opportunity to share your God-given voice and Love-Story songs with others. It is your fans who make it all possible," she added as she smiled at the people sitting beside them.

"Becca," Sunny sat up straight, "you are right. You are absolutely right." She turned and waved at some teenagers at a nearby table who had been giggling. They ducked behind the menus in their hands, embarrassed, and waved back with a few fingers. Sunny waved one of the pieces of pizza at them in agreement. "Great pizza, isn't it?"

The teens said nothing but nodded enthusiastically.

Sunny mouthed, "Thank you."

They grinned and nodded again.

"Hi, Sunny." April Stafford broke into Sunny's thoughts as she and Harrison approached the table. "Great pizza, right?"

"The best." Sunny nodded as she put a piece back on her plate. "Harrison, it's good to see you, too. I thought you were to be back in your office today."

"I am back in the office today," he agreed. "I took an extra hour for lunch since I have to stay two hours later for a meeting this evening." He smiled at April. "That gave me a chance to have lunch with my beautiful wife."

"Good thinking." Wiping her tomatoey fingertips on her napkin, Sunny said, "April, I've been thinking about the Investment Club you belong to." She stopped and blotted the crinkly napkin on her lips, hoping to approach the topic slowly so as not to alarm her. "I would love to attend a meeting of the group while I'm home. Are there any in the next few days?"

April's eyes shifted from the upper right to the lower as she mentally processed her calendar. "I don't think so."

Harrison looked at her and raised his eyebrows. "Sure, you do, Honey. You told me there's one tomorrow evening."

April's eyes continued to shift. "Oh, that's right, tomorrow. "But the meetings are just for those with families connected to teaching."

Harrison laughed. "I am sure Sunny Gaynor would be welcome. And, both her sister and soon-to-be brother-in-law are teachers. That's a family connection. Sure, Sunny, I'm sure you'd be welcome. Can April pick you up?"

April was rattled and stuttered a little, "S…sure, Sunny. I'd be happy to stop by." She reached into her pocket, took out a business card, and wrote a phone number on it. "That's my cell phone number. Call with directions to your house. It will be nice to have you along, Sunny."

"Thanks, April." Sunny slipped the card into her small purse. "I hope to learn a lot from your members. My New York investment counselor puts me in investments he thinks are good. I know little about them or the process."

"See you tomorrow, after supper." April smiled at Becca. "Good to see you again, too, Rebecca. Have a good afternoon."

"You as well," Becca said. When the Staffords walked to the back corner of the restaurant, she asked Sunny, "What was that all about?"

Picking up her pizza again, Sunny said, "Like I told April, I'm curious." But Sunny saw no need to pass on rumors and tell Becca exactly what she was curious about. She trusted Rebecca, but she wasn't a gossip. Goodness knows, there have been many untrue rumors floating around about her over the years.

All the possibilities of questions she might ask at the meeting came flooding in. Sunny was soon off again in a world of thought.

"Sunny, just be careful. Several years ago, I invested with Gus Walters. I have nothing against the group. It is made up of great people, but … Walters?" Becca whispered, seemingly embarrassed that she was talking about the man. "He gave off a sleazy vibration. Like a slithery snake, with the most winning smile you've ever seen."

Becca's words brought Sunny back, but she dragged along with her a little verse she made up a long time ago. It was to the tune of Old MacDonald.[8]

Gradually, a re-awareness began to take hold. The crowds around her weren't smothering her. She had enjoyed the cheers from the audience after a high school play or musical. What had changed? Being alone. She had become afraid in New York, afraid of walking down the street by herself and eventually, going anywhere alone. That made everyone a suspect. At home in Kettering, she felt different, like she belonged there.

"The pizza was wonderful, Becca. You chose the perfect place." As they finished eating, Sunny was ready to begin again. "Where is the other house? This is so much fun. I used to love going to the Parade of Homes annual events. I'd enjoy how all the rooms were staged. Then I'd think about what I might do differently. Thank you for inviting me."

Outside the pizza place, a fragrance of late blooming roses mixed with wisps of pizza that carried on the wind and clothing. It was perfume to Sunny's senses. "I feel free. I can run around the neighborhood for no reason at all, just like I did as a child." She put her hand to her mouth. "I'm sorry, Becca. I didn't mean you. You have a very good reason for running around the neighborhood. You're working. I'm enjoying your company, the community, and the beautiful day."

"Honestly, it's not work for me either." Becca led the way over to her car. "I love what I do." She checked her watch as they got in. "It's nearly 1:30. Good, we will have plenty of time. Shaneah will get home from school at about 3:30. We can walk around in the other house and

161

enjoy every room. You will recognize the neighborhood. The house is just a couple of blocks from Nick's."

"From Nick's?" Sunny was startled. It never occurred to her that the next house was near his place. "A couple of blocks? How many?"

"Sunny," Becca blurted out, "there is something going on between you two, isn't there? I see the sparks fly between you and Nick every time I see you together. We can talk about it if you want to."

"Sparks?" Sunny flashed back to the first time she saw Nick. "There was," she admitted. "I have no idea what is going on now."

Chapter Twenty-One
The House on Mulberry Lane

Rebecca pointed down the next block and whispered, "There it is, that house with the sweeping front yard."

The house on Mulberry Lane sat back from the road, with large red maple trees in the front yard that would turn crimson later in the fall. A winding sidewalk entered through the lawn from the front of the house and off the driveway, meeting in a swirling connection near the front door. The warm colors of the exterior were white, gray, and light rough-faced white stone. Just as Becca had said, or warned, it was two streets over from Nick's home, on a parallel street.

"Ah." Sunny put her hand to her chest in amazement and awe. "It almost takes my breath away." She was nearly afraid to speak. That house was her dream home, but one that was her private dream, alone. She didn't talk to anyone about it.

Rebecca said, looking at the house, "It is breathtaking, isn't it, Sunny. Those tapered front porch beams, with the stone pillars, are exquisite. Look at the rafters and those two gables. They're beautiful."

Sunny couldn't believe she was looking at the covered front porch and the gorgeous entry door she had always dreamed of. How could it materialize right there in front of her, on a comfortable street, there at home? She finally asked, "How big is the house?"

"Two thousand, three hundred square feet. Plus, a full basement," Rebecca answered. "Some realtors include the lower level in their advertisement of square footage. I prefer to list them separately, so the potential buyer doesn't feel tricked." She maneuvered the car and backed it into the driveway. "The current owner completed the lower level to get it ready to put on the market, but there's not much down there, just some books. They never furnished it. But you can imagine all sorts of clusters and placements of furniture, and maybe gym equipment, to meet your needs for the house." She turned off the engine.

Sunny couldn't turn her back on the house. She jumped out of the car with her eye on the prize. "Can we go inside?"

"The open house is Sunday afternoon, but I'll check." Rebecca walked up on the porch and knocked on the door. Sunny followed.

The lady of the house opened the door. "Hi, Rebecca. I see you have the sign."

"Hi, Nadine," Rebecca greeted. "Yes, we stopped by to put it in your yard. Today is a special day for you. I have an interested buyer along with me. Do you have the time to let us look around inside?"

Nadine hesitated. "A buyer? I was just leaving to pick up my mother. She has a doctor appointment in town in a little while. She hasn't been doing very well." Then she looked at Sunny.

Sunny took off her hat, shook out her hair, and smiled. "You're going to trust Becca with your beautiful home for the open house. If you're willing to let us tour today, this could be a dress rehearsal."

Nadine's mouth gaped. "Sunny Gaynor, in my house?" She reached out and hugged her. "Sorry for being too familiar. But I can't believe it. I love your music." She asked Rebecca, "You already have a key for Sunday, right?"

Rebecca dangled a key on a long chain in front of her. "Of course. And it's perfect." Dangling from a chain with the key was a small, smooth, ceramic art piece in the shape of Nadine's home.

"I love it, Becca. Good. Take as much time as you want, Sunny." Nadine checked her watch. "Right now, I gotta run. Please lock up when you're finished. Skeeter, our dog, is in her cage in the garage. She'll probably bark. But that's just because she thinks she's in charge around here. Bye."

"Will do," Becca called after her.

Sunny followed Rebecca's lead and stepped aside to let Nadine hurry out the door. The entry opened to an eleven-foot ceiling in the foyer and barn doors on the right leading into an office.

Sunny ran her fingers over the reddish wood of the doors and felt the polished surface. The wood was the same species as the towering red oaks in the front yard.

Rebecca highlighted the room. "This office is big enough to double as a recording and blogging studio. You can see all the built-in oak bookshelves. They aren't furniture. They'll stay."

"Look at this great room," Sunny said as she inhaled the smoky aroma of a recently extinguished fire in the fireplace. "I see she thought it was a little cool this morning, too."

"A fireplace can be very convenient," Becca agreed.

Sunny walked into the huge great room with a vaulted ceiling and the white stone fireplace that matched the stone on the pillars out front. "Rebecca, this is amazing. It's a very large room, but Nadine has arranged the furniture to make it feel cozy and friendly at the same time. There's plenty of room for party guests and family. Clustering a couch and some chairs around the fireplace also makes a place for intimate conversation between a few." She ran her fingers over the back of one of the light blue chairs covered in a wool blend for durability and a luxury feel.

"It is beautiful, isn't it?" Rebecca said. "The whole area is open concept, so the kitchen is right there. I'll be right behind you if you want to go into the kitchen. I left my phone in the car and the keys in the ignition. I'll get them, make a quick call while I'm out there, and set up the Open House sign." She looked at Sunny, who appeared to be enjoying the room, and the covered back porch she could see through French doors at the back of the house. "Okay?"

"Yes, take your time, Becca." Sunny walked into the large kitchen with a massive island and six chairs tucked under the cantilever, the overhanging part of the marble-covered island. Sunny touched every surface of the counter on the island and around the deep sink that was embedded in the middle.

"It's elegant, don't ya think? If a kitchen can be elegant." Mel walked in from the mud room. "My Josie cooks fantastic dishes on a stove much less fancy than this. Her browned and crispy chicken and fried corn are specialties that run around in your mouth and tantalize every corner. And her countertop is butcher block, not fine marble. This surface feels like cool silk," he said as he gently caressed the stone. "If I were to paint this kitchen, I'd put down extra drop cloths to protect it."

Sunny was surprised to see Mel in a stranger's house, but was always glad when she ran into him that week. "Mel? How did you get in here?"

Mel smiled and explained, "I was taking a walk. Then, when I saw you come in here, I wanted to say 'Hi.' I tried the side door to the garage." He sized up the six-burner range. "My Josie would love this."

Sunny got the first hint of where Mel lived. "You said you were taking a walk?" Sunny asked, "Do you live around here?"

Mel didn't answer the question but looked out of the window. "It's a beautiful neighborhood, isn't it?"

"It's amazing," Sunny said, walking into the adjoining pantry and turning on the light. Rows and rows of shelves lined the wall. The room smelled like cinnamon, ground ginger, and peanut butter. "Look at all of this storage. My apartment in New York doesn't have any of this. In fact, my kitchen isn't a whole lot bigger than this pantry."

~~*Memory*~~

Sunny's apartment pantry in New York consisted of two cabinet doors, high above the stove. She remembered when her phone rang one evening while she was standing on "*The International Who's Who in Popular Music – 2021.*" She was trying to reach a can of chicken noodle soup. Pulling her phone from her pocket, she saw Bruce's name on the screen.

"Yes?" Sunny squealed as she slipped a little. "Oh, ouch. I might have sprained my ankle."

"Sprained your ankle?" Bruce gasped. "You have a concert next week. Remember your dance routine? That's pretty rigorous."

"Thank you, Bruce, for your concern over my slip. Yes, I am fine. And yes, I think the ankle will improve with rest. And yes, I'll be able to keep my concert engagement. But, again, thank you, Bruce. Your empathy is underwhelming."

Sunny hung up on her agent and dialed a delivery service. She'd have a bowl of Chinese egg drop soup and a serving of sweet and sour pork for supper.

Limping slightly, she went into her living room, which she had decorated with Elizabethan antiques. She sat on the sofa and brought her legs up to rest them on the coffee table. With a soft breeze through the patio doors, where twinkling lights of the city were beginning to stream in, she closed her eyes and finally relaxed.

~~~~

Mel asked gently, "If your apartment isn't large enough, why don't you move to a larger one? You have been very successful."

Sunny couldn't keep it bottled up anymore. "I went to New York because I thought I needed to be there to be successful. I found out that wasn't true. My success is located everywhere."

Mel did not doubt her decisions. "If you know why you left Naperville … and Nick, maybe you could finally come home."

"I don't know why I left," Sunny said, but she knew that wasn't right. "That's not true. I do know why, or a piece of the *why*. I thought I might have to give up my dreams if I stayed with Nick. He never asked me to
~~~~

surrender anything, but he was so smart. I knew he would make a fantastic career for himself. What would I have to give up so he could succeed? Then in New York, nothing ever felt permanent. I never felt like I was home."

Chapter Twenty-Two
Possibilities

I always learn something from Mel, she thought, glad he had shown up at the Mulberry Lane house. A lot had been flooding her mind lately, and what made it a deluge were the flashes of memories from the past.

~~Memory~~

That spring so long ago at North Central College, Sunny didn't know if she could say goodbye to Nick. He had already captured her heart. It was his now. But the academic year was over, and they would both go back to Ohio. What Nick didn't know was that she would go home to pack.

When her cell phone rang, she checked the screen. It was Nick. "Hi," she stumbled through a flimsy greeting about being busy cleaning her stuff out of her dorm room to bring an end to her freshman year. But it was more than that. It was the end of *Sunny and Nick*, the perfect couple as she saw it.

"I'm almost ready," she told him. "You can come up to my room and help me carry my things down. That'll save time. I'm so tired. If I had to drag them down by myself, one at a time, it would take a while."

When Nick came to carry her things, he stopped at her door and asked, "Are you okay?" Nestling her in the crook of his arm, he said, "You look sad. Do you feel alright?"

"I guess I'll miss our time here." And she would. But Sunny was stepping out into a new life, turning her back on the complete Sunny Gaynor and choosing the famous and successful one-sided Sunny, the music side.

They were quiet in the car heading southeast, bypassing Chicago, and driving on through Indiana. Finally, Nick suggested, "After a few days' rest, I thought you might like to go for a walk, to a movie, or something."

Rather than facing the fact that she was leaving all that she knew and loved to begin a life of music, Sunny pretended to sleep. But sometimes her eyes were open, with a frightened, empty stare out the window, following the trees as they passed.

"Sunny," Nick spoke a little louder, with a teasing poke to the arm. "Are you awake?"

"Yeah," she whispered faintly. Without turning, she finally said, "Nick, I won't be home."

"You won't be home?" he asked in a tone of bewilderment. "We haven't set a day or time."

"Remember, we talked about that agent? The one who contacted me after the musical? I promised to think about his offer."

Nick drew out slowly, "Right."

"I've decided to sign the contract for an album with Title-Wood Records," she blurted out. Then she admitted, "I leave for New York in a few days. I'll stay with a friend of the family in Manhattan while I get settled."

"You're just now telling me?" Nick asked. The pain in his voice sounded like he was hurt, causing Sunny's own heart to break even more completely.

Sunny wiped away the flood of tears that ran down her cheeks. She turned toward him, but didn't look into his eyes. She feared there wouldn't be enough tissue if their eyes met. "I was afraid to tell you, Nick," she sobbed.

Nick's hands tightened on the steering wheel. "You were afraid of me?"

"No, never." She blew her nose. "I was afraid of me."

Nick was loving but frustrated. "I don't understand, Shine." Roughly running his fingers through his hair, he added, "You know I would have supported you. You needed to fulfill your dreams. I understand that. I wouldn't have stopped you. I would have driven you to New York myself. I love you, Shine."

"The sad part is, I love you, too, and I'm leaving." She turned again and buried her head in her arm. "Is it over between us?

"Not for me," Nick assured her, patting her leg. "It'll never be over for me."

They finished their ride home in silence.

~~~~

Mel touched Sunny's shoulder. "You've been afraid a long time, haven't you?"

"Afraid? How—?"

"I know how it feels to be away from family and friends. I feel like I'm only half a person when I'm away for a day or two, painting someone's house or business. You've been gone for ten years." Mel patted her cheek. "You left love to pursue fame. Honey, you can have both, as long as you know that fame isn't a representation of the real, complete you."
~~~~

She looked away to hide her feelings. "I was afraid love would hold me too tight. I would lose part of myself. It might sound silly now."

Mel smiled and said, "You did lose part of yourself—the family, loving, belonging part. You could find the rest of you if you find a partner with the same beliefs. He would have to let you be all of you, and he'd need room to be all of him." With his hand resting gently on her shoulder, he added, "Wouldn't that be wonderful, to be secure in love. Being held tight is not a stranglehold. It's just being embraced securely. It is a wonderful thing."

As salty tears gathered in the corners of her eyes, Sunny pulled a tissue from her pocket and blotted them. "I'm still afraid, Mel."

Mel's next words were like a saving breath, filling her with enough air to fly. "Lay your heart on the wind and let the love of God come in. His love will protect you and teach you how to love others. All kinds of love came first from Him: selfless love, romantic passion, deep friendships, and family love."

"Thank you, my friend," Sunny said as she hugged him. "It is strange, Mel. I've only known you for a few days, and I never even got your full name. But I feel like I have known you forever."

He turned to the great room and opened his arms to the majesty of it all. "The name's Mel Gaynor."

"Gaynor? What a coincidence. Why didn't you tell me?" As Rebecca came back into the house, Sunny turned toward the front door. "You won't believe it, Becca. My new friend, Mel, said his last name is Gaynor." She turned back and, once again, Mel had left the room. "That is so strange. He was here a minute ago. He came in through the garage door. I guess he went out the same way."

"Okay, thanks. I'll make sure that door is locked, too, before we leave," Rebecca said. She walked through the space and smiled. "Well, what do you think of the great room and the kitchen? Aren't they fantastic? If you want to take the time to see it, there's much more to the house."

Sunny stepped back into the kitchen and ran her fingers over the exquisite white cabinets and marble countertops. "The white marble feels like glass, with beautiful veining. Becca, it is breathtaking. Robin could sit at the bar while I'm preparing a family dinner. We'd talk just like we used to. There'd be room for Mom to join her. Grandma would want to help, of course. And there would be plenty of space for us all, and for Grandpa to get through the kitchen to fill his coffee cup."

"It sounds wonderful, Sunny. You've been away from your family, and it would be nice to reconnect," Rebecca said, checking her watch again. "We have plenty of time. Do you want to run downstairs and check out the basement? It's a large, open space with many possibilities. What do you think?"

"Yes. I'd like to. There is one thing I want to check for now. Then I don't have to take any more of your time. I can look at the rest of it later, if I have a burning need to see more." Sunny followed Rebecca down the steps to the lower level. When she got to the bottom of the stairs, she beamed. It wasn't really a basement like Sunny expected, with bare cinder block walls and a concrete floor. Sunny remembered when a basement was a cellar.

~~*Memory*~~

"Sunny, would you please run down to the basement and bring up a jar of green beans?" her grandmother had asked. *Run down* meant Grandma planned to make green beans, red potatoes, and large ham chunks for supper and would need younger legs to go down in the cellar to get them.

Sunny remembered her grandparents' basement on their farm. Truly, it was more of a cellar than a city girl would think of as a basement. At the bottom of the steps, a door led to a room that was located under the front porch. There wasn't a register to heat the room, and the open porch above made it cool enough to be ideal for storing food. Canning jars filled the stacked shelves on both sides of the fruit room. The room got its name because Grandpa bought a bushel sack of sweet yellow apples every fall and set it in the corner. They were there for months, allowing Sunny and Robin to reach in and pull out a delicious apple at any time.

Sunny knew the difference between a cellar and a basement.

<p style="text-align:center">~~~~</p>

"See." Rebecca twirled around. "The basement is finished, but there's nothing here."

"But what I wanted to see is over there." Sunny didn't even go into the larger space. She hurried around the corner where the steps came down, and walked straight to the bookshelves in the space beneath the stairs and along the wall beyond that. Opening several books, from the largest volumes to the small paperbacks, she sniffed a few of the pages. Slowly, she exhaled. "Perfect. There is no scent of mildew. My studio would fit right here if I chose this area rather than the office upstairs."

"Really? Do you think you could live here?" Becca became even more excited. "Could you make this your home?"

Sunny finally opened the eyes of her heart. "It is perfect."

Chapter Twenty-Three
The Patio

Outside, the sparkling warmth of the afternoon sun bathed her face in light, and a breeze kissed her brow. She breathed in deeply, taking in the amazing, sweet freshness of the Midwestern air.

"Hi, Shine." The familiar voice was low, like a breeze whispering in the leaves.

"Nick? What are you doing here?" Sunny closed her eyes and winced inside. *Why wouldn't he be here? It is Nick's neighborhood. His house is a few blocks away. He is the one who belongs here, not me.*

Nick's smile was the same old smile as always, and as recent as Monday. Nick was Nick. She could depend on him to be consistent. He didn't appear to be hurt by her behavior from the evening before, walking away in the middle of their dance.

He simply smiled and explained, "When I can get away from the office, I take a walk after lunch. It gives me time to think and to get some exercise, which I need, as you can see."

"You look great," she heard herself blurt out. And he did look very good indeed. He fit in his clothes like a catalog model and had the same poise and presence. Of course, he was filled out more than a college freshman. But it was muscle, not fat. He wasn't a boy any longer. He was a man.

"Thank you for the compliment. Coming from you, it's especially nice," he said, reaching for her hand. He was quick, wrapping his fingers around hers before she could stop him. That is, if she had an inkling to avoid his touch.

Sunny didn't have time to put her hand in her pocket or wave it around, gesturing to some obscure flower type. He joined Sunny and Rebecca as they walked around the flower beds. More roses bloomed along the side of the house, creating a lovely perfume. It felt homey walking together, hand-in-hand. But they weren't alone. "Nick, do you know Rebecca Raddner?"

"Of course," he said, offering his hand. "Mrs. Raddner showed me the house I now live and work in." He shook her hand and added, "You represented me, as a buyer, very well. You took the time to show me every house that was for sale in all of Kettering. It's good to see you, Rebecca."

"Hi, Nick," Becca said warmly. "Sunny and I were going to walk around the garden. There's a spot in the back I especially want her to see." She glanced at Sunny for a glimmer of permission, then looked back at Nick and added, "Do you want to join us?"

Sunny squeezed Nick's hand. He squeezed back, their old silent signal that said, "I'm glad you're here."

"Look at all of the giant zinnias." Sunny paused by the bed that flowed gracefully across the front of the house on both sides of the steps and up to the porch. Touching the blooms, the petals were delicately soft. "There is something holy about flower petals. They are gorgeous as a single petal, and magnificent as a full blossom. Like the individual Christian who sings praises to God and joins a full chorus, adding to the harmony of the group."

"The variety of flower colors is magnificent," Nick agreed. "They have beauty alone, and as part of a bouquet in a crystal vase."

Sunny looked into Nick's eyes and found the same message of long ago. *I hear you, Shine. I understand, and I'm with you.*

"Let's walk around to the back of the house," Becca suggested. "Sunny, you didn't get to see all of the house. There's still the covered back patio, the rest of the basement, and the bedrooms."

"How did you skip all of that?" Nick asked, quizzically. "Especially the patio. You spent most of your summers on your family's front porch."

Sunny looked down again at the scarlet and wine-colored flowers. "My friend, Mel, stopped by when I was in the kitchen. I asked him for his full name. After he told me his last name was the same as mine, I was overwhelmed with joy and confusion. He looked so familiar to me. It was eerie."

"Wow," Rebecca said, "what a mix of emotions." She touched Sunny's arm in support. "I know you'll be able to work it out." They walked around the corner of the house, past beds of more robust, blooming flowers. "There it is." She pointed to the inviting covered patio, complete with an outdoor kitchen in the back corner, and amazing, green furniture that looked comfortable enough for one to remain in the shade all afternoon.

Sunny couldn't wait to open the three drawers of the small prep area. "I can smell the steaks grilling already," she said as she ran her fingers over the large, shiny grill. "You could get food for a lot of people on this thing."

A small refrigerator was tucked under the workspace. Although not large, it was adequate for a party or to keep soft drinks cold on a hot day. The patio furniture was stuffed full of comfort and beckoned for Sunny to sit and enjoy the afternoon.

"Becca, I could live out here nine months out of the year. I can almost smell the hamburgers grilling over the open flame, and big slices of sweet onion waiting on the buns."

Nick laughed a little. "When are you moving in?"

"I haven't decided," she teased.

"Shine, that's great." Nick started to show his enthusiasm, then stopped. "No, I don't want to influence you. If a miracle like that did happen, it should be all yours. Right now, I'm afraid your decision could go either way."

Sunny said no more about moving to Ohio or staying in New York. At that point, she didn't know what she would do and was certainly not ready to answer questions. It wasn't because she didn't want another's point of view; it was because she processed ideas internally, not by talking unendingly about them.

Sunny walked over to the French doors and looked in. It was an opportunity to avoid Nick's excited gaze. She also chose to take one last look at the house she loved more each time she saw it. Without looking at Nick, she whispered, "I think I know how you feel, but I don't seem to have the right words to express my feelings."

Rebecca rolled her eyes and masked an expression of embarrassment. "Okay, Sunny. Is there anything else you want to see?" She checked her watch. "I still have time before Shaneah's school is out."

"Yes, there is something." Sunny put her hand on the door latch. "I'd like to see more of the basement. You said it was finished but not furnished. I just checked out that corner near the steps so far."

Rebecca unlocked the patio door, and the three went into the great room. They all smiled as they looked around again, even the two who had already seen it. "It's a happy room, isn't it?" Sunny said.

"Shine, this room is amazing." Nick moved around, taking in every corner and touching every texture that he passed. "Your whole family could fit in here with room to spare. It would be perfect for you."

"I know," Sunny agreed, "Isn't it great? Now, let's see, where was the door to the basement? I forgot."

Rebecca led the way to the door to the lower level. Once they got to the foot of the steps and saw all there was, it was hard to call it a basement. Even though Sunny had hurried down and darted into the small space near the stairs, she hadn't seen the entire lower level. A gasp rose from each of them as the huge space opened before them.

"Nadine said it was a nice, large space, but empty," Rebecca repeated. "But I had no idea. I didn't come down here. If you hadn't decided to see this, I would have missed this fantastic selling point."

Sunny walked around and sized up the space in her mind. She hadn't told Rebecca that a basement would be important to her. She especially wasn't ready for Nick to get bits and pieces of her thinking. Maybe he wouldn't want her to live so close to his house. Maybe he wouldn't want her in Ohio at all.

"Well, Sunny," Rebecca began cautiously. "What do you think?"

Sunny smiled and continued to create spaces in her mind. *My office and the recording studio would be perfect down here. There are no windows on that wall to deflect the sound. I could use the designated office upstairs for a music room and put in a grand piano. Over in that corner down here, I'll bring in toys and a slide for a playroom.* She was excited to think of future nieces and nephews enjoying the activities there. *They could have a complete indoor playground down here.*

"You aren't saying anything, Shine," Nick said as he silently walked around beside her. "But I can hear your thoughts."

Sunny wondered if her heart was pouring out all over the house. She thought, *Guard yourself, Shine, or you could have your hopes and dreams lying all over the floor. It could be a real mess to clean up.*

Chapter Twenty-Four
It Was Strange

"What ya need, Grandpa?" Sunny asked her grandfather, who stood at the door to her mother's busy kitchen.

"I'm on a snipe hunt," he said as he peeked around the corner. He wore a blue plaid shirt with a button-down collar and rolled up sleeves, ready to do any odd jobs if asked or offer help to a neighbor.

"A snipe hunt, is it?" Sunny asked, knowing her grandfather's playful nature. "You know there aren't any snipes, at least not in Mom's kitchen."

"I'm hunting for something I'm afraid isn't there. I wouldn't want to find a snipe in my son and daughter-in-law's kitchen." Grandpa John appeared reluctant to enter the room, already full of family preparing a meal. "I'll stay right here. I don't want to get in everyone's way. It looks really busy in there. Do you think there's a cup of coffee hiding anywhere?"

"I'll find some coffee for you," Sunny offered. She noticed that her grandfather stayed safely out of the way but close enough to survey the layout for any signs of a steaming cup of go-juice, as he called it.

"That would be much appreciated," Grandpa offered.

"I made a fresh pot when Gary was caffeine-deprived a half-hour ago," Sunny said with a laugh. "It's still pretty fresh and hot, Grandpa."

Sunny wiggled through the kitchen to the coffee maker. "Excuse me," she said as she hip-bumped Robin from in front of the carafe. "Pardon me." Sunny had originally gone to the kitchen to help, or at least, to be part of the hubbub. Her mother was working at the small counter space, and Robin was dueling with her elbows as she squeezed between her mom and her grandmother at the sink. It was easy to see that the problems of gathering to prepare a meal and enjoying fellowship would be solved in the spacious kitchen at the house on Mulberry Lane. As she neared the pot, the nutty, smoky aroma of the dark blend of coffee filled her with morning joy.

Robin stepped out of the way but didn't cease talking. "The bridesmaids have their final fitting tomorrow." She handed the cup of coffee to Sunny. "You'll be there, of course, won't you, Sunny?"

"Sure, but after that, I'll have to focus on finishing the song I started for you, until it's done." Sunny ran the obstacle course back to the kitchen door. "Here's your coffee, Grandpa," she said, handing him the colorful cup.

"Thanks, Dear," Grandpa John responded and started to go safely back into the living room, out of the bustle in the kitchen.

"Wait, Grandpa," Sunny called. As her grandfather took his first sips of java, she told him about her new friend. "I met him on the airplane coming home. He said he'd been in New York to put in a bid on a painting job. Then I saw him again around the Holiday at Home festival a few times. He even turned up at the house that Rebecca Raddner was listing and preparing for an open house."

Grandpa's eyes popped. "It sounds like he's been everywhere."

"But that's not the strange part," Sunny nearly whispered. "He said his name was Mel Gaynor and his wife was Josie. That name sounded familiar. What was your grandfather's name?"

It was easy to see that Grandpa John was stunned. His face went pale, and his hand shook so much he nearly dropped his coffee cup. He startled as the hot coffee splashes stung his hand. "My grandfather's name was Mel Gaynor. His wife, my paternal grandmother, was Josie." He shook his head. "That is spooky."

Sunny watched Grandpa John go back into the living room. He was slower than his usual zippy step. Maybe he was thinking about the super coincidence of Mel's name and his wife, Josie. Sunny pondered Mel Gaynor further, and she wondered if…but… *How could that be?*

Chapter Twenty-Five
Late That Night

Sunny sat on the couch in her parents' living room, attempting to finish the special wedding song she had promised. But as lyrics came to her, Sunny couldn't stop the bombardment of thoughts that pounded on her head about Mel and all he had said. She still couldn't believe his words. "I am from before," Mel admitted.

Sunny kept nodding off while trying to finish writing Robin and Gary's song. Everyone else had gone to bed. Grandma and Grandpa had gone home. Sunny was alone to create, but she would have to stay awake. She began wishing she could just write the song in her dreams and put it on staff paper when she woke up. But that wouldn't work either. Songs, stories, and scenes she dreamed about vanished within minutes of waking to a new day. At home, she kept a pencil and paper beside her pillow to capture the words and images as quickly as possible, before they vanished with the flutter of her eyelashes.

"From before?" Sunny's breath caught in her throat. She couldn't stay awake long enough to process what he meant. During her last nod into a bright, colorful dream, she saw images of Mel. In the misty garden of her sleeping thoughts, she asked the elderly man in the same coveralls he wore when she met him on the airplane, "Are you Jesus?"

Mel's smile filled his face. "No. You are a believer. Your heart would know it if I were Jesus, my dear Sunny."

When her cell phone blared, she was jolted out of that drowsy place where she was beginning to understand things. Confused, she rolled over on the couch and fumbled to answer her phone. "Hello?"

"It's me, Shine," Nick spoke hesitantly.

"Nick," she checked the clock on the mantel, "it's 2 a.m. No one makes a phone call at 2 a.m."

"I couldn't sleep," he said apologetically.

Fluffing the feather-filled pillow she brought down from her room to better support her head. Sunny settled back on the couch. "I tried not to sleep but did anyway. I was working on the new song."

"Shine," he began slowly. "I was hoping we could spend more time together while you're here."

"I know, Nick." Sunny had to confess her feelings, suspecting he knew she was afraid to leave this time. Then, words tumbled out that she hadn't decided to spill. "The rehearsal and rehearsal dinner are on Friday evening. Would you like to be my plus-one? I had already invited you and Maddie to the wedding. She's welcome too. You and she would be my plus-two if that's alright with you."

Nick's words flowed out. "You know I would. Thanks, Shine." Then a few seconds of silence. "Tomorrow, I plan to pick out some tile for the little powder room on the first floor, the kitchen, and the master bathroom. Those are jobs I want to do with my fixer this fall. I'll meet my designer at the tile store. I was hoping you would go along and help me select the right pattern. Your opinion means a lot to me. I kept worrying that you might say no."

Sunny wanted to spend that time with Nick, helping him to make his home a reflection of himself. But would she begin to daydream again about what could have been and get sucked back into a dream of what could yet be? That dream was hers alone. *And how can you get sucked back into feelings like happiness? Everyone wants happiness. That's not a bad thing to be avoided.* "Take some pictures of the bathroom so I know what you're redoing," she suggested.

"That's right. You were only on the first floor when you were here Monday." Nick paused for a minute. "If you have time, you could come to the house first. I'm scheduled to meet Nathan at 1:30 at his store. You could meet me at the house at noon and then ride with me to Nathan's Mile of Tile."

Sunny relaxed and laughed. "Is that really the store's name?"

Nick chuckled. "Isn't it something? Yep, that's it. Nathan's Mile of Tile. I've known Nathan for a few years. He has fun with everything."

Maybe she was so tired at that hour of the night that she would give in to anything. There was one thing she was willing to surrender. Maybe it was her exhaustion talking, but that was okay. "Nick, I need to apologize for acting as I did when I walked out on you at the dance. Some things are hard to face."

"I understand, Shine. I triggered a sore spot in you. I'm sorry, too." He paused and added. "I support all you do and all you decide to do in the future." After a few seconds of silence, he said, "I would love to have you help pick out the tile."

"Okay, that will be fine. Nathan's Mile of Tile. Hmm. See you at noon." She pressed the red receiver on the screen and scooted down more comfortably on the sofa.

Was she going to meet Nick again, for an event that wasn't connected to Robin's wedding? She couldn't believe it. In—she looked at the mantle clock again—less than ten hours.

"Who were you talking to in the middle of the night?" Robin asked as she came downstairs, wrapping her blue chenille robe around her. "Ignore the robe," she said. "I bought a fancy one for the honeymoon."

Sunny answered in one word. "Nick." She saw Robin raise her eyebrows. "I was talking to Nick. Okay? He called *me.*"

"At 2 a.m.? Conservative, well-organized Nick Sullivan called you at two in the morning?"

Sunny sat up, trying to clear her head. "Like I said, Robin. He called me. I didn't call him."

Robin sat on the couch beside her, leaning back into the cozy, pillow-filled corner. "You seem to think that makes the hour more logical. Talking on the phone at two o'clock in the morning is talking, no matter who called who."

"I was working on your song and had a breakthrough. I dozed off, and Nick called." Sunny's speech gathered speed as she explained, "He said he had wanted to call me all evening but was afraid I would hang up. We had a little kerfuffle after the holiday dancing. We both apologized. Then he caught up to me as I was helping Becca, and we got along fine. Tomorrow, he's going to pick out some tile for the kitchen and some bathrooms, and he wants me to go along to help select the pattern." Then her chatter took on a downhill pace. "He realized, when we were all there on Monday, I hadn't seen his whole house. So, he invited me to stop by to see where he plans to install it." She leaned toward her sister. "Do you believe the store's name? Nathan's Mile of Tile."

Robin's crooked smile couldn't be hidden. "Nathan's Mile of Tile? Yes, I've heard of it. Their advertisements are on the radio." She gently touched Sunny's hand. "Sunny, you're so excited."

Sunny blinked as she tried to make sure she was awake. "I feel like I'm still waking up. Like my life thus far has been half real, followed by the other half that is dark and fuzzy all around the edges. The world in the light is beautiful, but I haven't stood in the sun for a long time."

Robin looked deeply at her sister. "Honey, I'm not sure that makes sense."

"It's Nick, Robin. We were in love ten years ago, and it broke my heart to move away. And I never healed." She hung her head in confusion. "It seems Nick was in love with me and simply waited." She stood up and paced over to the mantle. "Robin, I don't know how to open my heart again. Now, millions who love me don't even know me. And I've kept a distance from those who know me and love me."

Robin gave Sunny a sisterly hug. "I am so happy for you and sad you're so mixed up at the same time. Where do you begin?"

Sunny tapped her lips. "I guess, at Nathan's Mile of Tile."

Chapter Twenty-Six
Nick's House

Nick's house appeared to welcome Sunny from the street the next day. Lights were on in the office and living room, even though the sun shone brightly on the house. Sunny guessed he may have waited for her in his office. Getting out of the car, a soft breeze felt good and helped cool the day. She opened Nick's office door and entered the waiting room.

"Good afternoon," the secretary greeted. "May I help you?"

"I'm here to meet Nick. We're going to pick out tile." Sunny sat down on one of the comfortable waiting room chairs.

The secretary stood up and leaned across the flat shelf of the half-door that separated her work area from the waiting room. "You must be Sunny." She stopped and covered her mouth. "Of course you are. I'd recognize you anywhere. He didn't say that Sunny Gaynor was going to meet him. Mr. Sullivan," she blushed, "Nick, will be ready in a minute. He's finishing a phone call."

"Thanks, ah —"

"Corene," the secretary said. "Corene Marsden. Can I bring you a cup of coffee or a soft drink?"

"Nice to meet you. I believe I met your daughter during the Gala."

"She said she met you. I wasn't sure. Perhaps it was wishful thinking," Corene said with a big smile. "So, it really was you."

Sunny nodded. "Yes, it was. She did a great job. If she needs a review for her club, let me know." She saw the table full of literature. "No, thank you for the coffee, Corene. I'll read a magazine." Sunny picked up two periodicals, looked at the covers, and put them down. Her own image was smiling back from them both. "I remember those interviews," she said softly. "I know the ending." She smiled at Corene and put earbuds in her ears to listen to the song she had worked on the night before. She was tapping out the rhythm on her knee as Nick came out of his office.

"Hi, Shine," he whispered. Seeming not to care that Corene was standing a few feet away, he pulled Sunny into his arms and stroked her hair. "I missed you."

Sunny surprised herself. There was no need to pull away from his warm embrace. It felt so familiar and safe in his arms. She could feel his muscles beneath his shirt. She was instantly reminded of how well she fit into his arms.

"I take it you know each other," Corene said, her eyes wide.

Sunny and Nick pulled back but stayed connected with his arm wrapped around Sunny's shoulder. Nick spoke first.

"We met the first day of college, many years ago," he said as he looked at Sunny.

"Can't be that long ago," Corene said with a laugh. "You two aren't old enough to have been college freshmen too many years ago."

"It seems like yesterday," Sunny said with a coy smile. "Maybe we'd better see where the new tile will go."

Nick led the way from the office to his house. The living room was as immaculate as it had been on Monday. The noon sun shone through the dining room floor-to-ceiling windows and the wide patio doors at the back of the house. The backyard and flower gardens dotted the image with color like an artist's masterpiece. The entire area was warm and homey, just like she imagined Nick's home would be.

"Let's go into the kitchen." He pointed past the elegant, curved staircase that flowed into the entry hall and spilled into the living room.

Sunny took a few steps on the stairs, holding on to the cherry wood stair rail. It felt secure yet soft to the touch, firm and dependable to her grasp as she ascended. It was all perfect. Everything about the house said *Nick Sullivan lives here.*

In the kitchen, Nick pointed to certain walls. "This is the area I want to tile." He pointed to the area along the entire wall behind the stove and up to the corner.

Sunny studied the placement of the cabinets and asked, "What do you do, dance from the stove to the sink, to the refrigerator, and back to the stove?"

Nick looked down at the off-white marble countertops. "I learned the Bunny Hop from some children the other day. I've been using that." He hesitated before he added, "I was always hoping to share the house with—never mind."

Sunny leaned her head on the back of his shoulder and whispered, "You've missed a lot of years."

"No, Shine," he corrected. "We've missed a lot of years." Running his fingers over the shiny marble, he said,

"Let's at least save this great house. I've painted the walls this dusty, gray-green. But I'm stuck on the tile."

"The paint color is beautiful." Sunny took her cell phone from her bag. "Let me take a few pictures so we get a nice match at the store." She blocked out several angles with her camera. "The light might cast the paint in different colors or hues. Sometimes, the same object or the paint on the walls of a room, shot in different lighting, will not look the same in a picture. We'll get a better match this way."

After she snapped several shots and put her phone in her purse, Nick put his hand on Sunny's elbow. "Ready?"

Sunny felt his touch and wanted to answer, "Yes, I've been ready for ten years." She didn't. "Okay," was her only comment.

Chapter Twenty-Seven
Nathan's Mile of Tile

Nathan's Mile of Tile was in the Town and Country Shopping Center. Nick turned east off Far Hills Avenue. The store was on the right, so he pulled into the parking lot. "Here we are."

The storefront was splashed with brightly painted colors that flowed from wide, decorative paint brushes. It looked bright and colorful from the outside and invited them in. Wall tile lined the left side of the store, with floor covering on the right.

"Wow, there are so many colors, finishes, and shapes," Nick announced as he surveyed the wall of tile.

Sunny got out her phone and pulled up the pictures. Holding up one image and then another, she slowly walked along the line of tile.

Nick stopped abruptly. "There. What do you think, Shine?" He pointed to a collection of white tiles with fine gold veining running through them.

"Nick, that is wonderful." Sunny grabbed Nick's arm and shook it gently in excitement. Then her gaze caught the softer version on the next panel display. "What do you think of the off-white? It's calmer. If you go out into the kitchen at night, you wouldn't be startled by the reflection that first tile might send."

Nick gave her a side hug. "I knew you would be able to select the perfect one. That's the one I want." He turned as a tall, thin man approached.

"Hi, Mr. Sullivan. May I help you?" Then he saw Sunny. "Aren't you—?"

"Marilyn Monroe?" Sunny spoke in the famous babydoll voice of the '50s movie star and batted her eyes. "Yes, I am."

Nathan laughed. "I heard you had a sense of humor, Sunny Gaynor. It's nice to meet you."

"Hi, Nathan." Nick nodded and tried to draw Nathan's attention away from Sunny. "I no longer need help with tile selection. You may help with the purchase. The decision has already been made."

"You brought your own interior designer. Good, let's write it up." Nathan walked over to the cash register.

Sunny continued looking at the porcelain pieces. "I'll be here, looking at all the beautiful tile," she told Nick.

She searched the display, not for a specific tile, but because she loved color. It was her theory that women become color-deprived, and that's why they love to shop. While in the mall, women's batteries are recharged by the energy from the vibrating colors. She never had her theory tested. She just felt it inside. She caressed the smooth surfaces of the tile. When her cell phone rang, she was jarred back from her dreams.

"Hello?"

"Sunny," the man on the line began, "this is Bruce. Are you enjoying your trip to Ohio?"

"Immensely," she said and looked over at Nick.

"Sunny," Bruce began again, cautiously. "I've been hearing a rumor." He paused.

"About what?" Sunny was impatient. It felt like her two worlds had collided, and she was trapped in the crash between them.

She heard Bruce tapping his pen on his cell phone. "I ran into an old music industry friend this morning. He had heard … that you may be nominated for another Grammy."

Sunny was stunned. She couldn't talk for a minute. Did that change anything for her? Not in her music career, although, it would enhance it tremendously. "When are the awards, Bruce?"

He explained, "The program is the first week of January. The nominations are early in November." He carefully added, "I'll reserve a suite for you at a hotel near the Crypto Arena in Los Angeles. No one would suspect that you were presuming anything. All the other voice artists will be making reservations, too."
Sunny felt defeated and didn't understand the negative emotion. How could a possible Grammy nomination be anything but wonderful? "Okay," she answered with little enthusiasm.

"All done," Nick announced happily. "They'll deliver it tomorrow."

Sunny smiled weakly but didn't speak. To Bruce, she said, "Gotta go."

"What's wrong?" Nick asked. "Who was that on the phone?"

She settled into his arms and said, "My agent. And, there is nothing wrong with you."

"That's good to hear," he said with a wink. "I know you have a busy schedule. I'll take you back to your car," Nick offered.

On the way back, Sunny didn't say anything. However, she worried a lot. *Will I lose Nick again if I leave to go to California for the Award ceremony? What am I talking about? I live in New York City. The celebrity world doesn't mix with the real one very well. There are too many demands. Too many absences.*

Nick broke the silence. "Will I see you tomorrow, lunch, supper, in the evening?"

Sunny didn't answer at first, but reached over and put her hand on his. "I can't. I'll need to finish Robin's song. I don't know how long that will take."

"Sure, I understand," he said, but his tone sounded disappointed.

Sunny nuzzled close to the console in Nick's car and searched the blue sky for answers to her conflicting feelings, her amazing yet smothering career, and her need to find a real home. As a child, answers would always be written in the clouds.

"There it is, Shine." Nick had driven to the house on Mulberry Lane on his way home. "Isn't it something?"

"Why?" Sunny was excited and anxious at the same time.

Nick turned his hands up like he was surrendering. "It's okay, Sweetie. I thought you might like to see it again."

His calling her Sweetie was not overlooked. Sunny felt like she was on a rollercoaster, slamming down to the depths of abandonment, then struggling up to the height of joy, only to fall again. She sat for a minute. "Do you think we could go around to the back again?"

"Sure. We'll knock first to make sure no one is home."

Nick jumped out of the car to ring the doorbell. No one answered. No light shone through the windows.

"Come on," Nick said in fun, opening the car door for Sunny.

She got out of his car, and together, they strolled around the flower garden in front of the house. The sweet, red roses still bloomed, and the grass smelled freshly mowed.

They continued past the glorious flower beds and rounded the corner. Sunny couldn't wait. She hurried to the covered patio and twirled around on the concrete floor with her arms out and her eyes closed. She sat on one of the deeply cushioned porch couches and patted the spot beside her for Nick to join her.

They sat in silence as the safe feeling of *home* overtook Sunny again. Birds flew into the feeders, fluttering and chirping at one another. Sunny thought she recognized a melody in their song. The warmth of the yard was like a fairy tale for her alone to see.

"Come here," Nick said as he reached out and put his arm around her.

Sunny slipped into his arms as she inhaled the fresh Ohio air. Honey bees flicked from flower to flower, collecting nectar for their hive, a source of food in cold winter months. Their hum filled the silence and reminded Sunny of her need for sweet honey on cold nights. A white rabbit hopped into the yard.

"Nick, look," she said without moving from her spot. "That rabbit is adorable."

The bunny cast a glib look at the patio and kept hopping since Rerun wasn't there to chase it. Its large, puffy tail bounced along from behind.

The song of a red cardinal sang from the top of a dogwood tree. Its music was so clear, it filled the yard with a tone as beautiful as any Sunny had ever heard. Her New York apartment was across from Central Park. But, sitting there in that magical garden, she didn't remember ever hearing a bird's song in New York.

"I don't want to move," Sunny finally whispered.

"Then don't," Nick answered, squeezing her gently.

To Sunny, that suggestion had a double meaning.

But of course, they did have to move to return to the activities of the world. They left the magnificent patio and drove back to Nick's office.

Corene was coming out of the office when they pulled into the driveway. Nick said, "We close the office early on Thursdays so Corene can care for her mother. Her mom has a round of appointments in the afternoon. I often spend that extra time with Maddie."

"You are a great uncle, Nick." Sunny reluctantly reached for the door handle.

"I won't see you until the rehearsal? Right?" Nick asked. It sounded to Sunny like he didn't want to let go either.

"Right," she said. Then she kidded. "If I need inspiration for my music, I'll call you. Oh, and this evening, I'll go with April to the Investment Club."

Nick touched her shoulder. "Thanks. I'll be interested in any information that might help Harrison's case."

Sunny didn't want to leave. Then she heard her old routine, "I better go."

Chapter Twenty-Eight
The Investment Club

April had called that afternoon and pulled into Sunny's parents' driveway later that evening. It was 6:30 p.m. The meeting was at 7 p.m. at Gus Walters' house, and April liked to be early.

Sunny was careful as she got in the car. She was finally wearing black designer pants with Irish lace down the seams, and she didn't want to snag them on anything. Anticipating an air-conditioned house, she wore a gorgeous, lightweight, black, three-quarter-length sleeve, cashmere sweater with a scooped neck.

"Love the car, April," Sunny said as she ran her fingers over the white seats and inhaled the earthy leather aroma. "It looks custom."

"It is," April said proudly. "Harrison bought it for me, and I added the upgrade items, like the white leather, a more advanced speaker system, and a better radio." She ran her long fingernails, painted with stars on red polish, over the dashboard.

"It is beautiful," Sunny said. However, she didn't add the additional questions and observations that were on her mind.

1. How much did the extras cost?

2. How long did it take her investments with the
   group to earn that much in returns?

3. She must have felt elated by her husband's
   generosity and her ability to add to it, since she
   was so poor growing up.

But Sunny didn't ask questions. There was no way to make it sound caring and supportive rather than a passive-aggressive putdown.

Pulling up to Gus Walters' home, Sunny studied it quickly. She memorized the address and surveyed the size and location of the home. It was a lavish, two-story house in one of those subdivisions where the wealthy live.

April knocked on the door, then turned the knob. Walters greeted her as quickly as they entered. When he saw her guest, his jaw dropped.

"Sunny Gaynor? I heard you were in town. Welcome! What brings you here? Don't you have investment counselors of your own, in one of those tall skyscrapers of New York City?" Reaching out his hand, he pulled her into the immense great room with huge beams stretching across the twelve-foot ceiling. "Well, mosey on over and have a seat."

Sunny smirked a little, then tried to hide her disgust over Gus's obvious fake Texas accent. *What's that all about?* she wondered. She scanned everything, taking in all the details. The club members wore casual after-work attire, but of the highest fashion and expense. April's dress came to mid-calf and flared when she walked. Sunny had seen one like it in a window display on Fifth Avenue in Manhattan. Calming herself, she took note of the rustic rock fireplace and the furniture. She knew the sofa and chairs were expensive because she had the same brand in her apartment. But she had to keep reminding herself that the club was not Gus Walters' only investment team. He could be a very successful investment counselor.

"Gregory is my great investment guide in the east," Sunny said, her eyes large. "But he's a seeing-eye money counselor, leading a blind person through a desert of numbers. I thought I could learn a little about the process here with this group."

Gus laughed a little and gave Sunny a side hug. "April, introduce your guest to the rest of the group, and I'll go get the coffee pot."

There were three high school teachers in the group, who taught algebra, history, and literature. An art teacher and a music teacher who directed both the band and the orchestra rounded out the group. April made six.

"Here is the wonderful blend of exotic coffees," Gus said as he pulled a gold serving cart into the room. On the mirrored tray were seven porcelain cups with saucers, and seven silver teaspoons for those who wanted cream and or sugar. A plate of chocolate chip cookies was also offered.

"Oh, I see," Sunny said with a smile and a wry glance. "You ply the group with mountain-top coffee so they will invest even more than they planned when they came."

"Oh no," he shrieked under his breath. "You know my tricks." He pointed to the coffee and added, "Well, enjoy your coffee, Pilgrim."

"I've met many like you," she said and couldn't help giving away a warning glance. But inside, she thought, *What a phony.*

Math teacher One, Jerry, commented with a set jaw, "I work the numbers before I get here and know exactly how much I'm going to invest. As the junior varsity football coach, I know how to plan play strategies."

Tiffany, number two, the algebra and trigonometry teacher, agreed. "I use the money I earned on the big deal from the previous meeting, and never touch any of my school paycheck. That way, I never overextend myself."

Number three, Lisa, said, "That's exactly what I do. I won't put my family income at risk."

The art teacher, Violet, added, "I don't know. When Gus reads the prospectus, I list four words that describe what he is saying in a colorful way. Deep down, I just know."

Instrumental music instructor Phil joined in. "Me, too. It has to ring true for me inside. Then, I'll know."

"That is amazing," Sunny exclaimed. "You all make decisions based on your interests and training." She wondered if she should ask the next question. After all, she had come with April. She was Sunny's ride home. Still, she plowed through the thick layer of various strategies. "How do you approach it, April?"

April sat down, took her cup of coffee, black, and swept a few strands of blond hair from her forehead. "I select the stocks based on which ones I can earn the most profit. I enjoy earning money."

Sunny smiled. "Gus, do you always make money?" She sipped from her cup to cover any tell-tale facial signs of investigation.

"Not always," Gus said. "But I put in large chunks of money, too. If they lose, I lose." He brought his cup up to his face. "How do you choose your investments, Sunny?"

"That's what I'm talking about. Gregory will recommend a stock and why he thinks it's good, and I authorize him to buy it." Sunny stared at the surface of her coffee as she stirred it for no reason. "I haven't really learned how to make a financial decision, not based on the math of the prospect, or a gut feeling inside." She drank a little and looked at each investor. As the group focused on their leader, Sunny reached into her purse and turned on her small recorder.

"Let's begin," Gus said. "Maybe Sunny will hear something she likes." From the stack of folders on the coffee table, he selected the one on top. "Okay," he began, running his finger down the page. "Ah, the first offering is the Color Me Happy Paint Company. They are also known as CMH Paint Company. They have been in business since 1955. They are a well-established company with solid numbers in their sales. That reality TV show, The Artsy Builders, uses that paint in every house they decorate. The show's host, Phylicity, has a favorite color from their line. It's Melody, a vibrant, positive color that sings across the wall."

Wow! Sunny's head was swimming. She couldn't have written a song that would press the buttons for each of the investors like Gus had. The math people received the assurance of the key words, "well-established" which probably translated into secure or safe to them. The other key words were "solid numbers," implying great earnings. The music and art people heard "decorate," "artsy," "melody," "vibrate," and "positive colors that sing." Gus had spoken the language of everyone there, even Sunny.

Sunny said, "That is a very creative way to describe the company."

"Those aren't the exact words in the prospectus," Gus admitted. "I condensed it for all of you, so you can make a wise decision."

Sunny didn't respond to his explanation. However, she suspected that the key words were not even in the prospectus, but were carefully crafted by Walters to meet the interests and talents of the investors in the group. That may explain why the group was successful, if you measure success by how much money Gus invests for them, not how much is the return on their investment.

April sparkled. "I like this company. We used Color Me Happy paint on our living room. I can increase my investment this month. It's too beautiful to pass on it."

Jerry scratched his cheek. "I have a little extra money this month. I'm going for the CMH Company. It sounds like a trusted pick."

"It sounds like we don't have to debate this company any longer," Gus said. "What about you, Sunny? Do you want to get in on the stock purchase?"

"It sounds like a harmonious product," she said, wiggling her finger in a conductor's beat of musical time. "I'll invest the next time I come." Sunny hoped that her withholding of money would not be misunderstood. "This evening, I'm being educated by professionals. Tomorrow, I'll open an account at a bank here in Ohio. When I get back to New York, I'll have a large amount of funds transferred to that account. Then, I hope I can come back here for another evening with the group."

"You certainly can." Gus welcomed her with open arms. "I can recommend a very friendly bank, Sunny. The Bank of Ohio, on Far Hills Avenue. My wife, Tamora, is the Vice President there. They are very cooperative." To the group, he added, "Does anyone want to hear another prospectus? Should we spread our investment money over several companies, or pour it all into CMH?"

Sunny was a bit startled. "I have a lot to learn. I would have thought it might be risky to invest in just one product?"

Everyone stopped what they were doing. Jerry said, "Sometimes you have to depend on one star player to make the touchdown."

Phil added, "A soloist can win over the entire audience."

"And a soloist can sing over the top of the entire choir," Sunny added. But the rest of the group didn't seem to get her meaning.

"Good," Gus said and went over to the cart again. "That means it's time for cookies and more coffee. In case you wondered, the coffee is decaf."

"It is?" Sunny asked, amazed by the true aroma rising from the cup. "It is wonderful. You'll have to tell me where you get it."

"Better yet." Gus hurried into the kitchen and brought back an unopened pound can of

Sacred Mountain Coffee. "Here's a pound for you. You can get it from the Mission Marketing Store on Salen Avenue in Dayton."

"Good to know," Phil said, finished his coffee, and bit into a giant cookie. "April, the Athletic Boosters would love these wonderful, chunky chocolate baked goods to be served at our next meeting. The fund is doing fantastically."

Sunny looked at April in surprise. "Are you a member of the Athletic Boosters?"

April did a little fist pump in the air. "Yeah, team!" she said, laughing and recoiling in embarrassment. "Harrison said, even though Micky is only ten years old, he is good at athletics. He'll probably make one of the high school teams. It'll take a while to raise the money for the new bleachers, but—"

"You should know, April," Phil said. "You check the books every week at the meeting. You even set up the spreadsheet on the computer your hubby designated for us."

She laughed. "I wanted it to be right."

"Anneta looks that stuff over every week. She's baffled by it all," Jerry said.

Sunny asked, "Anneta?"

"That's my wife," Jerry said as he ate some of his cookie. "She's a nurse. Works half days in Doctor Blaze's office. She's been coming to my office once a week to organize all the beginning-of-the-school-year stuff, like the athletic schedule, and the Booster Club's bleacher project. You know, all that kind of stuff."

"We're a busy bunch." Phil laughed. "April can even fix the computer program if something goes wrong. She's a computer whiz, but numbers aren't for her."

"Well, thanks a lot." April feigned hurt feelings. "I guess you're right, though. A page full of numbers is not my friend, unless those numbers are zeros and ones, the binary code. Adding a column of digits bores me."

"While April licks her wounds," Gus announced, "I'll take everyone's contributions. I'll meet with you, right over here."

Sunny kept watching April. She had to ask. Given her son's age, it could be embarrassing. "I didn't know you had a son, April."

"Yep," was all April said. She started to wring her hands and quickly put them in her pockets.

Sunny lowered her voice but kept it bouncy and full of fun. "April, your son is ten years old? What an exciting age."

At first, April didn't answer. She ate a bite of a cookie and then looked at Sunny. "Yes, he's ten." She looked away, biting her lip. "Yes, Sunny, I had him in my senior year of high school. That's why I wore sloppy, unfitting clothes and was out of school for a while."

Sunny didn't say more. She remained quiet and waited for April to explain. It was April's story to tell, or not to tell. There was silence between them, but neither moved. The conversation wasn't over.

April's face grew tight, revealing the pain she felt. "When I was seventeen, my stepfather got drunk and raped me. I became pregnant. Micky is the sweetest little boy you'd ever meet."

Sunny put her arm around April and comforted her. "Your stepfather?"

"Yes, Gordon was my stepfather," April admitted, her teeth gritting. "My own father died when I was very young, before we moved to Kettering. Gordon wasn't too bad most of the time. Just when he was drinking."

Sunny felt overwhelmed. She could not imagine how April felt. What else had she assumed about this young victim of poverty, humiliation, and sexual abuse? Coming back to the moment, she said, "His name is Micky? I would love to meet him."

April's eyes brightened. "You would?" April grabbed Sunny and wrapped her in a hug. "We were never really close in school. I had no friends. But … I can feel how much you honestly care now. I told people my husband was in the military and died in a training session. I told Harrison the truth: my poor beginnings, my awkwardness, what Gordon did to me … and Micky. Harrison loved the little toddler from the first time he saw him. After we were married, he adopted Micky. He's the only dad Micky has ever known. The next time you're in church I'll make sure you meet him."

"Great. I am so happy for all of you, April." Sunny thought about everything the group had said. Before she and April left, she went into the bathroom and deleted the last conversation about April's dad, Micky, and Harrison from her phone. She would keep that information to herself.

Chapter Twenty-Nine
Love Found Me

The morning sun had risen high enough for the front porch roof to bathe the glider in warmth but not glare, while leaving the yard aglow with the beauty of God's light. The porch was Sunny's choice to cozy down and finish composing Robin and Gary's song. It was late in the morning on a beautiful day. When she closed her eyes, she could smell the aroma of flowers that drifted up from the plantings in the yard. The spring peonies were gone by then, but the beds of zinnias and glorious chrysanthemums perfumed the air. She knew she was home. Suddenly, she was amazed by the realization that it was the same experience she had on the patio Rebecca showed her on Mulberry Lane.

"Hello, Nick," she said into her phone. "I wanted to hear your voice for a minute. I need to feel grounded. Is this a bad time?"

"No time is bad when I'm talking to you, Shine." Nick's deep, baritone voice floated through the phone like a sea of chocolate syrup. She found it soothing.

Sunny settled back on the porch glider. "I've had a fresh idea for the music, and I wanted to check in with you."

"I'm honored," he said warmly.

Sunny thought she could hear the blush in Nick's tone. His face often turned a warm red when praised, especially if it touched his heart a little.

He hesitated, then asked, "Are there any particular words you want to hear from me?"

Sunny knew what she wanted him to say. Since she couldn't utter the words herself, she couldn't ask Nick to be vulnerable either. "Nothing special," she said, knowing it wasn't true. Then she thought of something less personal. "You could sing the words to our college pep song if you want to," she said with a laugh.

"Well, let's see," he began. "I think I remember it."

"No, Nick, I was just kidding." She laughed.

Over her protestations came the familiar words, "I won't sing for a singer. But the words are,

> Go team, go
> down the field,
> even in snow,
> go team go."

"Hum." Sunny acted confused. "That's not the way I remember it."

"That's because you have all the musical talent, Shine. We make a good couple. You do the singing, and I listen with pride."

She finally found the courage to say, "That does sound like the perfect team." But then, that was why she had called Nick, to hear the voice that completed the other half of her heart. "I better get busy, or your pride will melt into your shoes at Robin's wedding if I don't finish this song."

"Before you get back to creating, the radio station's general manager said he would have time at 3 p.m. today.

Would you have the song done so you could go with me? He was impressed when I said I would bring a famous guest. I'd have to pick you up at 2:30."

Sunny laughed softly. "I'll make sure I'm finished."

"Great. I'll see you then," he said with a giddy voice.

"That will be fine. I'll see you." She gripped the phone more tightly. Her cheeks felt warm, like she glowed. Her smile was evident in her voice: "See you later." She knew that planning to meet Nick that afternoon would be the incentive she needed to stay focused and complete the song more quickly.

Her small musical keyboard waited for her over by the porch railing. It sat ready to play the chords she had already written. She touched the keys and played them again. The chords sounded all right. But just *all right* wouldn't be good enough for Robin's special song. Her major problem was in letting go and letting the music flow. Deep down, she knew she would have to allow herself to experience love to write about love. But how?

What did Mel say? "Lay your heart on the wind. Let the love of God in. He'll teach you to love others … like Nick." It's true, Sunny had added Nick's name herself. "Lay your heart on the wind," she repeated. And over and over, she pleaded, "How?"

Instantly, a feeling of knowing took over. Like God had laid an answer on her heart. Being able to use or understand her "knowings" began when Bruce suggested she attend a relaxation seminar. Sunny had been experiencing stress from months of travel and being surrounded by so many people. Relaxation was no longer a talent she possessed. Now, she would put what she had learned at the seminar into practice. She knew it would be an answer to her "how" prayer.

Sunny lay down on the glider and closed her eyes. A breeze from the yard brushed across the porch and blew some curls that caressed her cheeks. Breathing more calmly with each breath, she slipped deeper and deeper into a state of relaxation. "Lay your heart on the wind," she repeated. In her mind, she imagined an incoming breeze, whipping below and around her. Would she have the nerve to leave the security of being firmly planted on the ground? She prayed, "God, you are love. I choose to lay my heart on the wind, and let my heart fill with your love."

In her imagination, she saw herself stretched out like a mighty eagle, lying on the wind and feeling the wings of angels holding her up. She saw herself push off from the cliff, gliding and soaring on the breath of God. She felt inexpressible joy. Perhaps descriptive words might be elation and exhilaration.

"I can let go and embrace love," she cried out in the secret place of her heart. Then, her thoughts filled with:

> So, I lay my heart on the wind
> Letting love blow in.

Sunny picked up her phone again and punched in a series of numbers. "Hi, this is Sunny. I think I'm ready to give in."

Chapter Thirty
Marriage Takes Planning

"So, give them a WACK, folks. WACK them with love. WACK them with the truth. WACK them with songs. We'll be right back." The voice faded into a commercial. "Wrinkler Feed and Grain will be open an extra hour next week, as farmers begin to—"

Nick turned the radio down as Sunny fastened her seat belt. "Same Drive Home radio talk personalities as ten years ago."

"Really?" Sunny questioned. "Ben and Dan are still on?" Then the last ten years blew past like a tornado, making a pictorial director of her rise to stardom. "Of course, they would still be around if they like this market. I'm still around after ten years."

"Of course, you are." Nick reached for her hand and kissed her fingertips. "You will be around forever."

She blurted out, "You mean I'll never have a family, or a home, or a place to belong?" Then she wished she hadn't said anything. Maybe Becca could help her change part of that.

"What does one have to do with the other, Shine?" Nick rubbed her hand with his fingertips. "Everybody has a job, a career of some sort. Most people eventually get married. Many people want children. Some couples have more than one. They don't choose one and rule out the others. They do it all."

"But, how can they work eighteen hours a day and still be home to fix dinner for the family?" Sunny had struggled all week with how to manage it all. She still didn't know. "I might have a three-week concert tour out of the country, get home, and leave a week later for another one."

"That's why artists have a manager," Nick tried to explain calmly. "The singer or actor says, 'Plan my trips, but I want X-number of hours or days at home.' The artist doesn't do everything."

"Nick, I can't turn down opportunities," Sunny protested, leaning on the last ten years of fulfilling every commitment Bruce made for her. That's how she built her career. It was a formula that worked.

Nick was silent for a minute, then began, "Okay, let's think this through. If Bruce booked you into a big arena in Holland for Friday and Saturday, November 22 and 23. Then, sign a contract for another concert in London on the 24th and 25th. Next, he arranges for you to be in Paris on the 26th from 4 to 6 p.m., and Dublin, Ireland, on the 26th from 7 to 9 p.m. Would all of that be possible?"

"Wait," she grabbed her forehead with both hands, "I wouldn't be able to finish a show, change out of my costume, travel, and get to any stage in Dublin an hour later."

"But you're committed to perform on that schedule," Nick insisted. "Hurry, you can run and get it all done."

"The schedule has to be realistic," Sunny demanded, her voice a little louder.

"Shine, of course it does. You or a manager would develop a schedule that is possible for you. If you were married, you and your husband would make a schedule together. If sacrifices are needed, you would take turns making those adjustments. You would do that as a single person. And you'd do that as a couple. If you had children, their activities would be on the family master schedule, too."

"That life sounds full to me."

"I know, isn't it wonderful? Family life is packed with activities, exhaustion, exhilaration, … and love. And it only lasts about a third of your life. After the children are on their own, there will be time to spend with the grandchildren and travel. It is all full, Shine, full of love, full of joy, full of a sense of success and achievement, full of being all God planned for you to be."

Sunny took a deep breath. "That sounds like a fast life."

"You'd have to choose between fast with a family or fast all alone. Life is blessed, loving, busy, full, funny, challenging, sad, and so much more. The difference is inside the weekly planner, and where you spend your time."

Would she be able to ask the next question? Not asking meant another fast track to loneliness. She couldn't move forward without knowing. "What if my spouse wants me to make all the sacrifices, so his career can grow? What if he expects me to play the little woman, stay home, and scrub the floor?"

"I hope that you would know the man better than that before you married him." He paused. "Some families prefer that arrangement and make their plans accordingly. You would talk that over with your future husband before marriage. In your case, you have an agent and a manager to help with your career. You would also have help around the house, like a cleaning service. You shouldn't have to skip a concert because the laundry isn't done. They are all varied jobs, and one person can't do them all. You would have your job, and you and your husband's helpers would have their jobs."

Sunny looked out the window and watched a beautiful hummingbird. *Maybe, that's a sign of hope*, she thought. "What if my husband changed after a time, and became more rigid?"

"There are no guarantees in life, Shine. I know some people change over time. But if you are best friends, worship and pray together, and plan a cooperative life, that's the best you can do."

Then, in the parking lot of WACK Radio Station, he turned off the engine. Taking Sunny's hand in his, he said, "You know me." He stopped again and cleared his throat. "I am a man who would treat his wife as an equal, in all aspects of life. If she makes more money than I do, that's fine. She is probably in a different field of work, or has a different specialty than I, so she earns more. Money doesn't determine an individual's quality or knock the relationship off balance … unless one of you decides to sabotage the marriage." His voice grew soft and gravely. "Shine, if you were my wife, I would cherish you every moment of every day."

Sunny brought his hand to her lips and kissed it gently.

Chapter Thirty-One
Call Letters – WACK

"Good afternoon. How may I help you?" the lady in a light blue blouse and darker blue sweater greeted.

"We have an appointment with the station manager, Howard Thornton. I'm Attorney Nick Sullivan. This—"

"Sunny Gaynor," the receptionist interrupted. "I'm Amy. Mr. Thornton said you were bringing a celebrity with you."

Sunny smiled a generous hello and said, "Nick and I have been friends for many years."

"Wow," Amy sputtered. "My friend is Joe Schmuckatelli." She grinned and picked up the phone. "Mr. Thornton, Mr. Sullivan, and his friend are here."

She stood up from her desk, and Sonny could see Amy's blue shoes with their three-inch heels. "This way," Amy said.

Sunny stared at Amy's shoes as they walked into the inner office. "I like your shoes. I imagine they are shoes made for sitting."

Amy laughed. "You got that right."

"Mr. Sullivan," Thornton greeted, then he saw Sunny. "Are you who I think you are?"

Sunny reached out her hand. "It depends on who you think I am."

Mr. Thornton blushed. "Well, I believe you are Sunny Gaynor." He gestured to the chairs facing his desk. "Please, both of you, sit down." He looked at Nick and asked, "What can I do for you?"

"Thank you for seeing us." Nick touched the back of Sunny's chair. "As I said on the phone, I'm representing Elmer Hollingsworth, Mr. Thornton. I'm with the Innocence Project. If I may, I'd like to ask a few questions."

"Of course. Elmer was a great on-air talent and a good friend of mine." He sat back in his chair. "And, please, call me Howard."

Nick leaned forward with his hands on his knees. "Do you remember any of the questions the police asked you during their investigation, and, hopefully, what your answers were?"

"That's just it," Howard threw one hand in the air like a dismissal. "No one came to the station. They didn't ask one question … from any of us."

Nick looked at Sunny and shrugged. "Then, I guess we have a clean slate." He pulled a few three-by-five cards from his pocket and began. Reading the first question, he asked, "How long did Elmer work here?"

"Wait," Sunny interrupted. "I'm sorry. I keep a small digital recorder in my purse. Nick, would you like to record the session? I keep it to catch any music that comes to me when I'm out and about. Of course, with your permission, Howard."

Howard's eyebrows popped up. "That's fine with me."

Nick turned on the recorder. "I'm talking to Howard Thornton, September 5. Again, how long did Elmer Hollingsworth work here at WACK?"

Howard: "He was on the air from 3 p.m. to 6 p.m. Monday through Friday, for eleven years."

Nick: "Can you describe his work habits?"

Howard: "His audience liked him. He was honest, dependable, fun, and a good friend."

Nick: "Had you ever ridden in his car with him?"

Howard: "He was fanatic about safety. He always drove the speed limit, honored all traffic rules, and ensured the rider's comfort. I rode with him often. We bowled on the same league, and took turns driving to the alley."

Nick: "The afternoon of the accident, were you riding with him?"

Howard: "No. Elmer was still working. It was about noon. He had driven up to Englewood to interview the football coach at the high school. Elmer was a graduate of the school, and the coach was his friend. The interview that Elmer had with the coach was taped and played at about 4 p.m. on his radio show."

Nick: "Now wait a minute, when and where was the accident?"

Howard: "That's just it. The hit and run accident for which he was convicted was at 12:15 in Miamisburg."

Nick: "That's impossible. He couldn't have been north of town and south of town at the same time."

Howard: "That's what Elmer told the police. But they said he could have recorded the interview anytime: in the morning, or maybe even the day before."

Nick: "And the police never asked you?"

Howard: "No, I went to the police station and told them. They said Elmer had lied to me, too. They said someone had seen him at the scene of the accident. But thank you for coming in."

Sunny: "Don't they date and time stamp recordings in radio?"

Nick: "That should have been proof enough."

Howard: "Elmer didn't say anything about it?"

Sunny: "Sometimes that's done automatically by the equipment or the keeper of the recordings. Where is the tape? That would prove he wasn't anywhere near the accident."

Howard: "I'll have Amy track it down. I'll call when she finds it."

Nick stood up and turned off the recorder. "Thank you, Howard. This will help a lot."

"I hope so," Howard stated emphatically. "We were all shocked when Elmer was convicted. Not only would he not drive recklessly enough to injure someone, he was miles away from the accident."

"Thank you." Sunny offered her hand.

"We at WACK would love to get an interview with you, Sunny," Howard began, almost holding his breath. "Are you going to be in Ohio very long?"

"I won't be here much longer this time," she offered as she put the small recorder away. "I promise to come in for a talk ... after Amy finds the recording."

Nick was nearly bouncing with joy. "That may be all we need to set Elmer free. I'll look into the case further and review the court file again. I may have more questions, but this is great." Nick took Sunny's hand and rubbed it with his thumb. It told her, "Thanks. We're together in this."

Chapter Thirty-Two
A Rumor

"Hi Bruce," Sunny sighed slowly into her cell phone. She was trying to get ready for the wedding rehearsal and didn't want to be the last one to go downstairs. An interruption from her cell phone was not welcome.

"Sunny," Bruce began, "I just wanted to let you know. I made your reservation at the hotel closest to the event in L.A. You'll be next to the building for the Grammys. I might arrange to parade you to the red carpet in a limousine anyway. No one would know your driver just went around the block."

"That sounds like a lot of fuss." She put the phone on speaker while looking in the mirror. She raised her hands in surrender and decided to change her blouse.

Bruce sputtered, "Sunny, it's the Grammys. It is a big fuss. I'll check with an escort service—"

She nearly pulled a button off her shirt. "An escort service? Don't you dare!"

Bruce paused, then said stoically, "You write Love-Story songs, Sunny. You don't want to pull up to the ceremony alone."

Tucking the sleeveless shirt into her full-flare pants, she added, "But I *am* alone, Bruce. I've been alone for a long time. Having crowds of people around you all of the time does not mean you aren't lonely." Sunny heard Robin tapping on the bedroom door. "I've gotta leave, Bruce. The wedding rehearsal is soon."

It was obvious that Bruce was shuffling some papers. Sunny could hear the swish and scratch over the phone. Bruce gave in. "Okay, okay, but listen first. With you possibly up for a Grammy—"

"A Grammy? Again?" Robin squealed.

"No, it's not what you think." Sunny slipped on her brown sandals, those with the perfect height heel. "It's just a rumor right now. And it better not be spread any farther." She glared as she put on gold cluster earrings.

"Yes, Ma'am," Robin saluted, smiled, and stuck out her tongue. "But it is very exciting, even if it is a rumor."

Sunny looked in the mirror, and her shoulders drooped. "It would be exciting if I wanted to go back to New York."

Robin's mouth dropped open. "What does a music award have to do with where you live?"

Sunny went limp in surrender. "I don't know, but where I live has always *seemed* important."

"Sunny," her mother called from downstairs. "Are you ready? Nick and Maddie are here."

"Oh, good," she said as she darted out of her bedroom.

Robin yelled after her, "It's good because now you won't have to talk about this anymore."

"That's right," Sunny added as she danced down the stairs.

She looked at Nick and smiled, but spoke to the little beauty. "Maddie," she sang, gathering the little girl in her arms. "You look very nice this evening. It's so good to see you again."

"It's good to see you, too, Sunny," Maddie said and laughed.

"I agree," Nick added with a wink.

Doug began herding the family as he always had. "Pastor Morton will be waiting for us. Let's go. Head 'em up, move 'em out."

Nick held out his hand to Sunny. "Shine?"

Sunny didn't know how to respond. She was lost in maybes and ifs. Reaching down, she took Maddie's hand, then Nick's, hoping he would think they were all just friends.

Chapter Thirty-Three
The Key

"I'm glad we have this time together, Shine," Nick said, as they got into his car to ride the few miles to the church. Nick helped Maddie buckle up and then said, "I have great news. Howard Thornton called back. He said, since Elmer was his friend, he would call me himself."

"Nick, that's wonderful." Sunny took Nick's hand and held on. "Did he find out what you needed?"

"Yes, and no." He turned the corner onto Wilmington Pike. "They did a quick check and found the audio recorder that Elmer had used. The recorder was used in several other interviews since then. The other spots were recorded over Elmer's interview with the Englewood coach."

"Nick, I am so sorry," Sunny sighed, assuming that his lead with the audio recording had burned out.

Nick's smile grew. "That's the bad part. Thornton's positive information pertained to Elmer's friendship with Coach Washington. Elmer completed the audio interview about the team and their recent winning streak. Then they began to reminisce about their time together on the field, and Elmer took a few pictures of Washington with his cell phone. Then he asked one of the students to take a picture of them together."

"Nick, I think I know where you're going with this. It's amazing."

"The cafeteria began to serve lunch at 11:15, to be able to feed everyone. Hank Washington asked Elmer to join him for a meal before he had to leave. They would be serving sloppy joe sandwiches, one of Elmer's favorites in his years at the school."

Sunny chuckled lightly. "Umm, onion and barbecue sauce. It sounds good to me, too."

"Sloppy joes?" Maddie chimed in. "I love them. They're my favorite."

"Me, too," Nick admitted. "When they got to the cafeteria, everyone wanted to meet the WACK radio personality who had graduated from their school. He had always shown favoritism for his former team, even on the radio. But no one seemed to care. They liked the fact that he was a Montgomery County boy and a football hero."

"I like football, too," Maddie said.

"You do?" Sunny asked. She wondered about that. "Where did you learn to play football?"

"At your house, Sunny," Maddie said with a matter-of-fact shrug. "Bobby Blanchart taught me."

"Of course." Sunny looked back and gave Maddie a thumbs-up.

Nick had more good news. "While Elmer greeted teachers and shook hands, he asked one of the teachers to take pictures and short videos with the Coach and those in the cafeteria. The school clock on the cafeteria wall is seen in both the still pictures and videos. It shows that it's 11:22 a.m. After they ate lunch, more pictures were taken, and the clock was in the background of those, too. Of course, the pictures and videos are stored in his phone by day and date."

"Nick, you have proof of his alibi, right there in his cell phone," Sunny said, excitedly. "That's amazing. Why was he convicted?"

Nick shook his head in disbelief. "Thornton said, the police didn't follow up with phone calls, questions, or interviews with WACK. They said Elmer was guilty, and that was the end of it. Elmer was so shocked that he had focused on the audio interview and didn't even remember the pictures and videos. Elmer isn't married, so he didn't have that second memory backup that married people have."

Sunny sat back, admiring his conclusions. "Nick, you have found the key to Elmer's jail cell."

She didn't say that she recognized one more reason to face the world as a couple, to be each other's keeper of memories.

Chapter Thirty-Four
The Rehearsal

At the church, the sanctuary lights were bright. The clergy who had been the minister when Sunny attended and joined the church had been transferred to another congregation. But for Sunny, it was the congregation that made the church.

"Pastor Tom." Doug reached out his hand in greeting. "The herd is here."

The minister looked over at Sunny. "Thanks for coming last Sunday. Your sister said you would be her maid-of-honor, and you'll sing for her wedding." He shook her hand. "We will all try to make it as comfortable for you as possible."

Sunny was surprised by his comment. Still, she laughed in a friendly manner. "It's not about me, Pastor Tom. It's Robin and Gary's wedding. I hope to make it comfortable for them."

"That's what your dad said you would say," Pastor Tom said with a knowing smile. "And that's what we want for you. We've arranged for a private guard to be in the parking lot to ensure only guests come in. They will be very discreet. No one will be aware they're there. If someone does happen to see them, they will assume they are just watching the cars. Some kids like to come into parking lots and write all over windshields with soap. We want everyone to be comfortable." He paused. "Is that okay with you and Robin?"

Robin beamed. "I think it's wonderful."

Sunny was relieved. "If it is okay with Robin and Gary, it is perfect for me."

Maddie wrinkled up her nose and looked at her Uncle Nick. "Doesn't Sunny like to sign autographs?"

Nick squeezed Sunny's hand. "Sure, she does. But sometimes, she just wants to be Robin's sister and have family time." He patted Maddie's shoulder. "If you were having a birthday party, would you want a whole bunch of people to come into the yard, trample on our beautiful flowers, interrupt conversations and games, and flit around in your face like pesky mosquitoes?"

"No," Maddie announced with her hands on her hips. "Unless they all brought a present." She hugged Sunny and added, "I'm glad we're part of your family, Sunny, and not a stranger walking on the flowers."

"Me, too," Nick mouthed.

Sunny had no idea why she did it or where the courage came from. She rocked up on her tiptoes and kissed Nick's cheek. "Me, too."

"Let's all get ready," Pastor Tom said. "Two of the groomsmen will usher Grace and Gary's mother, Marie, to their pews. Steven, you follow Marie and her escort. Then, Sunny, you will be up there on the chancel. Once they are seated, you begin to sing. When you finish, the organist will begin playing one of the pieces Robin selected. Sunny, you come down and take your position as maid-of-honor. Gary, the best man, and the two groomsmen will come in and line up over there." He pointed to the opposite side of the steps. "As soon as they are in place, the procession will start with the ladies. Finally, Robin and Doug will start down the aisle." Then he asked, "Robin, will your attendants use the step - stop - step - stop walk down the aisle? It's not done often anymore."

Robin put both hands to the sides of her face. "Oh my, just walk, girls, just walk."

Nick and Maddie sat down in the third row and watched the marching and positioning. Maddie watched every move, but Nick had his eyes fixed on Sunny.

Sunny didn't practice her song. When she put the last note onto paper, the organist received the music by email. They rehearsed a few measures over the phone so the organist could get Sunny's timing. She wanted the music to be a surprise. However, she did walk through the staging as the pastor had directed, to make sure she ended up where she belonged, beside Robin. While the others went through their movements, Sunny went down and sat with Nick.

Gary hugged Robin. "Let's just call this rehearsal our marriage and forget all the fancy stuff. No tux, no tight shoes, no gagging tie, just athletic shoes, and shorts."

"I'm not sure you can get into the restaurant in shorts," Sunny said. "We'll eat off the evening menu."

Nick looked down. "I'm glad I wore my big-boy pants."

"I wore a dress," Maddie said, twirling around in the church's aisle. "They'll let me in to have my supper."

Sunny gave her a thumbs up. "You look precious, Maddie."

Doug whistled. "Okay, gang. Let's make this a perfect rehearsal. I'm getting hungry."

Sunny looked at Nick. "And you are one of those men who could eat all the time."

"I used to be," he admitted. "Now, I'm a little slower with shoveling it in."

"I used to like to watch you eat." Sunny patted Nick's stomach. "You looked like Rerun at her dog dish."

"I would be insulted about being compared to your dog," he said, watching the wedding party get into position again. "If I didn't know how much you love that little furry thing." He twisted one of Sunny's long curls around his finger.

Sunny closed her eyes as she savored the sweetness of Nick's touch. She didn't want to leave his gentle caress when her dad whistled again.

"Sooie, sooie," he called out slowly.

Grace rolled her eyes. "You aren't calling the hogs, Dear. It's a wedding rehearsal."

"Not yet," he said with a grin. "Move, move, move."

Sunny patted Nick's arm and went back up to the lectern to practice timing and location. She hummed into the microphone, then told the accompanist, "I'll bring my guitar, too. That will mellow everything out." To practice sound and volume, she began singing a favorite song:

be!   When we all
joic-ing that will be!   When we all
see   Je - sus,

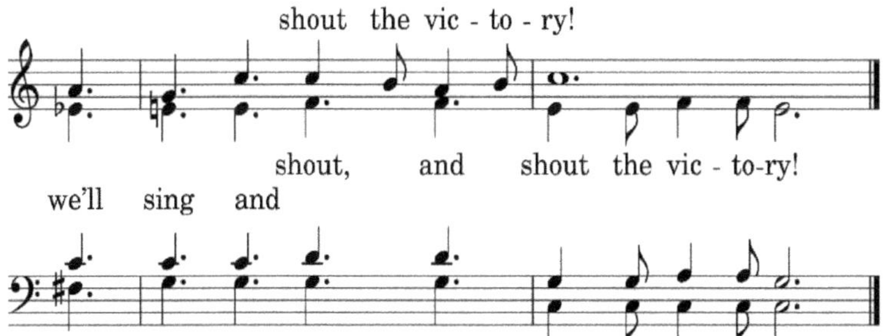

shout   the vic - to - ry!
shout,   and   shout   the vic - to-ry!
we'll   sing   and

Chapter Thirty-Five
The Rehearsal Dinner

The casual/elegant restaurant Robin and Gary chose for their rehearsal dinner had large windows facing a stand of breathtaking maples. In the fall, the trees would turn scarlet red. It was still the first week in September. But there was a tickle in the air that smelled like autumn. In the dining room, the meal the restaurant had prepared was a fragrant blend of barbecue ribs and filet mignon, laced with the perfume from the overflowing, flowery table arrangements.

After everyone was seated, Doug raised a hand and began one of his favorite quotes, "Of all the smells I ever smelled, I never—"

"Dad," Robin insisted playfully, "no! Not another dad-ism."

"Okay, okay," he surrendered, letting his best words fall on the floor. "Sit anywhere. There are no nameplates. Find a chair and claim it for yourself. We'll have grace before they serve the food."

Sunny wondered if her dad would pray the same mealtime prayer he did every night when she was growing up. She hoped he would. That would be a treasure for her.

Nick touched Sunny's waist, a small connection that made her feel like they were together. "Maddie and I will follow you," Nick said.

"We'll sit beside Robin and Gary. You, too, Maddie," she said, pointing to three chairs near the center of the head table. "Mom, Dad, and Gary's parents have planned to sit on the other side of the table. That leaves the chairs facing us at the next table, for the wedding party." Sunny put her lacy wrap on the back of the chair in case the room was chilly.

"Let us pray," Doug began. "We thank thee, Heavenly Father, for these and many blessings. Pardon, forgive us our sins." Then he added the precious words Sunny knew that Robin would love to hear. "And bless our princess, Robin, and her soon-to-be-prince, Gary. May their lives be filled with your joy and remain knee-deep in happiness forever. We ask in Jesus' name. Amen."

Sunny was surprised when Nick pulled out her chair for her. When he whispered, she felt warm.

"You look beautiful." His breath brushed her ear. "Sorry if I said something I shouldn't have."

"Nick, no. Thank you," she said when Holly Blanchart came up and rubbed her shoulders.

"Hi, Sunny," Holly greeted. Sunny would have recognized the lilt in her voice, even if she hadn't seen her coming. "Phil will be here in a minute. He's parking the car." She continued to massage Sunny's back. "I have a big favor to ask of you."

"Oh?" Sunny sat down on the comfortable dining room chair, surprisingly, well-cushioned in leather on the seat and back.

"Phil's fifteen-year-old niece heard that he was going to a dinner party tonight and that you would be here,"

Holly began slowly. "He is going to ask for your autograph for Candy. But he doesn't like the idea of bothering you. If he wants to be in good graces with his sister's family, he has to ask the intrusive question here at Robin's rehearsal dinner."

Nick blinked several times. "Phil is as confused as I am." As Phil approached the table, Nick had an idea. "Why don't I ask for the autograph? What's his niece's name?" He pulled a blank, three-by-five card from his jacket pocket. "I always carry cards with me in case I need to jot down some information."

"I understand." Sunny reached for her purse. "I carry some business cards, that I call fan cards, with me all the time. I'll write something on the back."

Holly got excited and looked for Phil, who had stopped to talk to someone. "Candy," she instructed Sunny. "Her name is Candy."

"Great." Sunny wrote, *Thanks for your friendship, Candy. Sunny Gaynor.*

Phil walked up. "Sorry. I hope I wasn't late. I saw an old friend. I had to stop and say, 'Hi.'"

"You're just in time. We haven't started eating yet," Sunny said as she handed Phil the card. "Here, this is for Candy."

With a sheepish grin, Phil raised his eyebrows at Holly. "I had finally decided not to bother Sunny with this."

"Oh, that's alright," Sunny said as she waved him off. "I heard Holly and Nick talking about it." Which she had, although it was a three-way conversation. "I had a card in my purse and jotted it out in seconds. No trouble at all."

Phil waved the card over his head. "Sunny, you are a sweetheart!"

Nick quietly took Sunny's hand under the table and rubbed her palm with his thumb. In a room full of people, they were together.

"Uncle Nick," Maddie interrupted. "I have to go to the bathroom."

"I'll take her," Sunny offered. "Come along, Maddie."

Sunny took Maddie's hand in hers. As they walked across the dining room, patrons stopped eating, stared, and buzzed about the musical star in their midst. "That's Sunny Gaynor."

Sunny didn't look back. In the few minutes she could claim as her private time, she didn't look out of the fishbowl she lived in, even though many looked in. Opening the Ladies' Room door, she checked to make sure no one was there. "It's empty, Maddie," she said. "You can go in. I'll be right here. I see someone I know."

Sunny waved a little and walked over to Mel, who stood beside the checkout counter. The cashier had stepped into the room behind the counter, and Mel was there, leaning on the glass top, as if waiting for her to return.

"Hi, Sunny. Have you thought more about the house?" Mel asked and smiled.

"I've thought about it a lot." She looked at him with a smile. "I told my grandfather about meeting you. He told me his grandfather's name was also Mel Gaynor."

Mel looked over at the wedding party's table and smiled. "John? Yes, he's a fine man. And Claudia is a sweetheart."

"You know them, then?" Sunny concluded.

"A little," was all he admitted. "I like to stay close to those I care for." He patted Sunny's hand where it lay on the counter and changed the subject. "You would be close to Nick in that house on Mulberry Lane. That is, if you have decided to let him get close, to fill out the rest of you... your personal life."

Maddie burst through the restroom door. "Sunny, I'm ready."

"Good," she answered and hugged the girl. "Did you wash your hands?"

"I did. Uncle Nick told me to sing a whole verse of 'Mary Had a Little Lamb' while I washed, to make sure they were clean."

"What a great idea, Maddie." Sunny turned to Mel, but again, he was gone.

On the other side of the room, Nick was smiling at them with those eyes that warmed her heart.

When they got back to the table, Nick smiled and whispered, "When you started back to the table, it's like they turned the lights on. I remember Lawrence Leininger, our Psych professor, saying that you have quite a sensual glow. I was standing beside you after class, so I know he wasn't flirting. He was making an honest statement about the way you shine when you come into a room. It isn't your celebrity. You were eighteen years old at the time, Sunshine Sullivan. You were just ... mine."

Sunny didn't look at him. She wasn't afraid of his closeness this time. But her own "glow" might give away her feelings before she completely knew his.

Nick looked at others around the tables and saw that they were involved in their conversations. "After the parade last Monday, we had a hiccup, a kerfuffle, and you walked home. What happened?"

Sunny's grin was sheepish. "I didn't walk all the way home. Rebecca saw me and picked me up."

"Whew..." Nick relaxed. "Why didn't you tell me?"

Sunny looked into Nick's eyes. He was smiling. "I sent a text. Besides, you didn't ask me," she admitted.

He put his arm around her and pulled her close. "Are you finally home?"

She received his embrace and returned his love by letting go of that first brick in the wall between them. "Nick, do you remember, in that first year I was away, when I called from New York because I had to hear your voice? A girl answered your phone."

"I sure do, Shine." Nick looked at her intently. "It was the last time you would take my calls. What happened?"

In a low, trembling voice, she slowly continued, "You and the woman were playing around with the phone." Sunny reached out and tenderly touched his cheek. "Nick, who was she?"

"That silly lass who teases and pushes me around?" Nick took Sunny's hand from his cheek and kissed her palm. "Shine, that was Emma, my little sister, Maddie's mom."

At that moment, Sunny's wall lay in crumbles at her feet, leaving her with no bricks to hold her up. Her heart rose from the rubble, freeing Sunny to love again.

Running on a collision course with her reborn feelings of love, the Grammy Awards ran through her mind like a tornado alert. The gilded gramophone on top of its base shone brighter than anything around her. Then she thought of Nick, and he shone more brightly. The phone call she made the day she completed Robin and Gary's song rang loudly. And Mel's words flooded her mind.

Chapter Thirty-Six
The Big Day

Robin and Gary's wedding day blew in on the fluffy white clouds of a beautiful September morning. Sunny woke up and stretched. Wafting up the steps was the smell of frying bacon and the sound of her mother singing "Oh What a Beautiful Morning."[11] Was it any wonder why Sunny broke into song without notice or warning? She jumped into some shorts and a T-shirt and hurried down to all the family activities.

"You're up early," her mom sang out. "Your dad and the rest of the men are still on the links. Robin is sleeping, I guess. I haven't seen her yet. Your grandparents will get here about eleven."

Sunny was amazed. Her mom could make an impromptu meal out of the contents of her refrigerator. "Are you going to fix lunch for everyone?"

"Yes, and no," she said with a chuckle. "I have bread and buns, sliced ham, and roast beef from the deli. I picked up potato salad and coleslaw while I was at the store. Served on paper plates and eaten with plastic forks, it will be nutritious, filling, and quick."

"Mom," Sunny began and hugged her, "you are fantastic."

"Thanks, Sweetheart. A long time ago, I found that you can accomplish things without complicating your life."

"Thanks." Sunny nodded. "That helps a lot with some of the things I've been thinking about."

"Helps with what things, Dear?" Grace put bacon on two plates and scooped up some scrambled eggs for each. "Here, take them over to the table. I'll keep Robin's breakfast warm."

"This looks wonderful, Mom." When her mother joined her, she tasted the food. "These eggs taste amazing."

"*You* are amazing, Honey." Her mother put her fork in the eggs and blew on the bite. "I heard you finishing the wedding song the other day." She paused and cleared her throat. "It is beautiful. It should do very well with the public."

"You have always been my greatest fan," Sunny admitted. "You're the canary in the coal mine. If you like it, everyone will."

Grace reached down and gave Rerun a tiny piece of bacon. "Honey, I wish you were closer so I could tell you more often."

Sunny wondered if she should tell her mother about the struggles she had been having in recent days. Rehashing confusion didn't seem productive. There wasn't anything certain to tell anyone, only some ifs and maybes.

Grace asked, "Are you going to see Nick before the wedding?" She paused. "I like him. But the important question is, do you?"

Do I? Sunny tried to come up with an honest answer. *Like* was a very mild word to describe her feelings for Nick. But how could she admit her feelings about Nick when she had to sort out some major issues that surrounded their relationship? "I do, Mom. A lot."

When her cell phone rang, Sunny didn't want to answer. It was probably Bruce again, and she didn't want to complicate the day with more talk of awards and movie deals. Stealing a glance at the screen, she smiled. It was Nick.

"Shine," Nick spoke cautiously, "I picked up the tile for the kitchen backsplash. The wedding isn't until this evening. Would you have time to come over and advise me on the layout pattern?"

Shine was glad she would have a few hours of creative distraction. She was feeling anxious, and it would help her to relax. Sunny had entertained thousands, but hadn't sung a note for family and friends in years. "I'd love to."

Chapter Thirty-Seven
Working Together

Boxes waited on the island at Nick's. "Here it is," Nick said, as he opened one and removed several pieces of kitchen tile. "What do you think?"

Sunny smoothed the surface of the matte finish, off-white tile. "Nicky, I knew it was the right one there in the store, and I'm positive now that I've seen it with the cabinets and flooring. It is beautiful."

A darker shade of cream tile had already been installed on the floor and the front of the island. With a shade of warm blue on the island's paneling, everything was coming together, with the same harmony that Sunny put into her music and art pieces with which she surrounded herself.

"Do you think I should stack them?" He put a few in place, all lined up vertically. "Or another pattern?"

"They are gorgeous. Any arrangement would be nice. I do like the double basket weave pattern." Sunny laid two tiles, side by side, at a right angle. Then two off the center, going northeast, and two off the other side, going southwest. She

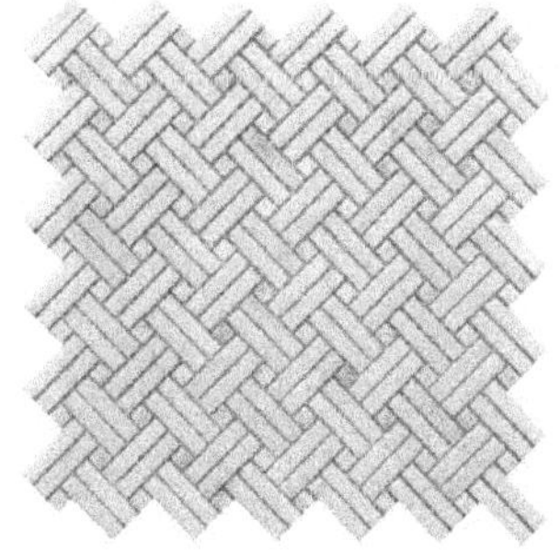

continued the pattern until she had a square for Nick's inspection. "The time-consuming part will be filling the little square that will have to be cut to place in the space. How about this one?"

Nick smiled and patted the completed square. "I love it."

Sunny studied the tile and the floor. It was amazing. Nick had taken all of her suggestions and applied them to his home. "I love it, too."

"Do you want to see the rest of the house, Shine?" Nick asked cautiously. "When you were here before, you didn't see the second floor or the basement."

Sunny looked around the room, inhaling the sweetness of the house. Then she took in the colors and the style of the furniture. Nick had been redecorating, and Sunny would like to see it all. But the second floor, the bedroom floor, might be too intimate for her. That freshman year in college, she had dreamed of someday marrying Nick Sullivan, but she couldn't immerse herself in wishes and regrets on the day of Robin's wedding. Her sister's celebration should be a joyous day. "I'd like to see the basement." Maybe he would understand.

"Sure, Sunny. I get it." Nick took her arm and ushered her to the open stairs. The handrail had wonderful wooden turnings that were finished in the same tone as the floor.

Walking down the steps, Sunny ran her fingers over the balusters like the strings of a harp. At the bottom, she stopped and took in all the fun areas that Nick had placed there. "Oh, how wonderful!"

Nick spread out his arms for Sunny to take in the entire room. "Maddie spends a lot of time here. This is her space." A large television hung on the wall. "Right now, at her age, I have videos for her and the friends she invites for a Saturday afternoon. I don't want to let her have access to everything on TV until she's a little older. In a year or two, I'll have cable installed, with parental controls, even though I'm not her parent."

Sunny watched his face light up and asked, "You've missed having children of your own, haven't you?"

"Shine, it's not too late. I'm only thirty-two. Maddie lets me practice on a seven-year-old." He took her hand. "It's not too late for —"

Sunny's heart was ready, but part of her wasn't. She changed the subject. "Nick, you built Maddie a basketball court over in that corner, and an art studio in the other. Thick pillows and stuffed animals are everywhere." Turning to another nook, she bent over in laughter. "Maddie even has a play kitchen."

Nick smiled. "The stove doesn't work. But the sink has running water, and the small refrigerator is cold. She keeps orange juice bottles in there for her friends."

Sunny clapped her hands and turned around. "And there's a short balance beam over there," Sunny said as she walked over to the wooden beam, six inches off the floor. "This looks like fun. I might have to play down here with Maddie sometime."

"Does that mean you'll come back home more often?" Nick asked, giving Sunny the space she seemed to need.

Sunny picked up a little basketball that lay in the corner and made a shot. "I'm working on a plan." Before Nick could say more, she checked her watch. "We'd better leave. I have to get my hair done today."

Nick wrapped one arm around her as they started toward the steps. "It looks beautiful just the way it is."

Sunny curtsied a little. "Thank you, kind sir. The queen for the day has a specific coiffure in mind for all her subjects."

Chapter Thirty-Eight
A Fun Run

Nick backed out of his driveway onto the street, which was lined with magnificent maple trees. The graceful limbs formed an arch above the sturdy, red oak trunks.

Sunny and Nick were quiet, with only the music from the radio to fill the car with song. As Nick turned onto Mulberry Lane, Sunny sat up a little straighter. "My street."

"I like the sound of that," Nick said.

"Well, I meant, this is the street with my favorite house on it." She quickly turned and looked out the side window. How was she going to explain herself?

"There it is." Nick pointed down the block as he slowed the car. "Looks like there's a sign in the yard."

"It's probably the For Sale sign." Sunny craned her neck to see better.

As they nearly coasted into the next block, Sunny smiled. The sign read, Sale Pending.

"What ya thinking?" Nick asked.

She grabbed Nick's arm and squeezed. "I'll tell you later."

She began singing the lyrics that came to mind. They were little rhymes that were fun to her and allowed her to speak, without really saying a word.

A secret is precious to me,
It's a surprise that was meant to be,
Be patient, my love, I'll tell you in time,
It's a secret message from your Shine.

Nick reached over and took her hand. "My love? My Shine?"

"That's part of my secret," she said, pulling down the sun visor and checking her lipstick. It gave her something to do and filled the lovely silence with … anything. Before she replaced the mirror, she noticed a fancy red sports car behind them following their every turn.

"Anything wrong?" Nick asked.

"It's just me. It looks like that red car is following us." Sunny quickly turned around to see behind them. "You would think, if he were a stalker, he would have chosen a less conspicuous color."

"Is one really there?" Nick adjusted his rearview mirror to check how close the car was to his own.

"No. It's just that it feels like everyone is looking at me or following me." Sunny looked into the rearview mirror again. There was no suspicious follower. "I'm not paranoid, Nick. I'm … I just want to be a normal person who happens to write music and sing songs."

"You already are, Shine. Everyone is a normal person with certain talents and gifts." Nick patted her knee. "Remember, you even played a spy at Gus Walter's house."

Sunny laughed. "I sure did."

"Did you get any information that would help Harrison's situation?" Nick turned into a full parking lot at the dealership where he had purchased his car. He waved at a salesman. "Hi, Sam. I want to have my tires checked. I'm going to pull around."

Sam waved him on, and Nick zipped to the back where the air pumps were. "I'll be right there," Sam called after him.

"I saw some things. I'll tell you about them as soon as I gather my thoughts about that night," Sunny said.

When Nick parked by the air pumps, Sunny jumped out of the car and stretched. He hooked up the gauges and tapped the air hose. "It's good," he said and replaced the cap.

Sunny recalled an evening in Naperville during Homecoming. After the parade and a great football game, several friends, along with Nick and Sunny, headed to an ice cream parlor in town to celebrate with huge banana splits. Gordy, a freshman commuter with a legal car on campus, let Nick borrow his Jeep to drive Sunny back to the dorm. As she slid over in the car, she felt him beside her and admired the way he handled the vehicle, strong and confident, not reckless. That day in Kettering, she dismissed the nostalgic thoughts. She couldn't keep flashing back to the past.

"Now, to the hair salon, my Dear," Nick announced. "Your appointment to join the Gaynor Sisters quartet is coming soon."

Sunny opened the car door. "Nick, we won't all look like paper dolls of the Gaynor quadruplets. Robin has a general idea of our hairstyle, but we will instruct the hairdresser in our style, whether short, medium, or long hair is our preference."

Nick shook his head in admiration of her individualism. "Somehow, I knew that."

Nick put up the air hose, and Sunny jumped into the car. "We are all individuals," she reminded him.

"I'll be along this evening, too." Then he snapped his fingers. "If there's time, be sure to tell me what you discovered about the investment club."

"While I'm waiting for the others to get their hair done, I'll gather my thoughts and take some notes."

Nick pulled into the shopping center parking lot. "I had fun."

"Me, too." She touched the door handle. "I always do when I'm with you."

Chapter Thirty-Nine
From Top to Toe

Sunny was the first to have her hair shampooed and "done," as her grandmother would say. Jen, the hairdresser, took extra time letting the warm water work the fresh lemon-smelling shampoo into her hair and massaging her scalp.

"How does that feel, Sunny?" she asked. "Wait until I tell my family and friends, I did Sunny Gaynor's hair."

"It's true," Sunny agreed. "But I prefer to say you did the bride's sister's hair."

When she completed the blow-dry and styled her hair, Jen spun Sunny's chair around and let her see her reflection in the mirror. Sunny was pleased. Her long hair had been swept up into a beautiful puddle of curls.

"If you go shopping, Dear," her mother warned, "your upsweep might meet its downfall."

Sunny laughed. "Mom, you're funny. No, I'm not going out. I'll sit over there and get my pedicure." She transferred to the manicure and pedicure station. "When Lilah is finished with me, I'll go over to that corner," she pointed, "and make a few notes."

"What are you going to write about?" Grace asked.

"When I give away the plot or melody I'm writing, it takes away all the urgency of getting it down on paper. Like a pierced balloon, the idea will wilt and wither to the ground."

"Oh my," Grace said, holding her hand to her chest. "The death of a developing song. We wouldn't want that."

"Alright, alright." Sunny put the back of her hand on her forehead. "No, Ma'am. I'm going to sit right here."

Sunny opened her folder and took out some lined paper and a few sheets of musical manuscript paper. "I contribute my feet to this endeavor," she said to the pedicurist, "but I'm going to jot down some ideas." The tension in her shoulders melted as she felt the warm water on her feet, while her toes dissolved into the foot bowl.

"You just relax, Sunny," Lilah said. "I'll take care of your feet."

Sunny smiled but was too relaxed to speak. The investment characters danced in her head. *If I were creating a song using these characters as the beats and rhythm, what value would I give each note?* At the top of the music staff sheet, she drew eight zeros, symbolizing the notes of music. *Now the values.* She sketched a treble clef symbol and smiled.

- *Gus would get two beats, including the downbeat. He selects the items for the group to invest in. And, he disburses the profits. He has the greatest influence as a leader and a professional investment counselor.*

- *But there's something about Anneta. She's also involved in this mess in several ways. She works in the athletic office organizing the entire schedule and program, and she's the treasurer of the Boosters Club, in control of the funds. She deserves two beats.*

- *April is a member of the Boosters Club but has no control of anything, except perhaps the coffee. Still, she is very gifted with computers and computer programs. She might be able to hack into the Club's funds. She would have a half beat.*

- *Jerry teaches General Math and should be aware of the investment process. He's also the JV football coach, but has no personal access to the Boosters Club funds. His beat value would be one beat.*

- *Tiffany, Lisa, and Violet are respected teachers, but have no contact with the Boosters Club. Violet has no contact with any of the investment discussions. She didn't care. Phil directs the band and supervises their march patterns, but has no connection to the Boosters Club. The first two get eighth notes, and Violet gets none. She'll have a rest.*

Sunny studied her notes and closed her eyes. Musical scores and the faces of the club members sang in her head like a choir. In her mind, she arranged and rearranged the 4/4 time into an answer. Relaxed and surrendering her will to God, like composing Robin's wedding song, Sunny laid her heart on the wind and let the music tell the story.

As the music sang in her heart, she stacked the two, two-beat notes on top of each other, with Gus on the top, creating a chord.

April's half beat stood alone.

Violet had the rest.

The four other members represented eight notes in 4/4 time

"By George, I think I've got it!" Sunny looked at the notes. "Now, let's see. Da da, de, rest, da da da da."

"A new song, Sunny?" her mother asked as she sat down beside her.

"Well, sort of." Sunny held the folder tighter. "It's short, but sweet."

"Care to share?"

"Not yet," Sunny said and smiled. She was thrilled with the small bar of music she had created, but she couldn't share it. She had been writing music for years. She had outgrown the need to sing every short piece she had written right away, unless it was one of her short fun-with-life pieces. She changed the subject. "Have you heard from Grandma and Grandpa? Will they be able to drive down in time?"

"Oh sure. Your grandmother called. She said they were leaving soon. They'll get here really early, so she'll bring her knitting. She's making a soft prayer blanket for her church. And your grandpa will play solitaire on his cell phone."

Sunny laughed. "Typical of them."

Grace asked slowly, "How was your time with Nick this morning?"

"You know, Mom," Sunny shifted a little on the hard chair. "I always have a good time with Nick."

Grace gave her a little hug. "It's too bad you and Nick—" But she didn't say more.

Chapter Forty
The Sleazy Man

Holly and Quin went to the church carrying all of their wedding clothes, makeup, fancy shoes, and hairpieces. Along with Robin, they chose to get ready in the nursery room. There they'd sit on little wooden chairs with their knees to their chests as they put on their shoes. Sunny wondered how they would stand up after sitting with their knees higher than their backside. With all that had happened in recent days, Sunny arrived at the church completely ready.

Her beautiful dress fit perfectly with a flowing mid-calf skirt. Although her performance outfits were custom-made, she felt more comfortable in her bridesmaid dress than in any costume she'd ever worn. Her shoes slid on like Cinderella's slippers.

Sunny checked in with the rest of the wedding party when she arrived. "Robin," she sang out as she opened the door into stacks of colorful blocks, doll beds, and very short tables and chairs. "I'm here."

"Sunny," Robin put her hand to her chest and exhaled deeply, "you are here. You look beautiful." She hugged her.

"Thanks." She kissed Robin's cheek, knowing how special it all was for her. She had waited so long, with Gary beside her all the way. "But you're the center ring attraction of this show. You even look special in your silky, bridal slip. I suggest, however, that you wear your wedding gown over it. Is there anything I can do to help you?"

"I don't think so," Robin said as she looked around at her prep station. "I brought everything I need and probably far more."

"As your maid-of-honor, it's my job to be your Lady-in-waiting. I want to do what I can." Sunny was getting excited about so many things; how would she handle the whole day? She would introduce her new song during the wedding. Launching the maiden voyage of a new piece was always a thrill for her. There was also her report to Nick about the investors' meeting. What would he think about her composed jingle, and would it help Harrison Stafford? She might even hear from Bruce about the award ceremony during the wedding. But, most of all, she couldn't wait to hear information about the house on Mulberry Lane. And there was the question of Nick.

"Honey," Robin said as she reached out and touched Sunny's arm, "you look like you're getting anxious. I've never seen you like this before. Are you worried about singing your new song?" She looked into the mirror, checked her teeth, then smoothed some cucumber-smelling Exquisite Lady cream on her face before applying the foundation.

"I'm never nervous about singing a new song," she said as she twirled around, allowing the bottom of her skirt to flare out. "If you don't need me, I'll check out the sanctuary. I saw the florist leaving when I got here."

"That would be great. You saw the diagram I drew for the layout of the flowers. I'll feel better if you look over the placement. Go. Besides, your nervousness might be contagious." Robin waved her hand, shooing Sunny away.

Sunny went through the sanctuary's swinging doors and paused. The beauty of the room was inspirational. Enormous blooms of blue chrysanthemums and white dahlias in crystal vases were on each side of the altar. White chrysanthemums overflowed their planters in short flower stands, creating a path to the focus of worship. Tall, white candle stands with festive blue bows were on both sides of the steps leading up from the sanctuary floor to the chancel. Every other pew had a single white candle stand attached to the end of the seat back.

Organ music began to fill the sanctuary with heavenly music. At the rehearsal, Sunny had shared with the organist her appreciation for his complete preparation. Hank had played the organ at the church since Sunny was a little girl. She knew that he loved to fill the world with music. She inhaled the melodies, the floral aroma, and the beauty with reverence and awe.

"Pretty, isn't it?" a familiar voice spoke behind

"Gus?" Sunny gasped.

"You seem nervous," he observed. He had changed. His friendly approach was absent. Walters sounded more like a predator than a concerned friend.

She fumbled for an honest answer. "My sister is getting married in a while. I'm not nervous. I'm excited."

"I wasn't invited," he said through hissing teeth.

Sunny's mind raced. She didn't feel comfortable with Gus. The sleazy vibration he exuded at the meeting had mutated. Now, Sunny felt extreme caution and deep distrust. "I didn't know that you knew Robin and Gary."

"I don't," was his only answer.

With Walters standing between Sunny and the sanctuary exit, she began to edge up the aisle. Looking around, she saw no other way out, except the door on the other side of the room. But she was already trapped in the aisle, away from the second exit. Even the times she played hide-and-seek as a child with her Sunday school friends, no one had discovered another exit.

"Uh," Sunny tried to come up with a reason to get past Walters. She felt like he was a stalker moving in on his prey. "I'd better go back and see if Robin needs anything."

"You just checked. She's doing fine without you." Gus stepped closer as Sunny backed up. "You and I need to talk."

"Oh?" Sunny asked. "About what?"

"You know about what, Miss Gaynor. You weren't at our meeting as an interested learner. You were there as a mole. Why? Who do you report to? What do you think you found out about our little group?"

"April invited me," Sunny answered, now getting more frightened.

"I've seen you around with Nick Sullivan," Walters said and inched closer. "Now, what would a lawyer send you to find out?"

"Nothing," she denied backing up more. She tried to lead him away from whatever he was thinking. She turned and spread out her shaking hands. "Isn't it all beautiful? The flowers are lovely."

"Yes, beautiful," was all he said in a flat tone.

Sunny turned back to Walters and tried to appear friendly and open, hoping it would help calm him down. But he was now in her face, just a step or two behind her. Sunny was startled and tried to smile. "Oh, Gus, I didn't know you were so close." She brushed an imaginary piece of hair from her forehead. "May I help you?"

Walters grabbed Sunny's arms and shook her. "Tell me what you plan to tell Sullivan. Since you came to the meeting, the police called and asked me to come into the station on Monday."

Sunny squealed and tried to free herself. "Let go of me," she demanded while struggling to pull away.

At that moment, Hank nearly stood on the organ's foot pedals and blared minor chords into the room.

"What do you think she should tell me, Walters?" Nick bellowed from the back of the sanctuary. He quickly looked at Maddie and pointed to the door, indicating that she should leave the room. He snapped back at Gus. "Take your hands off Sunny."

Walters released his grip, surrendering his hands. "Just as I thought," he seethed. "Where Miss Gaynor is, there is Mr. Sullivan."

Nick glared but did not touch the intruder. "I have no authority to throw you out of the church. But the police will have the authority to arrest you for assaulting Miss Gaynor if you don't leave immediately," Nick warned.

Gus hissed and hurried out of the sanctuary, his face tight with anger, and his head down. If he could have slammed the outer door, he would have. It had slow-close hinges, however, and gently reseated itself.

"Nick." Sunny sighed. "You came. Thank goodness you got here early." She fell into his arms, holding on tightly.

Nick didn't say anything. He just didn't let go.

Chapter Forty-One
Robin's Wedding

As wedding guests began to enter the sanctuary, Nick gathered Maddie and got out of everyone's way. They seated themselves without benefit of usher, mid-way to the front, on the bride's side of the sanctuary. He knew them both, Robin and Gary. Even after Sunny left for New York, Nick continued to go to college events with them. Robin and Nick had graduated from high school during the same year, although at different schools. The trio didn't add another member to the threesome because Nick didn't date after Sunny left.

"Look, Uncle Nick," Maddie said, all excited as she held up his cell phone screen. "I put the puzzle together."

Nick took the screen in his hand. A nine-piece puzzle of a dog appeared. "That dog looks like your, Frosty Dog, Maddie."

"That's what I thought," she giggled. "Look." Maddie pointed to a family who was being seated at the end of their row. "There's Shaneah and her mom and dad."

Nick nodded at Rebecca and Kevin as they seated themselves in his row, with the girls side by side. The girls whispered and giggled some more.

The room began to fill quickly as the time of the wedding drew near. Ladies in lightweight dresses or pantsuits carried sweaters or fancy covers over their arms. Men wore summer-weight suits or slacks with casual, button-neck knit shirts. All were smiling.

Robin and Gary had been in love for a long time and had been engaged for several years. They were devoted to renting a good-sized apartment, or perhaps buying their first house, so they watched their money closely. Sunny had offered to give them the down payment on a home, but the wedding couple had refused, preferring to create their own home, as well as their future. They decided to make a challenge of their savings. Each found fun ways to reuse materials rather than purchase new until they had a key to their front door. They saved for their wedding in the same manner.

Hank's music changed to one of Gary's favorites as Jerry Tuttle, Quin's husband, seated Marie Foxworth on the groom's side. Steven followed and sat beside her.

Phil Blanchart came down the aisle with Grace on his arm as Hank played one of Sunny's songs, one that Robin especially loved. Doug would walk Robin down the aisle and then sit with Grace. Gary and the groomsmen entered from the side aisle and stood facing the guests.

When the introductory music finished, Sunny stood at the lectern to sing "Love Found Me." This time, rather than avoiding his gaze, she smiled and focused on Nick. She was finally honest with herself. The song was for the only love she had ever known.

After she finished, she made her way down to her spot as maid-of-honor. When Robin and their dad started down the aisle, tears gathered in Sunny's eyes. Robin's happiness filled Sunny with joy.

Chapter Forty-Two
Sunny's Report

On the ride back to the Gaynor house, excitement filled the car. By the warmth that exuded from Nick's every pore, she knew he got the meaning of her song. She felt connected to family, not just her parents and sister. Home was all around her. Maddie had finally wound down and sat quietly in the back seat watching the sky turn brilliant colors of rose and lilac.

Sunny decided that Nick was speaking softly because Maddie was tired, or he was respecting the intimacy of their time together, following her song.

Nick took Sunny's hand and said, "It's nice that Robin and Gary chose to have their reception in your parents' yard. A large tent is perfect for everyone, and the evening is beautiful and cool."

"It's funny." Sunny wiggled in her seatbelt, trying to face Nick. "When Grandma and Grandpa were dating, she could snuggle under Grandpa's arm as they rode along. Now, car companies build wide consoles between the seats for cup holders and a place to stash stuff, blocking any skin-to-skin contact between sweethearts." She was quiet for a minute, then added, "Robin would talk about her wedding when we were teenagers. It included the reception in a tent. Maybe she saw one on TV."

Nick inhaled slowly, "Sweethearts?"

She answered courageously, "Sweethearts."

The car was quiet again for a minute, except for the slow breathing of a sleeping seven-year-old. It all added to the comfortable feeling in the car.

Sunny filled the silence. "You said you're going to research Elmer's case tomorrow?"

"Yes, and no." Nick's enthusiasm began to rise. "I'll finish reviewing the trial transcript. That shouldn't take long. They rushed to judgment faster than any case I've seen. With the information you helped me get about Elmer's trip to Englewood and his lunch there with the coach and the students, I'm ready to approach the appeals court. We have solid evidence that Elmer was miles away from the car accident. None of that was allowed into court."

"Nick, that is wonderful. Let me know what the court says."

"I'll call you right after I let Elmer know." Then, Nick seemed to remember something else as he thumped the steering wheel with the heel of his hand. "Sunny, what were you going to tell me about the investment meeting you attended with April? If you don't want to tell me, that's okay."

"Kinda like," Sunny began with a chuckle, "I'm not talking until I consult with my attorney?"

Smiling mischievously, Nick raised his eyebrows. "Well, I hadn't thought about that answer."

"Just teasing." She patted his shoulder. "Yes, I did find an impression, a theme. I tend to think in musical terms. Here's how I see it:

"Gus Walters chooses the investment portfolios he presents at each meeting. He influences the group with keywords he selects. At payout, he is the payee, so he controls the money. In 4/4 time, he gets two beats.

Jerry is a math teacher and the JV football coach. Anneta, Jerry's wife, completely organized the Athletic Office and the Boosters Club schedule. She is also the treasurer of the Boosters Club. So, she gets two beats.

April is great at computers. She could probably hack into the Club's funds. But, according to some, she's not good with numbers, or she's not interested. And, she doesn't control anything but the coffee pot. Like the rest of the group, she'd know which specific investment they were talking about. Due to her ability with her computer, I'd give her one beat.

Jerry is the coach but has no access to the Club's funds. I'll give him a half beat. That's true of Tiffany and Lisa, so they also get eighth-note beats. Violet isn't left-brained at all. She's artsy and creative. I give her an eighth-note rest.

The little jingle I came up with is Gus and Anneta have the same beat, so they make a chord, played twice. Then, a quarter note, then four eighth notes, then a rest. So ... play the drums, please ....

First two and nobody else. Harrison Stafford had nothing to do with any of this."

Nick nearly ran off the road. "That is brilliant, Shine. We'll delve into these people, using your jingle, and present it to the police. They'll take Harrison off their Person of Interest list. He had no connection to any of it. Neither did April. She doesn't manage, enter data, or have any other connection to the money. The detectives can investigate how Gus might have gotten into the boosters' fund. When Walters intimidated and threatened you before the wedding, he revealed his nefarious intent. The police will be very interested."

All seemed settled as Nick pulled up in front of the house. Due to the evening hour, lights were strung across the wide driveway, creating a sparkling cover from the corner of the porch to the tent set up in the side yard.

"It is glorious," Sunny praised.

Chapter Forty-Three
The Reception

An enormous white tent was draped from the center top in measured sections. Each section simulated the banded glass in the ceiling window of the beautiful, downtown Dayton Arcade, but on a much smaller scale.

"Isn't it beautiful? And the big one, the Arcade's rotunda, is huge." Sunny inhaled the space with joy. It was just as Robin had planned so many years before.

"Wow," Maddie gasped. "It's like a princess's great big doll house. Look at the ceiling," she said, sparkling like a nursery rhyme fairy as she twirled around with outspread arms. "And all the white tables, and sparkling stuff all over!"

"It is amazing," Nick agreed, his eyes dancing to every ceiling window. "Maddie, why don't you look for our place cards?"

Maddie wrinkled her nose. "Place cards? What's a place card?"

"See those?" Sunny pointed to a table as they passed. "Those little cards were propped up at each place. They are the place cards. It tells the guests where they're supposed to sit."

Nick watched Maddie pass one of the tables and added, "Do you know how to spell Sunny's name?"

"Do I know?" she rolled her eyes and plopped her hand on her hips. "Of course I do. Sunny signed an autograph for me, S-u-n-n-y. I'll go on a Sunny-hunt."

"A Sunny-hunt, is it?" Sunny echoed. "A great idea. Then, we'll go on a Maddie-hunt and Nick-hunt."

"I'll race ya," Maddie called out, skipping toward the head table. "I found you, Sunny! Right there!" She pointed to a place card near the center of the long table.

"You sure did," Sunny said, hugging her. "And you, Miss Maddie, are there, too, along with your Uncle Nick."

Robin and Gary's place cards were in the center of the table. As the maid-of-honor and the bride's sister, Robin had seated Sunny beside her, then Nick, then Maddie.

Maddie studied the arrangement, then grabbed her uncle's place card, and her own, and switched them. "There," she announced. "Now, I get to sit by Sunny."

"Sweetheart," Sunny began, "I would love to sit beside you. But this isn't my party." She looked at Nick out of the corner of her eye. "Robin arranged all of the seating and put everyone where she wanted them."

Nick silently took Sunny's hand and squeezed it. A message that Sunny could easily read.

They would spend the evening together, just the two of them, amid a roomful of about one hundred and fifty people.

All the guests began milling around, searching for their seats, and greeting one another with laughter. People who didn't know each other talked together and included everyone around them in the conversation. The evening was filled with love.

After everyone was seated, Sunny stood and tapped her butter knife on the side of her water glass, sending a *ting, ting, ting* into the room. "Take whatever glass or coffee cup you have near you, and let's toast the bride and groom. Ready?" She held her glass high. "I'd like to offer a toast to the greatest older sister in the world, and the man she chose to spend her life with. Robin, you have everything: a job you love and a husband you love even more. You have found a way to do it all. And Gary, thank you for letting my sister complete herself. That will require an equal partnership between you. I know you two are already life companions. Now, may God richly bless your life together."

The guests tapped the raised glass nearest them, sipped, and cheered. Then the best man stood up.

"My toast will be a little shorter." He held his glass high. "To this great couple. May your fridge always be full, the electricity always working, and future children not run amok with the law. Cheers!"

Everyone laughed and clicked their glass together with the friends around them.

"And now," Doug announced, "while the final details of our meal are being prepared, our wonderful Robin and her Gary will dance their first waltz as a married couple."

Gary took Robin's hand and led her to the dance floor. The music started slowly, then … it changed into an old-fashioned Jitterbug. They did the swing dance and laughed. Three chord progressions later, the tempo and meter slowed to a waltz. Gary drew Robin close as they eased into the three-count rhythm and the step-step-close pattern.

Sunny was mesmerized by the couple's movement. Leaning toward Nick, she said, "I am so glad she's happy."

He put his arm around her shoulder. "Shine, I'll be happy when you are."

Bobby Blanchart came over to their table, holding his breath. "Mm…Maddie," he stammered. "Would you like to dance with me?"

Maddie snapped a look at her uncle. "Can I? Can I?"

"Of course," Nick said with a big smile, shaking Bobby's hand. "Good to see you this evening, young man. You two have fun."

When Sunny's cell phone suddenly rang, she jumped. She was embarrassed. What kind of sister would answer her phone at her sister's wedding reception? She pulled a little purse from her lap that didn't fit more than her phone and a tube of lipstick.

"Hello?" Pause.

"Yes, hi." Pause

"You're where? Oh, yes, I see you." Pause

"What? Really! Praise the Lord. And, thank you, thank you." Pause

"Right, will do. Thanks again, Rebecca. Bye."

Nick's eyebrows raised. "Sounds like a cryptic message."

Sunny looked at him with an excited sparkle in her eyes. "It was," she said, smiled, and patted his hand. "It was a great cryptic message." She slowly stood up. "If you'll excuse me for a minute, I'll be right back."

Chapter Forty-Four
A Decision

Sunny met her friend near the table dedicated to wedding presents. She was excited and grabbed her hand. "Rebecca, repeat, please." They jumped up and down, nearly knocking some of the fancy wrapped boxes, with flowery bows in white and robin's egg blue, off the table. "Oh no, Aunt Julia's present nearly landed on the floor. What if a fine crystal bowl or candy dish were inside? That's the kind of beautiful gift Aunt Julia enjoys giving."

"It wobbled," Rebecca said with a smile and a shrug, "but didn't fall to the floor."

Sunny carefully restacked the few gifts precariously stacked on the corner of the table and patted them like a small puppy. "Stay," she commanded.

"Okay, this information is very time sensitive," Rebecca began as she looked around to see if anyone was listening.

"Time sensitive?" Sunny began to think of all the pieces of her life that stood behind a clock, ready to demand center attention.

"Yes, time sensitive." Checking for nearby ears, Rebecca began again. "Nadine called me. The open house is tomorrow. She was hoping she could accept your generous, all-cash offer before the event. Or, if you need a little more time, would you outbid the highest offer if the quotes had already started coming in? Here's another catch. Her husband is going to France for a business meeting next Friday. If you want the house, you would have to stay home another week and close before he leaves."

"Oh, my." Sunny closed her eyes and shook her head. The images of her responsibilities beginning on Monday overwhelmed her. Her airplane ticket was booked and paid for, for her return to New York, departing the Dayton airport at 11:15 a.m. Her new album was waiting for two additional, original songs. Also, Bruce told her that she should be on a flight to Hollywood on Monday at 9:47 a.m. That's opposite coasts on the same day. None of it seemed to be Sunny's choice. She would have had a linear path in some direction. It was all orchestrated by others, mainly Bruce. Perhaps it was time to find a new agent, or make clear to Bruce his responsibilities and hers.

"Sunny, what do you think?" Rebecca asked, touching Sunny's shoulder as if gently trying to bring her back from wherever she had run, chasing an overzealous agent. "All four of us, Nadine, her husband, you, and I, need to sit down, sign all of the papers, and you submit your financial offer by Thursday at noon."

Sunny's head raced out across the start line of life's fast track. First, she was confronted with being on both coasts at the same time. The next problem was the wonderful opportunity to have one of her songs featured in an upcoming movie, but it meant dealing with an impossible schedule. If she chose to ignore her family again, as she had in the past, she would give the regret speech … "Sorry, I can't stay. Love you all. I must honor my commitments. I'll be back in another ten years."

But that apology wouldn't work with Nick. Her family would always love her; they were family. But Nick would have to move on. If he were going to have a family of his own, he would have to find a partner who was committed to the relationship. That would mean that family would have to take precedence over career most of the time. It would take careful scheduling, and those details would have to be Sunny's, not dictated by her agent. It would all have to be discussed, negotiated, and scheduled by Sunny if she were to grow the other half of her life.

Regardless of all those career details, for Sunny to have a balanced, complete life, filled with belonging and love, meant Nick. And it started with the house on Mulberry Lane.

"What do you say, Sunny?" Rebecca asked, with wide eyes and a giant smile. "Nadine wants me to call her back after you say yes or no. They know they'll have no problem selling the house. It's a great place. But she would like to sell it to you." Rebecca watched Sunny's expression.

"That's very nice of Nadine and her husband," Sunny said and beamed.

"Honestly, Sunny, I am not pushing you or trying to trick you into buying the house by putting such extreme deadlines on its purchase. It's just the circumstances. If you leave without buying it, it will be gone when you get back. If Nadine doesn't also leave on Friday to go to Columbus for a new position, she'll lose the job. When Gordon gets back from France, he'll arrange for everything to be packed and moved. Then he also has a wonderful new job waiting for him in Columbus. Those are facts, Sunny, not blackmail demands."

Sunny relaxed. She hugged Rebecca and said, "I understand. That's an adult's life, making choices. So far, to get my career into full swing, I've let those who know the business tell me what to do and when. I'm ready to make my own decision. I'll fly out on Monday and return Wednesday, if we can close on Thursday. Becca, I want to choose Home. Tell Nadine, Yes!"

Chapter Forty-Five
Shall We Dance

When Sunny returned to the head table, Alissa Bowser, Nick's part-time event partner, was sitting in Sunny's chair, between Robin and Nick. Sunny thought, *for an English teacher, you sure can't read body language. Of course, that topic isn't in a stuffy textbook. Even when I first met you, you could see my interest in Nick.*

"Sunny," Alissa cooed, "it's good to see you again." But she didn't move out of the chair.

"It's good to see you, too, Alissa." When Sunny saw the warmth in Nick's eyes, and it was all for her, her anger subsided. "I'm so glad you came to Robin's wedding."

Alissa's smile was more genuine as Sunny's welcome became friendly. "I work in the same school as Gary. He's a good guy. I met Robin at a faculty Christmas Party about eight or nine years ago."

Robin had returned to the table for a drink of water. She put her arm around Alissa. "We hit it off right away. We have many things in common. She began attending our church four years ago and joined the Bible study group I have participated in for several years. In warm weather, we both like golf. Well, she plays. I play at golf." She tapped Alissa's hand. "Tell Sunny your handicap."

"Robin," Alissa blushed, "no."

"Okay, then I'll tell her. Alissa's handicap is twenty. That's a lot better than mine. We won't even discuss my handicap." Robin gave her a little hug. "But most of the time, we just enjoy the long walk from one green to the next on a beautiful day."

Alissa looked up at Sunny and blushed. "Oh, I'm in your chair." She jumped up and pulled the chair back for Sunny, smiling, "Ma'am, may I seat you?" Turning to Robin, she said, "I am so happy for you two, Robin. When you get back from your honeymoon, maybe we can get in a few holes of golf before the cooler weather sets in."

"I'd love it," Robin agreed. "Gary will be out late many evenings for football practice. That will be a good time to hit the links. I'll give you a call."

"Great," Alissa said and kissed Robin's forehead. Turning, she added, "And Sunny, I am so happy for you and Nick."

Nick smiled a relieved smile and stood up. "Shine, are we going to let the kids have all the fun?"

Sunny joined him on the dance floor, where Robin and Gary were continuing their waltz. Many of the guests followed them. Maddie and Bobby were trying to jitterbug to waltz music. Somehow, it looked to Sunny like they had succeeded. As a composer, she wondered how that was possible. The jitterbug is in 4/4 time, and the waltz in 3/4.

On the smooth dance floor, with the magenta, blue, and purple lights from above simulating a sunset, Sunny allowed Nick to pull her close as they danced like they had so many times before. She laid her head on his shoulder, closed her eyes, and found she was finally home. As Nick waltzed her around the floor, she caught a glimpse of Mel on the sidelines.

His overalls were as clean and sharp as they had been when she first met him on the airplane. He was mouthing a message to her, like he didn't want to interrupt her time with Nick. What was he saying? She watched his lips closely.

His words became as clear as though she could hear them. They were the same, and yet new every time she heard them. Lay your heart on the wind. Mel waved, blew a kiss, and left.

Lay your heart on the wind, Sunny repeated silently. She talked with herself as fast as she could. *The Grammy Awards are held at the Crypto.com Arena in Los Angeles, California. Airplanes fly to L.A. out of Dayton just as they do from New York. It doesn't matter where I live anymore. My music is worldwide. I have concerts everywhere. It's irrelevant where my home base is located.*

"Did you see someone?" Nick asked as he looked in the direction Mel had been. "It looked like you recognized somebody."

Sunny smiled. Who was Mel? How could she explain him? "I would say that I saw my great-great-grandfather, but that would be silly." Still, she wondered.

"If anyone could see a distant relative, it would be you, only you, Shine." Nick pulled her closer.

"I wish I could see the future," she moaned, leaning her forehead on his chest. "Oh Nick, I wish I knew for certain what to do."

Nick stroked her hair and kissed the top of her head. "If you are waiting for certainty in this world, Shine, you'll wait forever. Why are you worrying?"

Remaining in the folds of his slick, dark suit, she wanted to hide until she could figure it out. "I don't know how to be all of me. As a teenager, I thought pursuing my musical career would complete me. I would be everything I always wanted to be."

Nick didn't try to confront her, but gently caressed her back as she hid safely in his arms. "Do you not want to sing anymore?"

"No, no, I love singing. That's my language." She brushed away the tears that ran down her cheeks and threatened to drop on Nick's suit. "But, since I've been home, I've discovered that music is only half of me. My songs have become the public Sunny, and it's so time-consuming that there is no private me, and hasn't been for many years. But I don't know how to be complete, get married, have a family, and still fly to California or Italy."

"Many married women and young moms commute to work," Nick revealed, with a smile in his voice. "My cousin, Jeannie, gets up at four a.m., Monday through Friday, to drive fifty-nine miles each way so she can teach in a school she loves."

Sunny stayed in his arms, with her hand clinging to the lapel of his jacket. Her voice snapped and cracked as she asked, "What does Jeanie's husband think when dinner is late?"

Nick put his hands on her upper arms and pulled her back where he could see her. "It has to be a team effort, Shine. Jeanie didn't marry a self-centered, lazy little boy. She married a man who entered into the marriage with a clear idea that he wasn't getting a live-in servant. He was marrying an equal member of the family of God."

To Sunny, Nick's closeness was warm. His shoulders were firm, yet gentle. There was a faint aroma of masculine hair cream. He always fought with his waves and tried hard to hold his hair in place. Sunny rubbed her nose in his clothes and inhaled the essence of Nick.

As Sunny whirled around the floor in Nick's arms, the music filled her with hope and excitement. It may take more courage to complete herself than it did to find her place in the music world, but she was determined to do it. She had laid her heart on the wind, and God had supported her as she stepped out into the mist of her future life.

She thought of the sweet face of her friend, Mel, and imagined a picture of his family: his Josie, and their six children. *Lay your heart on the wind*, she repeated his words. Closing her eyes, she saw herself lying out across the sky, letting go of all that tied her down—her apartment, California, everything—and flying into the freedom of the breeze. The wind beneath her was as strong as Nick's arms. She felt like she could fly anywhere, on the wings of love.

Chapter Forty-Six
Sunday Morning Plans

The next day, Sunny waited for the pastor as he greeted those who came to church that morning. She stood back, not wanting the church family to assume she was waiting for praise or attention.

"Thanks for waiting after service, Pastor Tom." Sunny offered her hand in friendship.

"Of course, Sunny." He touched the top of their joined hands.

"I wanted to say, Robin and Gary's wedding ceremony was beautiful, and your contribution to that service was immense."

Tom smiled. "Your family is a blessing to the church."

Sunny removed a handkerchief from her pocket and blotted a few tears that had started to fall. "I also had to tell you how much your message touched me today. It put a blessing on some plans I've been making. You read from 1 Corinthians 9:5, 'Do we not have the right to take a believing wife along with us, as do the other apostles and the Lord's brothers and Cephas (Peter)?' You explained something I had overlooked. It's Paul's discussion about having the rights of some of the apostles apply to all of them. Some of them, like Peter, and those considered to be 'brothers of the Lord,' had their believing wives along with them on their ministry journeys. Paul says that all of those in Christ's ministry should have that same right." Sunny patted Pastor Tom's shoulder. "That helps me see that those in His service can have a balanced life. It tells us all that a complete life includes family, our immediate family or one of our own."

Pastor Tom touched his heart. "I appreciate your words of encouragement, Sunny. We all feel blessed when we've been heard. And someday, maybe you'll share with me your new plans."

"I sure will," she said as she started to turn to leave. "Everyone will know. Now, I promised to have lunch with Nick Sullivan."

• • • • •

Nick looked at Sunny warmly and laid his fork on his plate. "You're quiet, Sunny. Is your grilled salmon good?"

"The fish is great, and I'm feeling wonderful. It's just that," Sunny paused. "I need to tell you that I'm leaving for a few days. Trust me, I am not running away. I have to fly out late this afternoon, but I'll be back Wednesday evening." Sunny searched his face for disappointment.

"I trust you, Shine. I'm only disappointed that I won't see you for a while." Nick stroked her hand where it lay on the table. "Disappointment is not the same as despair."

"Nick, you are my rock," she assured him as she laid her hand over his. "I have a lot of details to take care of, and I'll tell you about each one of them when I return. Right now, I'm holding them close. Part of the excitement is that they are mine, and I'll grow into the person I want to be by proving to myself that I can work them out on my own."

"I want you to do what you need to do. Then come back. Always come back."

"That's part of my plan," she said, holding up two fingers to show she had told him a pinch of her plans.

Chapter Forty-Seven
A Contract of Her Own

The flight to L.A. was different from her trip to Dayton. Mel didn't suddenly appear to make Sunny's trip entertaining. She wondered if he had come into her life to say what she needed to hear and then had gone home. Wherever he was, it would have been nice to have him along. He simplified things, making them easier to understand. During her short visits with Mel, she had learned to open her heart and become a more complete person, and not permit others to plan her life.

Sunny watched the clouds off in the distance and thought of Nick. She wished he had come with her. Sharing the palm trees of the West Coast and the sparkling ocean of the Pacific would have been a joy. But making the trip to California alone was the point. She would have to make sure her career fit into her life, rather than letting her career *be* her whole life

• • • • •

Monday at 1 p.m., Sunny walked into the production office of Jason Streeter's Production Office. It was warmer in California than it had been in Ohio. She dressed as the weather suggested. Her mid-calf dress was a pale green, accenting her auburn hair. Sunny was not one to make deals using her neckline to influence the contract. The scoop at the top of her dress was enough to welcome the sun and still present herself as a professional. Small seed buttons ran down the front to the waist. Her straw wedge sandals were high enough to be fashionable and low enough to help her feel secure.

"Sunny." Tall, lanky, gray-haired Jason stood up and walked around his desk to greet her. "Your agent isn't with you? Or is he parking the car?"

"He's not with me this time," Sunny explained with a straight back and a keen eye. "Bruce doesn't know that I came on my own. I'll let him know about our conversation."

Jason directed Sunny to two leather wingback chairs that sat in front of a large window. "It will be more comfortable here, Sunny."

Sunny watched a reddish brown and green Allen's hummingbird flit from one blossom to another in the gardens beyond the window. "This is beautiful."

"It is, isn't it?" Jason's eyes narrowed as he studied his guest. "Is there something wrong between you and your agent?"

"No, not at all." Sunny crossed her legs and relaxed. "I wanted to come on my own so we can talk one-on-one. I want to understand what you need from me regarding my song. I will work with you better if I can ask questions myself and get the information firsthand."

"That sounds like a good idea. After we agree on contract details, shall I send the proposal to Bruce first? Then the two of you can talk." Jason leaned forward.

Sunny nodded. "Please send a copy to me at the same time, so Bruce and I can read the agreement together."

"Okay, good." Jason sat back and stretched his feet out in front of him. "I assume Bruce told you, we want to use your song, 'What If.' It will be the theme song and the premise of the movie. We're ready to start filming."

"Yes, that's what Bruce said." Sunny paused and tried to think of how she might word her next question. "What will the Motion Picture Association rating be for the film?"

"It will be a major film for the Wholesome Family Studio and will be rated G: General Audiences, Suitable for all ages. Bruce said that it was important to you. We are committed to wholesome films, so the contract will be carefully worded to protect your interests and ours. You will receive a copy of the full script before you sign the final contract." He paused and smiled reassuringly. "I hope you're a fast reader. Sunny. We also plan to provide the dailies for your review. If you find anything offensive, we'll reshoot."

Sunny was getting excited about everything Jason was saying. "Goodness, that is fantastic."

Jason lowered his head and looked at Sunny over the top of his glasses. "With your permission, we're naming the movie, 'What If.' With that much commitment to your song, we won't just pay you for the rights to use the music; we'll offer a considerable amount for the inspiration that prompted the entire storyline. I can go over those figures with Bruce or with you. You decide."

"Jason, I'll admit, I'm excited. Except for recording the song, reading the script, and watching the dailies, what other time commitment will I have?" Sunny shifted her legs. "Bruce led me to believe I would have to move out here temporarily."

"Good question," Jason said, and smiled. "We would like you to be here for about a week to record the soundtrack for the film. We'll send the dailies to your computer, and you can review them anywhere. In addition to your song, we will need about twenty to twenty-four more measures of music. You don't need to write lyrics. The measures will provide the musical theme that will flow under the action and the warm scenes. You can compose it, or we can find someone to create it in your style. Another possibility is that you and the collaborator could work together. Whichever you have time for. Some of the measures could be alternative, compatible themes, or slight variations on the song."

Sunny's mind filled with music. "That sounds marvelous, Jason." She added up the various time commitments. "I'd be here for a week recording the song. Then I can review the dailies, compose the additional music, and send it to you, all from home." She thought about the additional songs she needed for her next album and realized that she could also compose them at home.

"I hope you can attend the premiere," he encouraged. "Everyone will look forward to seeing you."

Sunny was excited about the idea of a premiere. "Will that date be set before I have concerts scheduled? I wouldn't be able to cancel a show."

Jason clapped his hands together. "We'll work around your schedule, Sunny. Your being there will be too important to risk double-booking."

Together, she and Jason worked out many more details. Bruce usually presented contracts to her as if they were cast in stone. This time, she was able to ask questions, interject her opinions, and negotiate her needs.

Sunny was excited. She liked the idea of her song being the inspiration for a movie. And the best part was, she didn't have to live in New York for any of it.

Chapter Forty-Eight
New York, New York

"Bruce? I'm glad I caught you before you went home for the day." Sunny covered her right ear so she could hear over the noise of two small boys as they chased each other around the air terminal.

"Where are you, Sunny?" Bruce raised his voice to be heard above shouts of, *Tag, you're it.* "It's so loud on your end, I can barely hear you."

"It's louder on this end," Sunny said with a laugh. "Listen, I'm leaving here and will get to New York later this evening. Meet me tomorrow morning at my apartment. Say, 'Yes' and I can hang up."

"Yes," he agreed. "I'll call tomorrow before I leave."

"No need. Just be there at 10 a.m. Bye." Sunny tapped the screen and settled back to watch the boys as they played. They seemed to have no end to their energy.

"I'm letting the twins wear themselves out so they might sleep on the flight," a woman with a sweet smile explained. "Before boarding, we'll see who can do the most push-ups."

Sunny sparkled. "Thanks, I'll remember that. You're a smart mama."

When some teenagers passed, Sunny tipped her ball cap lower, shading her face.

"And, you're a smart celebrity, Sunny," the woman whispered.

"Oh, sorry," Sunny apologized to the boys' mother as she answered her phone. "Hello? Mom?"

Sunny's mother asked quickly, "I just had to call and find out how things went in California."

"Perfect. It will be a whole new experience for me," Sunny said as she dodged a wadded-up paper ball one of the boys threw. "Missed," she whispered to the child.

Sunny's mother sighed deeply. "I won't keep you any longer. It sounds like you're at the Roller Dome. I just had to find out."

"Thanks for calling, Mom. I'll be back on Wednesday," Sunny said as she disconnected. She studied her phone screen and began texting. *Hi Nick. I had to know you are out there, but didn't want to call. I wasn't sure where you would be right now. My meeting with Jason Streeter went great. I'll fill you in when I get back. Shine.* She changed her phone setting to Airplane Mode and slipped it into her carry-on.

"Our flight to New York is now boarding," a voice announced.

Sunny pulled her carry-on from the chair beside her, got into line, and found her seat in first class. With the boys and their mother in business class, Sunny settled down for the flight east. She thought about Maddie and how much the little one would have enjoyed playing tag with the boys. She imagined Robin and Gary's future children playing in the yard. But most of all, as she dozed off, she thought of Nick.

• • • • •

Her apartment was chilly when she arrived. September weather in New York could be either extreme or a cozy medium. But that night when she opened her door, it didn't seem cozy inside. Hurrying over to the fireplace, she lit the gas flame. Even though it gave no heat, the flickering flame took away the chill she felt inside.

She clicked the TV remote and tuned to the late news. After seeing depressing images of a car pile-up on the George Washington Bridge, she changed the channel to a delightful comedy movie, using it as white noise as she began working on the tasks she wanted to accomplish. She pulled a small suitcase on rollers from the hall closet. It would be perfect to transport the music she had already written, as well as the two pieces she had partially completed for her new album. A packet of blank music staff paper was added to the other materials, along with her contract with Bruce, and some of her more recent awards.

"There," she talked to the empty room. "At least I got started. I'll finish in the morning." Setting the suitcase aside, she went into the bathroom, took a long, hot shower, and put on fresh short pajamas. The next day would be the start of everything new.

•••••

Sunny was up, dressed, and had started organizing her clothes before Bruce arrived. "Thank you for coming." Sunny held the door open for her friend and agent.

"I didn't even know you were coming back so soon until you called from the airport." He went into the kitchen and helped himself to a cup of coffee. "How was Ohio?"

Sunny topped off her cup with more coffee. "Robin's wedding was wonderful, and being with my family was a real blessing. It was so good to be home." Sipping carefully, she took the coffee into the living room. "Let's sit in here, Bruce."

Bruce sipped from the hot liquid and set it on the coffee table. "You seem different, Sunny. Did something happen? Were there delays in Dayton?"

"I don't know." She hesitated, not knowing how to explain all that had happened. "I didn't fly out of Dayton. I left yesterday morning from Los Angeles."

Bruce nearly choked as he tried to swallow. "California? I didn't know we had an appointment. I am so sorry I missed it."

Sunny spoke softly, "No, Bruce, you're fine. You and I didn't have an appointment with Jason Streeter. I did."

Bruce's shoulder drooped. He didn't sound angry. He sounded hurt. "Are you firing me, Sunny? We have a contract."

"No, of course not." Trying to stall and gather her thoughts, she finished her coffee and put the cup down. "Bruce, I had to negotiate my time commitment with Streeter. That wasn't something someone else could do for me. I know the limits of my strength and energy. I had to be the one to decide if the project was possible for me."

Bruce didn't say anything, but he didn't turn away either.

"When you agreed to represent me, I was only nineteen years old. I knew how to write songs and sing them. I knew nothing about the music business, any aspect of it. I needed you to do it all for me."

Bruce opened his mouth to speak, then stopped when Sunny raised a finger to continue.

"Bruce, I still need you," she assured him. "But now, I have to be part of the planning. I mean, I tell you how much time I can commit to a quarter or even a year, and how many trips I can take out of the country. Then, you plan it all, make all of the contacts, and handle every detail." She started to reach for her coffee again, then waved off the empty cup. "I will handle my personal life, like where I live, and the amount of time I need for a relationship, family, church, and community."

He threw his hands in the air and shouted, "Hallelujah! Honey, you don't know how many times the family and I have prayed that you would slow down and find love."

"I found love, and I wrote a song expressing it for my sister's wedding." She checked her watch. "I have a lot to do, and so do you. I have to go to the bank and be ready to catch my plane for home at four this afternoon. And, I need a lot from you. I'll leave most of the furniture here. I may keep the apartment until I see how much I might use it. You need to call a mover who will pack all of my non-furniture items, except in the kitchen and bath. I'll need dishes, cooking pots, and bath towels if I visit from time to time. The movers will need to carefully pack it and leave on the date I'll give you later. I will need you to go through all my files and materials and pack them. We can burn up our phones with the multitude of questions and answers I'm sure we'll both have." She waited for an answer. "Does that seem possible?"

With a furrowed brow, Bruce asked, "And our relationship is still good?"

"It is still great. We do most of our communicating by phone now anyway. The only changes will be that I will decide on commitments and time involved."

Sunny's new life was in her hands.

• • • • •

Sicily Sherwood came out of her office at Treadway Bank when Sunny entered through the revolving door. "Miss Gaynor, good afternoon. May I help you?"

"Mrs. Sherwood, it's good to see you. I'm here for two reasons. I'm going to pay cash for a house and need to know how to transfer those funds to the appropriate place. And I'll be opening a bank account in Ohio, where I'm moving, and wondered if my account here could somehow be connected to that bank. Since Treadway doesn't have out-of-state bank locations, how can this be solved?"

"I am so pleased you trust us to leave your account in Treadway Bank. Before you leave today, I'll give you the bank transfer numbers you'll need to purchase your house. As to combining your new account at an out-of-state bank with our bank, we already have banking systems in place for you to continue using our bank here in Manhattan. Or, you can transfer money monthly or quarterly to your other account. We only have to wait for your routing and account numbers from your new bank."

Sunny felt relieved. Inside, she knew the bank would handle it for her, but she had to hear the words. "That's why I trust you and Treadway Bank. Thank you."

Mrs. Sherwood picked up the receiver. "Tony? Prepare the necessary process and numbers for Sunny Gaynor to pay cash for a house she will purchase in Ohio very soon. Thanks." Sherwood pulled out a special leather folder from a cabinet behind her desk. Inserting her business card in a notch inside, she said, "Call me directly for whatever you need. I can assist with any of your purchases. I can answer any questions you may have regarding finance. I'm here to help."

"Thank you so much." Sunny was thrilled. Every item on her to-do list was done.

A middle-aged man with a mustache and large glasses came in and handed Mrs. Sherwood a packet of papers. "The material you requested," he said.

"Thanks, Tony." Mrs. Sherwood placed the papers in the folder, zipped it shut, and handed it to Sunny. "Good luck. I look forward to hearing from you. If it's okay with you, I'll call once in a while to make sure things are going well."

Sunny stood and extended her hand. "I am sure you are very busy, but I would be happy to hear from you."

As she stepped back outside, she clung to her folder and smiled at the sun. It was a beautiful day with the bluest sky she had seen in New York in years. She felt God smile on her as she hurried to a taxi. She would go back to the apartment for the last time in a while. It would always be there if she needed to be in New York. It was a good decision…for now. She didn't want her apartment to be a crutch, a place to hide if she didn't want to face something. She'd talk it over with her family. But most of all, she'd ask for Nick's opinion.

Chapter Forty-Nine
Good Morning

"Hello?" Sunny was still asleep in her parents' home when her phone rang. She couldn't focus her eyes on the screen to identify the caller. Glancing at the clock, it was 9 a.m.

"Shine?" Nick questioned. "I'm sorry. You were still sleeping. I'll call back later."

"No," she said as she quickly sat up. "I got in late last night and fell into bed." She flipped her sheet off to see if she had changed into her pajamas. "Yep," she mumbled to herself. "Don't hang up, Nick. I want to hear your voice."

"Just hear my voice, or can we have a conversation?" he teased

Sunny yawned. "You go first, but don't wait for me to catch up."

"Let's see," he dramatized. "I was busy while you were away." It sounded like he was making himself comfortable while he gave a full report. "Monday, Harrison, and I went into the police station to talk to the detective in charge of investigating the money that's missing from the Boosters Club. I presented your hypothesis. I wondered if Detective Young knew what I was talking about. His eyes glazed over, and he just nodded. When I simplified it for him, he understood. After we talked, he said that Harrison and April are no longer persons of interest. They'll focus their investigation on Gus Walters and any other name we might think of."

Sunny stopped holding her breath and said, "What a relief. April and her husband are good people. What about Elmer Hollingsworth?"

"Oh, I get it. I go on and report the local news so you can close your eyes and rest."

"Sounds right to me," Sunny laughed.

"Okay. Major story, number two. I contacted the Appellate Court on Tuesday and presented Elmer's case. We hoped to have his conviction overturned or at least get a new trial. The people I talked to were shocked that some evidence had never been seen. They said the case had merit and directed me to the people who will receive our petition to vacate his conviction. They saw no reason why Elmer wouldn't be released."

Sunny woke up fast. "Nick, that is wonderful! You're brilliant."

Nick lowered his voice to a soothing whisper. "Shine, you are the one who began to look at the case differently. Elmer said he will be eternally grateful to you."

"I'm glad I could help him." She swung her legs around to the side of the bed and said, "Nick, can I see you in about an hour? I can meet you at the house on Mulberry Lane."

Nick's voice melted into the phone. "Of course you can. But I thought Nadine and her husband wouldn't be home. Didn't they have to be away?"

"Yes, but Nadine said I could sit on the patio whenever I wanted to while they were gone. I love it back there." She pulled some clothes from the closet and continued. "Becca said Nadine and her husband have a meeting here in Kettering tomorrow." Sunny tried not to sound excited. "So, they'll be back for a few days. We won't bother them if they're home or away." Hesitating, she added, "I don't want to hang up. It's so good talking to you. I'll see you in about an hour."

Sunny jumped into the shower and washed fast enough that the water didn't have a chance to heat. She put on a flowing, full-skirted sundress with blue flowers delicately placed on the fabric, and slipped on sandals.

Chapter Fifty
The Patio

Nick's car was parked in Nadine's driveway when Sunny arrived. She felt giddy even though she hadn't seen him yet. She jumped out when she guessed he was on the patio.

Every flower she passed on her way around the house seemed to smile at her. The same red cardinal she had seen before sat in the dogwood tree, then spread his wings, and swooped across the yard.

There was a dependable consistency about the home and yard. The bees still filled the silence of the morning with their buzz as they flitted from blossom to blossom. And the white rabbit with its large, puffy tail continued to hop in the yard.

"That rabbit is fun, isn't it, Shine?" Nick said as he walked toward her.

Sunny filled with excitement as she hurried into his arms. "Nick, you came."

Nick stepped back, looked into her eyes, then held her close. "Shine, I said I would. I'd come to you wherever you are."

Sunny hugged him dearly. "That's perfect, Nick. I may be up for another Grammy. They'll announce the finalists in November. I want you to go to the awards ceremony with me."

"I would be honored to be your plus-one. I know you'll win it," he said, squeezing her with a loving touch.

"Nick, you would be my only-one." She kissed his cheek again and again. "Thank you for believing in me. It would be nice to win a second Grammy. But I don't have to win to know that fans appreciate my work."

He gently stroked her back and whispered, "You're my Shine, and I'm your Santa. I want to always be here for you … and not just as a friend." Nick breathed softly.

"That will be easier than you think," Sunny admitted and smiled. Looking into his eyes, she drew close and brushed his lips. "Nick," she whispered, "Nadine accepted my offer on this house. I'm home."

Nick kissed her forehead, the flutter of her eyelids, then he found her lips. Gently touching her hair, he whispered, "I found my home that first day at North Central College when I saw you walking across the quad, Miss Sunshine of My Heart. I love you."

Sunny nestled close and felt the warm breeze of love. She had found her home on the breath of the Lord.

Glossary

1 "Grab Ahold of Jesus" Copyright 2025 Doris Gaines Rapp.

2 "What If?" Copyright 2025 Doris Gaines Rapp.

3 George Mathews (Lyrics) and Albert L. Peace (Music). "O Love that will not Let Me Go," Hymnary.org. In the Public Domain.

4 New York, New York. This song is the theme song from the Martin Scorsese film *New York, New York* (1977). It was written for and performed in the film by Liza Minnelli. Writer(s): John Kander, Fred Ebb. The theme song, "New York, New York" was composed by John Kander, with lyrics by Fred Ebb.

5 Pitts, William S. (1830-1918). "The Little Brown Church." Copyright cr. 1857. In the Public Domain.

6 William M. Backer. Backer and Spielvogel Ad Agency. Ad for Beech Nut Gum.

7 Car Show: vintage cars (1919-1930), antique cars (over 45 years), and classic/muscle cars.

8 Thomas d'Urfey (1706) "Old MacDonald Had a Farm." In the public Domain.

9 "The Sleazy Man" Copyright 2025 Doris Gaines Rapp.

10 E. Hewitt (1898) Refrain: Emily D. Wilson. "When We All Get to Heaven." In the public domain.

[11] Rodgers and Hammerstein (1955) "Oh What a Beautiful Morning." *Oklahoma!*.

[12] "Love Found Me" Copyright 2025 Doris Gaines Rapp. A few notes in a musical progression in one of the measures is similar to a few notes in "You'll Never Know" by Jos Clauder, arranged by Reginald De Koven, and published by Harris in 1898. "You'll Never Know" is in the public domain. "Love Found Me" was written for this book and is Copyrighted (2025) by Doris Gaines Rapp.

Other Books by Doris Gaines Rapp

<u>Novels:</u>

Tucker McBride and the Trumpet Call

Tucker McBride and the Christmas Gift

Tucker's Perfect Day

Tucker McBride's Many Lives

Tucker McBride

A Man of Significance

The Boy with the Golden Horn (A Novel)

The Boy with the Golden Horn – A Picture Book

Escape from the Belfry

Escape from the Shadows

Murder, She Blogged – Just in Time

News at Eleven – A Novel (Prequel to Murder, She Blogged - Just in Time)

Length of Days – The Age of Silence (1ˢᵗ in the trilogy)

Length of Days – Beyond the Valley of the Keepers (2nd in the trilogy)

Length of Days – Search for Freedom (3rd in the trilogy)

Hiawassee – Child of the Meadow

Smoke from Distant Fires

Children's Picture Book:

Shyloe and the Mayor

Lincoln's Christmas Mouse

Collection:

Christmas Feather, one of eight short stories by eight different authors in a collection titled, Christmases Past

Non-Fiction:

Prayer Therapy of Jesus

Promote Yourself

Waiting for Jesus in a Can't Wait World – Advent 2014

Internet Presence

Facebook: facebook.com/doris.gaines.rapp – Author Page

Website: www.dorisgainesrapp.com

About the Author

Doris Gaines Rapp, Ph.D., is an author, psychologist, educator, and speaker. Doris and her husband, Bill, met during their freshman year at North Central College in Naperville, Illinois. She has written five novels about Bill's growing up years in Dunlap, Indiana, the Tucker McBride books. His niece asked her to continue the story, writing about when they met. As a private person, that would be very difficult. "Lay Your Heart on the Wind" is a novel based on their love, set in Doris' hometown of Kettering, Ohio, during a Labor Day weekend, with memories of Naperville. The book, however, has a fictional storyline.

Doris and Bill have been married many years, have six children, twelve grandchildren, and soon to be four golden-grans.

Doris enjoys writing her books and hopes you enjoy reading them. Always remember her desire for you: "I hope you live all of your life."

www.ingramcontent.com/pod-product-compliance
Lightning Source LLC
Chambersburg PA
CBHW070518310726

48976CB00002BA/465